Andres & Blanton

I0629540

Done with Men Forever

S. Jane Scheyder

Andres & Blanton
Niantic, Connecticut

Done with Men Forever

Published by Andres & Blanton
Niantic, Connecticut

ISBN 978-0-9830318-9-5

Printed in the United States of America

www.andresblanton.com

10 9 8 7 6 5 4 3 2 1

Acknowledgements

My heartfelt thanks to:

Jacob, my cover designer and fearless editor, promotions coordinator and website specialist. I simply can't express how profoundly you affected this book. You would never allow this cliche, but it's absolutely true: I could never have done this without you!

Jan, Linda, Katie, Mary, Hannah, and Ellie - my tireless reviewers. I've learned so much from you! Thank you for your attention to detail, and for embracing Becky and her story. You've given me much-needed encouragement and made this story an infinitely better read!

Bob and Sandy - my sports and medical experts. I love doing research over dinner with you! Thanks for your interest, knowledge, and support!

Daniel - my football expert, along with Michael and Jacob - my sometimes intentional and often unwitting models for male behavior, from Parker to Tank. You've helped more than you know - thank you!

Paul - my renovations go-to guy, and the one who keeps me believing that romance is worth celebrating. Thank you! I love you!

All of the wonderful people who helped to make Clairmont a living, breathing community, and Maddy's Inn a warm and happy place to visit in Cafenova - thanks for coming back with me to tell Becky's story!

Finally, thanks to my mom, Judy, and Linda, Becky, Jisue, Donna, and many others who prayed this project through to completion.

Done with Men Forever

Andres & Blanton

one

Becky Jacobs climbed the steps to the porch of the old Victorian inn, debating whether she should knock or just go inside. She peered through one of the parlor windows and then immediately pulled back. One didn't look in the windows of the newlywed's house, even if it had been one's home for the past six weeks.

She sighed. Maybe her sister, Maddy, was having coffee on the beachside porch with her new husband. Becky circled the house and found the porch empty. She glanced at her watch. *Ten o'clock.* It sure wasn't her idea to show up this early.

Might as well take a walk. She started down the beach, waving to the occasional neighbor - people she'd started getting to know over the past few weeks while she lived with Maddy. Not many were left; most had returned to their real homes in the real world.

Funny, Becky had left her real home in the real world and now hovered on the edges of someone else's reality, with no real direction of her own. At twenty-seven, she wasn't quite ready to panic. Despite recently losing her teaching position and now working a pity job at her perfect sister's inn, Becky was not about to give up hope. She wouldn't be stuck in this tiny, coastal Maine town forever.

She reached the Clairmont public beach, remembering the day she'd spent there with Maddy during the summer. They'd worn fabulous new swimwear and had the attention of nearly every male on the sand. Not that Maddy had noticed. She was so heartbroken over her little fight with her boyfriend, she didn't realize she had guys waiting in line to take his place. That was just another difference between them. Maddy was irritatingly single-minded. Becky believed in variety.

She circled back toward Maddy's Inn. Nearing the house, she couldn't help but wonder what it would be like to wake up on the day after your wedding in the arms of the one man in the world you had waited for. Becky slowed and approached the porch. Her thoughts were positively maudlin. She would not think about her sister or how she'd spent the last twelve hours. It was none of her business. She wouldn't give it another thought.

***

"But seriously, tell me."

Maddy Fordham didn't even spare a glance for Becky as she put the carafe back in the coffee maker. "The water's so choppy today. Must be windy."

"You can't distract me," Becky pressed. "How was ... everything?"

" 'Everything' is none of your business, and you know it," Maddy said with more of an edge than Becky expected.

Maddy did look a little haggard. Must have been a long night. "You look pretty rough. Long night?"

Maddy poured cream in her coffee and put the carton away in the fridge with a sigh. "John will be back any minute with the boys."

"Okay, we'll make this fast."

"I'm not telling you anything."

"You don't have to. I'll guess, and then you can, you know, correct me if I'm wrong."

Maddy rolled her eyes.

"I know. So this is what I imagine. You had a romantic ride home in that horse-drawn carriage ..."

"Didn't work out. The driver got the flu. We came home in John's truck."

Becky smiled, undeterred. "He carried you over the threshold and up the stairs ..."

She waited for Maddy's revised version, but only received a scowl, so she went on, " ... into the Captain's Quarters, which was full of balloons." She glanced at her sister. "Nice touch, huh?"

"Hilarious." Maddy's expression did not suggest that she was amused. "I just asked for some cheese and crackers and maybe a bottle of," she choked a little, "champagne."

"I did all that, too. And the chocolate covered strawberries," Becky pointed out. "And the ..."

"I know, I know," Maddy interrupted her. "You thought of everything."

Becky smiled smugly. "Yes, I did. And really, you don't seem very grateful." She sat back with her coffee. "Maddy, what happened?" It suddenly occurred to her that Maddy might not have had the memorable night that she'd tried not to imagine.

"Nothing."

"Fine, don't tell me. But really, Maddy, 'nothing' on your wedding night is a bit of a stretch, even for you."

Maddy swirled the coffee in her mug.

A few more minutes of strained silence confirmed Becky's growing suspicion that all had not been magical at Maddy's Inn the night before.

"Please tell me that 'nothing' means you don't want to tell me. I mean, I know you don't want to tell me, but tell me this is your way of not telling me, and not that there's nothing to tell."

Becky watched Maddy's face carefully and felt an incredibly unwelcome sense of remorse when her sister teared up.

"I'm sorry, Maddy, I shouldn't have ... It's none of my business. Just tell me that John isn't ..."

Maddy blinked. "Isn't what?"

Becky stalled. "I don't know. He was interested, right?"

"I wouldn't know. I assume he was, but I wasn't ..."

"*You* weren't?"

"No! Yes! Of course I was! I just didn't, I couldn't ..."

"Oh Maddy, of course you could!"

"Just let me finish!" Maddy sighed. "Everyone kept refilling my champagne glass last night - congratulating us and toasting us - and you know how tired I was, and I don't drink much."

"And you passed out." Becky bit back a smile.

Maddy slumped over her coffee. "Yes," she whispered.

"And you didn't ..." Becky inhaled. "Was John mad?"

Maddy looked up. "Of course not. At least not that I could tell." She stared at her coffee. "I vaguely remember coming home, and yes, he carried me, but only because I couldn't walk."

Becky shook her head in wonder.

"The next thing I knew, the sun was streaming through the windows - killing my eyes - and John was getting ready to pick up his boys."

Becky considered her sister. There were so many ways she could respond to this unusual dilemma - very few of them charitable. She opted for gracious. "It's not such a big deal," she ventured.

"It's a huge deal!" Maddy moaned. "It was going to be so perfect, being together for the first time in the place where we met."

"I thought you met at the post office."

Maddy lifted her head long enough to glare at Becky. "You know what I mean."

Becky sipped her coffee. "It's kinda funny, really. You got married and didn't - ah ..."

Maddy continued to glare.

"Whereas *I* ..." Becky's smirk was a little forced.

Maddy raised her eyebrows. "You what?" She shook her head. "Oh, Becky. Who?"

A shriek and a stampede of little footsteps announced the arrival of John's two young sons, Blake and Parker, through the front door. Maddy, eyeing Becky with concern, stood and set her mug on the counter in preparation for the body slam hug that was in store.

"Miss Maddy!" Parker burst into the room with a five-year-old roar. "We're here!" He ran into her arms and hugged her fiercely.

"Hey, Parkerpants! Thanks for the heads-up. I would never have known!" Maddy hugged him back. "Where's Blake?"

"He's helping Dad get something out of the truck. And Burt, too."

Becky smiled at the idea of Maddy's huge Irish wolfhound helping John and Blake unload.

"Well, we'd better get out the donuts," her sister replied.

"Yes!" Parker released her and jumped up on the bar stool, noticing Becky for the first time. "Hi, Miss Becky! Your hair's messy. What happened?"

Now used to Parker's candid observations, Becky smoothed her hair. She didn't do messy, by anyone's standards. "I walked on the beach this morning. What's your excuse?"

Parker grinned and turned as the door opened. Burt trailed Blake into the kitchen, and both approached Maddy for their requisite hugs.

"How are you, Blake?" Maddy smiled at his proper, 'Fine, Miss Maddy,' while Burt greeted her effusively.

"How is he ever going to make it two weeks without you?" Becky asked, eyeing the dog with concern.

Maddy laughed and scratched his ears. "He loves you, too, Becky. You'll have a great time together."

"Right," she replied doubtfully, as Burt finally left Maddy's side and walked past in search of his water bowl.

"So, Blake," Becky addressed John's older son. "You're hanging out with your aunt and cousin for the next couple of weeks?"

Blake nodded. "They're coming to stay at our house with us."

"Yeah, we don't get to go on vacation with Dad," Parker explained. "It's for grownups."

Becky smiled, glancing over at Maddy. "Well, maybe next time you can go."

The familiar sound of John's boots on the dining room floor drew the girls' attention. Maddy shot Becky a warning glance as the door swung open.

John Fordham stopped in the threshold, apparently unprepared to be the sole focus of the two women in the room. "Everything okay?"

Becky smiled, biting her tongue as she considered the six-foot-something, handsome guy her sister had married the day before. *Lucky girl.*

Maddy reached up to kiss his cheek. "Hi, John."

He wrapped his arms around her and gave her a compelling kiss. Becky rolled her eyes and looked over at the boys, who'd walked over to mess with Burt. *At least they're occupied,* she thought, drumming her fingers on the counter.

"Hey, Blake and Parker," she finally said. "Let's go hunt for treasures on the beach."

They jumped up immediately. "Can Burt come?"

"Burt's the only one who can lead us to the treasure," she assured them. Sparing a quick glance at Maddy and John, she said, "We're going on an adventure. It'll probably take a while."

With that, she was out the door, herding her three very energetic boys onto the porch. She grabbed Burt's leash, and led them down to the sand.

"Better bring those buckets, guys. We've got some digging to do."

two

One more broken nail, and she was going to quit. Becky stopped scrubbing the bathroom floor and looked down in dismay at her right hand. Where were her perfectly manicured fingernails? She should have taken the time to find those stupid, ugly, rubber gloves, but she'd been too lazy. She'd always taken pride in her hands, and this cleaning up after people business was taking a toll.

Straightening up, she looked in the mirror and blew a wisp of hair out of her face; another part of her that had taken a hit. *No highlights - not a decent cut in months.* She reached up to tuck the blonde strands behind her ear, then recoiled in disgust. No way she would touch her hair with that hand. Groaning, she leaned on the sink and looked out through the bedroom windows to the ocean. How did she end up cleaning bathrooms in her sister's B & B?

Maddy and John had been on their honeymoon for a week, and Becky refused to think about them. She had enough on her plate running the inn while her sister started her wonderful new life with her gorgeous contractor. There was no point in bemoaning their very different life directions.

She washed her hands and walked out into the bedroom. Stepping onto the balcony, she breathed in the unseasonably warm-for-mid-October, salty air. She tried to see the ocean through her sister's eyes. Certainly, she admired it from an artist's point of view. That particular blue-green of the waves would be fun to recreate on canvas; the white caps broke up the color with a rhythm she thought she could capture. Still, Maddy seemed to draw a kind of inspiration from the water that Becky simply didn't understand.

She looked down the beach at the neighboring cottages and homes. How could Maddy stand being out here by herself?

But Maddy wasn't by herself, anymore. She had John now, and Blake and Parker. She wouldn't be tormented by the quiet. Becky shuddered despite the warm sun on her skin. She didn't like being alone. For someone who'd lived on her own for the past five years, she'd spent very little of that time by herself. These past weeks at Maddy's had been very eye-opening, and she wasn't sure she liked what she saw.

Becky drew in another deep breath. She'd go crazy if she spent another minute alone. Even Burt would be a distraction. She left the balcony, disheartened by the fact that she, the girl who used to have it all together, who always dressed perfectly and surrounded herself with interesting people, was reduced to wearing sweats, cleaning bathrooms, and seeking out the company of a dog.

It was better than the human alternative.

Becky tip-toed past the door of the only other person in the house on her way to get bedding from the Anchor Room. It wasn't likely that the obnoxious, ex-pro-football player would show his face on this Sunday afternoon, but she wasn't in the mood to take any chances. Hearing nothing as she leaned toward his door, she turned to the room across the hall. She'd be so glad when he finally left.

Her own shriek startled her. "What are you doing in here?"

The hulking former athlete turned from the window and scowled at her. "Same thing you are. Nothing."

Becky drew a calming breath and imagined herself perfectly coiffed and wearing Versace. Her confidence rallied a bit, and she started pulling sheets from the bed.

"I'm cleaning. I run the place, remember?"

He snorted. "Right, the maid. Nice pants."

Becky's dressed-to-kill fantasy evaporated as she looked down at her oldest pair of striped pajama pants. Not even sweats. She hadn't expected to see anyone this afternoon, least of all the Neanderthal from the Seashell Room. She pulled her T-shirt down to no avail. The gap exposing her midriff would normally escape her notice, but it drew his gaze, and she was determined not to give him any more of a show. She grabbed the sheets and stalked toward the door. She reached back and awkwardly hiked up her pants - holding the sheets in front of her didn't protect her backside - and immediately dropped half her load.

He actually laughed. She kicked the sheets out into the hall, refusing to bend down and pick them up while he was in viewing range. Safely behind the door, she leaned back in.

"I'll be back here in ten to clean. Please be gone. I've already taken out the trash."

***

The woman drove him crazy. Tank Kimball stepped into the hall and made sure she was gone before heading back to his room. He couldn't even have a few minutes to look at the ocean without her barging in on his peace and quiet. Why'd she give him a room without a view, anyway? It wasn't like she had any other guests.

He walked into his room and slammed the door, rattling the silly seascape painting on the wall. A tiny twinge of conscience made him walk over and adjust the picture. He loved the water, but this painting irritated him. The artist didn't get it, somehow. He glanced at the bottom right corner, and for the first time noticed the name - *her* name. She painted? He grunted. No wonder the picture made him mad.

He stretched and yawned, prowling the room. He'd come back to Clairmont to clear his head and plan for the future. He wanted to get away from people who knew him and who knew football and what a mess his career had become. He came to be alone and to think. The last thing he wanted was to be at the mercy of a blonde know-it-all who brought out the worst in him.

The bed groaned under his weight as he sat down. When had ignoring each other become open animosity? And what was his sister thinking, sticking him out here with this paper doll who knew nothing about running an inn and everything about irritating him? It's not like he was known for his charm, but for some reason, he found himself determined to be nasty to the woman whose job it was to take care of him - *for another whole week.*

He lay back on the bed and moaned. He'd never make it.

Footsteps sounded in the hall; she was probably returning to clean the room they'd just left. Was she getting ready for more guests? Who else would he have to try to avoid? He pulled himself off the bed and walked over to the window. *Nice view of the neighbor's house.*

He moved restlessly around the room, tempted to cross the hall and mess with her some more. Why did he feel the need to harass her? He'd managed to stay out of her path for the first few days, and everyone else at the inn as well. He'd taken the plate of food she left in the dining room for him every morning, timing his arrival to avoid interacting with anyone. It had worked until she decided to hassle him about his bill.

Did she honestly think he wouldn't pay? She'd come to his door, insisting that he sign some forms. *He'd been there for so many days and she didn't have any proof of his ability to pay.* He hadn't actually spoken to her before that point. Grace, his sister, had handled everything; he'd just moved his things into the room while the women talked. He'd seen enough of Becky to know she was just like all the women he'd spent the last eight years trying to avoid; surface, self-absorbed, determined to suck everything she could from one man before moving on to the next.

He had no problem giving her a wide berth, until she'd had the nerve to come up to his room. Didn't she know he wanted to be left alone? He'd decided to cash in on his size and make quick business of intimidating her.

It didn't work.

He'd come to the door in a T-shirt, sweats, and a scowl. He'd braced his hands high on the door and the frame and leaned toward her in a way that made most men squirm. She'd taken a step back initially, wide-eyed and a little disconcerted, then she'd thrown her shoulders back, lifted her chin, and asked him for his name.

His name! No one called him anything but Tank, and he wasn't about to tell this nobody his real name. Did he have a credit card? Not likely. She kept pressing him until his blood boiled. People rarely ever dared to push him, but this little ... innkeeper just wouldn't quit.

Her big brown eyes didn't work on him, and he'd never cared for blondes. She could take her little act elsewhere; he wasn't interested. Maybe that's why he felt he had to drive her away every chance he had. Her kind was dangerous.

***

Becky actually flinched when she heard the door open across the hall. She took a deep breath and braced herself. Whatever hostility had developed between them over the last few days had to stop. She had to find a way to be civil to him for Maddy's sake. Determined not to rise to his bait again, she flipped out the sheets. Let him come in and give her grief. At least she had pants on.

Tank did his 'arms on the frame, lean in the door' thing. Becky glanced up and refused to be intimidated or impressed by his size. She offered a carefully bland expression.

"Can I help you?"

"Are you expecting anyone else this week?"

She swallowed her surprise; a normal question? She hardly knew how to respond.

"You're it until next weekend." *Gonna be a long week*, she added silently. She blew the hair out of her eyes and smoothed the sheets before adding the comforter. *Please go away.*

"Can I move into this room?"

She turned to him with her hands on her hips. "Why?"

He shrugged, probably getting a workout, just moving those traps up and down. She focused back on his face; his disagreeable, perpetually frowning face. His crew cut only made him appear more formidable. She couldn't even tell the color of his hair with how short he kept it. Darkish, anyway; just like his personality. She raised a brow, determined not to snap.

"I like the water."

Three non-combative sentences in a row. The man was capable of conversation! She eyed him speculatively. No expression touched his fearsome face. Actually, his face wasn't so fearsome at the moment - just moderately scary. If she was being very generous, she'd admit that when the dark brows weren't crowding over them, the deep-set eyes just might be ... interesting.

Back to the question. He wanted to change rooms. Well, as long as he stayed out of the Captain's Quarters, the only room booked for the following weekend, she couldn't care less where he slept. She had to clean his other room, anyhow.

"Fine. Since you're asking so *nicely,*" she smiled at him without warmth, and stuffed a pillow into the pillow case. She grinned genuinely as she considered the peach-colored bedding. "I'm not changing these sheets again. They manly enough for you?"

Okay, stupid remark. No need to stir things up.

She glanced at him but he said nothing. Did she imagine the color touching his cheeks? Probably. The man had no soul.

"Okay, well, I'll be out of here in a few minutes. You can move in any time."

"Thanks." He turned and left.

Becky stared at the door. *What was that about?* He was almost human. Laying the bedspread out, she suddenly felt strange about having her hands all over his sleeping space. She fluffed the pillows and gave the room a quick once-over. Cracking the windows open to let in the fresh air, she left him to his new room.

***

Tank walked along the beach, glad to be out of the house and away from the innkeeper. Apparently, she wasn't even that. It was just his luck the real owners were gone while he was staying there. He shrugged out of his jacket. At least he'd have a better room for the rest of the week. The view from the Anchor Room, or whatever she called it, was much better than his current room. It was smaller, but that didn't matter. As long as he could stretch his limbs on the beach during the day and hear the waves at night, he didn't care about his sleeping space.

In a few days, he could move into his own place, and he was looking forward to calling someplace home. He'd been running since early spring, and he was tired. He'd sold his condo and traveled, seeking distraction; anything to keep from confronting the truth that he'd probably never play football again.

The truth of it ripped him up inside. Football had been his life for as long as he could remember. He'd wanted to be a running back or a wide receiver, but he just kept growing. No one expected his speed to keep up with his height and weight, but it did, all through high school and into his pick of colleges. His formidable size made him a linebacker to be reckoned with, right into the draft his senior year.

He rubbed the back of his neck as he walked. Stupid concussion. He'd felt fine after that last hit, he just needed a few minutes to catch his breath. Turned out it was hours before he came back around, and by then the game was over and his future decided. You could only have so many concussions before they put you on the bench, permanently.

His appointment two weeks earlier - his last ray of hope - had confirmed it. Another concussion would put him in a really bad place, might even kill him. While any concussion was potentially life-threatening, Tank had maxed out on his luck. No way his team would take him back now. No one would take a chance on him. He was a walking time bomb.

His gaze swept the water - funny how that could always soothe him - and he wondered how he'd ever come to terms with a life without football. What would he do? Money wouldn't be an issue for a while, that much was good. He'd been conservative and invested well; didn't party as much as some of the other boys.

He picked up a piece of driftwood and heaved it into the water. All the money in the world didn't make a difference. He wanted to play football.

three

Becky put Tank's breakfast on the warmer and finished cleaning up the kitchen. It felt much more like fall, but the weather was still great for a jog. Burt would be happy; she'd missed taking him out the day before.

"Alright, Burt, time for a run," she called as she walked onto the porch.

The dog lay under the table pining for his owner, but he did open his eyes when she said 'run.' He stood, stretched, and lumbered over to her.

Becky scratched his ears. "You've got less than a week, buddy, and she'll be back. You'll make it." She stepped down to the beach, and after stretching briefly, started her jog. Burt kept up, distracting himself with the birds and the beach treasures. He trotted on ahead.

Becky concentrated on breathing evenly and avoiding driftwood and rocks. These runs were a mixed blessing. Now that everything in her life was uncertain, it gave her much-needed, and much-feared time to think. What was she going to do?

Planning for her future, uncertain as it was, was better than thinking about the past. She'd really liked her job at the academy, and had hoped to be offered a contract for another year. The board had debated cutting the art program all summer long, but the headmaster had gone to bat for her. She'd been thrilled until she found out why.

He'd wanted to sleep with her, of course. Said she'd sent all those signals and was sure they had an understanding. He'd even come to her home to tell her the good news about her three-year contract. When she declined the offer, the art program suddenly lost its funding.

Becky tossed her head. She was tired of the assumptions that men made about her. She was tired of men, period.

She focused again on her surroundings. Burt was behaving and trotting happily just a couple yards in front of her. She picked a spot ahead on the beach for her turn-around point and amped up the speed a bit.

While she was glad for a place to come and sort things out, spending time with Maddy had been challenging in its own way. Thankfully, planning and helping to run the inn while Maddy got ready for the wedding had filled almost every waking moment. Becky had had little time to think about how very happy Maddy was, and how very empty her own life had become in comparison.

For the last week, however, she'd had plenty of time. After seeing Maddy and John off, she spent the day with her parents before they returned home, then prepared for the couples due to arrive the Monday after the wedding. Tank had been a surprise, but she figured Maddy would be happy for the business, and since he was pretty low maintenance at first, it had been no big deal.

Once she got into the routine of making breakfasts and doing the minimal clean-up after the guests, she was left with all kinds of time to contemplate where she'd been and where her life was going. The one thing she really didn't want to contemplate was how she spent the night of Maddy's wedding, but that seemed to haunt her the most.

It was almost a relief when she'd picked a fight with Tank. At least she had someone to be mad at besides herself, and there was a whole lot to be mad at with Tank - physically and emotionally.

All she'd done was ask for a credit card. Any reasonable person would have given her one at check-in. When she'd asked for his name, you'd have thought she asked him to cut off his right arm. What kind of name was 'Tank,' anyway?

Since it was Grace's brother, she'd initially given him space and figured he'd come around to take care of business. She liked

Grace, loved her coffee shop, and figured her brother would be an interesting distraction, at least.

Interesting was hardly the word.

Men like Tank made her want to be done with men. She warmed to the thought. Maybe if she swore off men, they'd stop harassing her, both the ones haunting her dreams, and the all-too-real ones roaming the halls of her sister's house.

***

"I'm done with men forever." Becky sipped her Americano as she relaxed in the booth of her friend's coffee shop. The more she said it, the more right it felt. Who needed men? They caused nothing but trouble and regret. She'd had enough of both.

Grace Kimball looked at her apologetically. "Is my brother driving you crazy?"

"Well, yeah, but it's not just him. He's just a great big reminder of how terrible they all are." Becky sipped her drink again. "Okay if I vent about him?"

Grace laughed, her green eyes dancing. "Of course. I told you to keep me posted. There's really not much you can say that would shock me." She sipped her tea. "I'm just sorry he's been so difficult for you. I should have had him stay at Maplewood."

"Yeah, well, he needed his privacy, you said."

"I doubt it would have made much difference. It just seemed a little more off the beaten path out there. Besides, I thought Maddy could use the business."

"She'll be happy he was here. I'll be happy when he's gone."

Grace laughed again. "Do you want me to talk to him?"

"No, we're actually doing okay for the moment. He switched rooms yesterday, so at least I got in to clean the other one."

"Charge him extra for the trouble. He can afford it."

"Oh, I will."

"So, Maddy's back on Saturday?"

"Yep. Late. I've got a couple coming in on Friday, but that's it. Should be a quiet week if your brother behaves. He leaves on Saturday, right?"

"Yeah, his cottage should be all set by then - furnished and ready to go. It's the place my family always rented for vacations when we were kids."

"Oh, that's right. You didn't grow up here, either. I always feel like I'm the only one from out of town."

"Nope. There are a few of us. I just kind of came back on a whim, well, and on a really good real estate lead." Grace smiled. "I can't believe they're still renting the house out. I hope that makes it feel more like home for him."

"I'm sure he'll be happy to have his own space," Becky replied. "Now that he's found his way out of his room, he does a lot of prowling. It would be okay if he weren't so scary big, and *quiet*. How does he do that?"

"I don't know, but it's a well-honed skill. When we were little, well, when *I* was little, he used to sneak up on me and scare me all the time. It never got old for him." Grace furrowed her brow at the memory.

"At least we don't have that kind of relationship," Becky conceded, relieved. "He mostly tries to avoid me, but if I ever have him cornered, he's like a caged animal, ready to attack."

"Well, not all men are like Tank. You don't need to write them all off."

"Yeah, I think I do," Becky replied. She narrowed her eyes at her friend. "You're looking a little dreamy-eyed. That's not like you."

Grace grinned. Grace, her serious businesswoman friend, *grinned.*

"Is it that guy from Saturday? The high school friend?"

Grace continued to smile. "Yep."

"Really? Wow. Well, he *is* gorgeous," Becky conceded. "But you didn't seem so happy with him when I last saw you."

"I wasn't. I was overwhelmed - Tank had just thrown me a curve ball about the shop, and I just didn't think I could handle a new relationship." Grace shrugged. "Anyway, we talked yesterday. Alex came back to the shop and was very ... compelling," she smiled. "We're going to try the long-distance thing. It may not work, but," she sighed happily.

Becky rolled her eyes. "You were the one person I thought I could count on to be rational." She shook her head, but couldn't help smiling a little. "I'm happy for you. When will you see him again?"

"He's coming back this weekend. He may be in touch about staying at Maddy's."

"Well, if you're sure you want him around Tank." Becky picked up her empty mug and slid out of the booth. "Just have him give me a call."

"Great - thanks." Grace followed, gathering her dark brown hair back into a pony tail. "Take care of him, but, you know, not too much." She grinned sheepishly and tied her apron.

"Done with men *forever*," Becky reminded her with a determined smile, and made her way out of the coffee shop.

***

Becky neared the house with trepidation. She didn't like feeling this way about coming back to her own home. Well, it was more her home than *his*. Tank's Jeep was still parked in the drive. Why didn't he go out to eat or something? Did he really think the whole town would fall apart over an ex-football player? *Big deal.*

She walked around to the oceanside porch and paused when she saw Tank and Burt out on the beach. They were a perfect pair; neither one looked abnormally huge when they were together. Tank was tossing pieces of driftwood and Burt was having a great time chasing them.

Tank was in short sleeves and had worked up a bit of a sweat heaving the large pieces of wood around. His arms were huge. Becky was not about to take in the spectacle for another minute. She turned to sneak back around the front of the house before either one of them saw her.

Too late.

Burt loped around the side of the house. Becky tried to urge him back, to no avail. He ran right up to her, tail wagging, and she had no choice but to greet him. Tank followed a moment later. Rounding the corner, he simply stopped and stared with his dirty hands on his hips. Then he turned and walked back to the beach.

Becky grabbed Burt's collar and walked him into the house. "We need to find you better friends."

four

Since Tank had yet to show up for breakfast during the last week and a half, Becky decided to take it easy on Tuesday. She'd had coffee and scones or muffins on by seven a.m. every other morning, and a hot breakfast available between nine and eleven. Since there was no way he'd be getting out of bed, she wasn't going to, either. She hadn't slept well, and there was nothing compelling her to get up, except preparing food that was going to get cold, anyway. She sure wasn't eating it. Resetting her alarm, she snuggled back under the blankets.

Fifteen minutes later, a gentle bell sounded. John had rigged it to ring in several places throughout the inn, and one of them, of course, was Becky's bedroom behind the kitchen.

Did she have a new guest? She squinted at the clock - just past eight in the morning, mid-week, late October; not likely. The only alternative was Tank, and she could hardly imagine that he'd suddenly become an early riser. Curious, she threw on some jeans and a T-shirt, quickly combed through her hair and brushed her teeth. Make-up would have to wait.

She opened the door between her room and the kitchen. Her one and only guest paced like a wild animal, turning when he heard her enter.

"Breakfast ready?"

Her dislike of him multiplied exponentially. What kind of person didn't even say 'hello'? Becky walked to the fridge, yanked open the door, and pulled out an orange. She tossed it to him while she rummaged for other ingredients. Tank caught it, of course; stupid athlete reflexes.

"Homemade orange juice this morning, compliments of you." Deciding not to wait and see if he was going to heave it back at her, she pulled out the eggs, bacon, and butter. *Coffee, first.*

"By the way, I've had breakfast ready early every morning this week." She glared at him. "Coffee will be ready in five, the rest will follow whenever. Why don't you wait outside?"

The rain beating against the windows almost drowned out his reply. "Hospitality business really suits you."

"Yes, I was born to take care of helpless grown men. It's what I live for."

She ground the coffee good and long, hoping that the noise would irritate him and he would leave. *No luck.* She made a production out of measuring the coffee and pouring the filtered water. He still hadn't moved. Finally she turned around with arms crossed.

He was gone.

Becky glanced out to the porch - had he gone out to sit in the rain? She refused to look for him, or be curious about how he'd escaped the kitchen unnoticed. She didn't care how he did his disappearing act, as long he kept doing it.

Fifteen minutes later, the omelets were finished and sitting in the warmer. Of course, Tank was nowhere to be seen. This time she did hunt him down. If he was going to get her out of bed, he was going to choke down the food she'd made for him while it was hot.

He wasn't in the parlor, front office or dining room, and she knew he wasn't in the sunroom next to the kitchen. Had he really gone out to the porch? She walked to the window and peaked out. *No one there.* She followed the route he must have taken up the back stairway to the second floor and all but stomped down the hall to his room.

Knocking sharply on the door, Becky waited with her hands on her hips. She knocked again, and was just about to call out when she heard the bed creak. She waited an eternity for the beast to make his way to the door.

He didn't even open it. "Yeah?"

He actually sounded like he'd been sleeping. For the briefest moment Becky doubted that he'd even awakened her, but she shook that off. He'd been down there alright. No way she'd imagined that whole debacle.

"Your breakfast is ready, *Mr. Kimball.*"

Hearing no response, Becky grew impatient. What was his deal?

"Fine."

Fine. *That was it?* He got her up early to make his breakfast just so he could go back to sleep? "You've got five minutes, then I'm giving it to Burt."

The door creaked open, and she kept her eyes averted from his too-tight T-shirt.

"Leave it in the warmer."

"No."

"Leave it in the warmer."

"No. They're omelets."

"They'll be fine."

"Why did you get me up if you're just going to sleep?"

He shrugged, yawning.

"You are *impossible.*" She bristled with the urge to shove him, which must have been evident, because he half-smiled.

"You gonna take a swing at me?"

"I'd love to, believe me, but my sister wouldn't approve."

"Your sister, the real innkeeper."

"I really, really can't stand you."

Tank smiled.

Burt whined from down below, giving Becky her out. "Sounds like I have another animal to feed. You have four minutes."

***

Becky tried a new dish on Wednesday morning. Tank didn't deserve it, but she figured it was a good time to try a new recipe. If it didn't turn out, no big deal. She had no doubt she'd hear about it one way or another.

The blueberry french toast bake that she left for him disappeared before noon, and Becky shook her head with a grudging smile. The man should be a spy, the way he could sneak all that mass around, undetected. She wondered what kind of football player he was. It seemed like he was too big to be a running back, and he didn't have the charisma she thought necessary to be a quarterback. *Probably some kind of lineman; big, scary, and mean.*

She was happy that the big, scary, mean guy had taken to playing outside with Burt. Besides her morning run, she hadn't really spent any considerable time with him. The poor dog missed Maddy so much it was almost comical. Becky was glad that Tank distracted him. At least he was good for something.

She decided to take some leftovers to Maddy's neighbor, Otis Jensen. He rarely cooked for himself, and a warm meal might be appreciated. Walking out onto the porch, she winced as the door *banged!* behind her. She noted that Burt's leash was missing; Tank must have taken him for a walk.

Otis was on his screened porch, reading the newspaper, and Becky called out to him as she approached. "Hey, Otis! Want to try one of my latest experiments?"

He stood with a smile as she let herself through the door. "I'd love to. Thank you, Becky."

"It's a new french toast bake I tried." She set the plate on the table. "Beats making individual pieces, especially when the house is full of guests."

"Sounds delicious," Otis said. "Been busy over there?"

"It's slow this week. Just one guest. Had several couples last week; that's probably good for mid-October."

"Well, word will get out, and Maddy's Inn will take off. I just feel sure of it."

"You don't mind the extra neighbors?"

"At my age, it's fun to watch life still happening around me," Otis replied. "Everyone coming out to a B&B on the water is here to relax and enjoy themselves. That generally makes for good neighbors." He reached for the plate and lifted it close. "Mmmm ... smells wonderful. I think I'll have it for lunch."

"I hope our current guest hasn't given you any trouble," Becky said.

"Tank?" Otis looked up with concern. "Why would he be trouble?"

"You've met him?" Becky wasn't sure she liked the idea of Tank helping himself to her friend. Besides, she didn't want him bringing Otis down.

"Tank's been good company the last few days. I'll be sorry to see him go."

"Really? You've spent time together?"

"Sure. He introduced himself, oh, a few days back while he was out walking on the beach. He joined me one evening for a meal and we play cribbage in the afternoons."

Becky was absolutely stunned. Tank had been Mr. Sociable with eighty-year-old Otis, but had barely shown his face around the inn?

"Well, I'm glad he's been, um, friendly."

"He's a fine young man. Always out there playing with Burt, which is no small thing. Too bad about the football. Can't imagine how disappointing that must be."

Becky clearly didn't have the right audience for venting about Tank. "Well, I hope you enjoy your lunch. I'd better get back and, well, get busy," *doing absolutely nothing* ...

"Thanks so much for stopping by - and for lunch." Otis stood, always the gentleman. "Have you heard from Maddy and John at all?"

Becky shook her head. "I don't suppose they're thinking about me right now."

Otis chuckled. "I suppose not. I'm sure they know you've got everything under control here."

Yes, everything was going perfectly.

***

"Can you move your Jeep? I need to water the yard and your vehicle is about to get doused."

Tank didn't even look up from the book he was reading. His long legs stretched to the middle of the wicker coffee table. *Irritating*. The man just took up too much room.

"It rained yesterday."

"Yeah, well, it's been dry lately and the grass needs water."

He eyed her cynically. "And where will my Jeep be safe from your horticultural expertise?"

Big words for the dumb athlete. "Bar Harbor."

The corner of his mouth almost lifted, but Tank caught it in time. "How 'bout I water the lawn and you go to Bar Harbor?"

The three-hour trip sounded very appealing. Tank had made it a point to be underfoot all afternoon, which is to say he'd been hanging out on the porch, and she'd had enough. It was another unseasonably nice day, and Becky wanted the porch so she could paint. If she couldn't paint, she was going to water his Jeep.

"I'll go set up the sprinkler. We'll see where the water falls, and then you can decide."

That got him to his feet. He was surprisingly quick for a big guy. "You'd enjoy that wouldn't you?"

He trailed her around the house to where she already had the sprinkler attached to the hose. She bent to turn the water on and he reached for her arm.

"Easy! I'm not really going to spray your car - yet."

He backed off, leaving her plenty of space. "I have to go inside and get my keys. Do you think you can hold off that long?"

"I really couldn't say. You'd better run."

Tank gave her a look of utter exasperation and jumped up the front steps to the porch.

Becky smiled, thoroughly enjoying having the upper hand for a few, brief, satisfying moments. Tank returned in record time, and Becky made sure she appeared nice and relaxed as she leaned against the side of the porch, filing her nails.

He barely spared her a glance as he hopped into his Jeep and roared out of the driveway. Becky watched with surprise as he peeled down the street. She hadn't really expected him to leave altogether.

Well, good riddance.

She scanned the yard. Who watered their grass in October? She went back to the porch to paint.

five

Tank walked onto the porch and stopped short. A pair of long, bare legs, crossed at the ankle and perched on the far railing, caught his eye. Even in the dim light from the few flickering candles, Becky's outline was clear. He'd been inclined to think of her as too skinny, but there was nothing wrong with the legs that graced the porch this evening.

He contemplated going back inside, but there was no way she hadn't already heard the *bang!* of the screen door. He was tempted to fix the silly thing himself; it drove him crazy every time he left the house.

Tank sighed and waited for a moment to see if she'd react. *Nothing.* He took a tentative step forward. Finally, a wineglass swung into view, then Becky's arm, shoulder and head followed. She waved him over with her beverage.

"Mr. Kimball!" she said, with much more enthusiasm than he'd ever heard from her mouth regarding him. "It's you! Come and sit. It's beautiful out here tonight."

It really wasn't. It was chilly, almost cold. He didn't know what she was doing in shorts. Becky sipped her wine and waved her glass again. She barely seemed to have a hold of it with her two fingers. Tank wasn't sure he wanted to be around to clean up after her.

"I have more wine!" she said, as though he'd won the lottery.

He advanced slowly. Becky had turned to face the beach again. She wore a big, baggy sweatshirt, but the rest was still uncertain. She'd definitely made a dent in that bottle she was offering.

"Sit!" she said, slurring the word a little, and making the invitation sound a bit like an expletive.

Raising his eyebrows in surprise, he found himself obeying by perching on the edge of a hardy Adirondack chair. The wood creaked and groaned. There would be no perching. Tank sat down in the chair and waited. This was probably not the time to hassle her or pick a fight. In a few minutes she might even need to be hauled to bed. He decided to see how things played out.

"You never talk," Becky complained, reaching for the bottle on the table. "Here, have some." She looked around and giggled. "No more glasses!"

It was much funnier to her than it should have been, but Tank found himself smiling, in spite of himself.

"You can use mine, if you like," she offered, almost dropping her glass, again. "Or just drink from the bottle. That's what real men do, right?"

He eyed her and considered the offer. Then he reached over and picked up the bottle. Shiraz. *Figures.* He lifted it to his lips and took a swig.

"It's good," he lied.

Becky grinned, and he found her smile almost attractive in the candlelight, especially since it wasn't filled with venom.

"I'm just having a little party," she informed him, sipping again from her glass. "We have new guests."

"I noticed." The couple, probably in their late thirties, had arrived early in the evening. The husband, or so he assumed, had been very attentive to Becky. Tank wondered what she made of that constant attention.

"They're very nice," she went on. "Verrry friendly," she snickered, though the amusement had left her eyes. She took another drink.

"Where are they now?"

"All tucked in," Becky sighed and blew the hair out of her eyes. He'd seen her do that before. It was distracting.

"Mr. Reynolds said he'd be down later, you know, in case I was *lonely,*" she told him, swinging her glass some more. "I thought maybe it was him," she stopped and tried to focus, "*he,* when you came out just now."

Drunk and grammar conscious. Tank shook his head. Apparently, she was planning to hook up with her married guest. Here was the Becky he'd come to dislike so intensely. He took the glass from her hand.

"Do you want me to leave?"

She looked at him wide-eyed, almost fearful; the first honest response he'd seen from her. She caught herself and shrugged. "Do whatever you want. I'm done with men forever."

"Excuse me?"

"I'm done with men, *forever*," she repeated, as though talking to a very small child.

"Got it. Does your friend know that?"

"Dunno. Where's my glass?"

"Here," Tank said, replacing it gently between her fingers. "Careful."

Becky swung the glass to her lips. "Men are so predictable. They all want one thing, even if they're married." She glanced at him. "Except you."

"I don't?" Tank asked, his mouth curving up a little. He might as well have some fun at her expense.

"Not with me, you don't." She shifted in her seat so she was facing him. "That's why I'm safe with you." She pointed unsteadily with her glass. "You don't like me."

"I see." The fact that Becky felt safe with him kicked in his protective instinct. He wished he could kick it back out.

"Most men like me. Actually, *all* men like me," she leaned her head back and rolled her eyes. "I'm done with men forever." She swung her gaze back to his. "But we can be friends."

"We can?"

"Yeah, cuz you're immune to me."

That was probably true.

"You should probably stop drinking and get some sleep," he suggested.

She turned with a pout and faced the water again. "Maddy loves the water. My sister, I mean. The *real* innkeeper, remember?" She raised a brow. "Maddy would not be drunk on the porch while she had guests." She sipped her wine. "Maddy would not be drunk on the porch, *ever.* Good ol' Maddy," she sighed. "Too bad for you, huh?"

Tank shook his head and let her talk.

"She can look at the water and and just calm right down. I don't get it." Becky ruffled her hair and took another sip. "I need this to calm down, so don't bother telling me to stop."

An admission of weakness? *Interesting.* "Okay," he replied.

She narrowed her eyes. "Don't pretend to be nice. I like not liking you."

Tank grinned and reached for the bottle. Might as well get rid of some of her supply.

"I mean, what's not to not like?" Becky continued, looking at him a little too intently.

He took another swig and grimaced. *Nasty stuff.*

"You're big and scary and mean." She cocked her head. "Well, you're bigger than most. Why are you so big?"

"Wait!" She waved her wineglass, as though to stop him from answering her question. Like he would.

"Football, right? Big, fancy, po-fressional football flavor."

Becky started to giggle at her string of mistakes. "Bet no one's ever called you a flavor before." She leaned back and laughed.

"Nope." He shook his head again, trying to ignore her laughing smile. It was unaffected and ... he decided not to think about it. Just like he wasn't going to think about her legs. What he did allow himself to think about was the fact that she wasn't going to be in any kind of shape to make breakfast for her guests in the morning. Then he wished he hadn't thought about that, either.

"I don't think I ever dated a football player," she chattered on, "but I went out with everyone else." She closed her eyes and the smile left her face. He had the feeling she was about to pour her heart out, and he wasn't sure he wanted to hear it.

"*Everyone.*" She opened her eyes and swung her head in his direction. "No one's safe from me." Her gaze was surprisingly piercing for her inebriated state.

Tank shrugged. He wasn't much of a conversationalist to begin with, and this was definitely uncomfortable territory. He really didn't want to know anything else about her. Not this way.

"Of course, you have nothing to say. What can you say?" She squinted at the water, as though she was still trying to extract some of her sister's magic out of it. "I slept with someone after Maddy's wedding."

That got his attention. He watched Becky's face as she continued to recount something that clearly pained her. She kept her eyes closed, but her delicate brow furrowed as she unloaded.

"Someone. Didn't even know him. That's what I am now."

Tank fought the urge to feel sorry for her. Wasn't she just confirming everything he'd suspected? He played with the label on the bottle, mostly to keep it out of her reach.

"People sleep around all the time," he finally replied, not sure why he was trying to comfort her.

"Not my sister. Not her hubs ... hubs ... John." She shook her head. "Not even on their wedding night." Her hand flew to her mouth. "Oops! I wasn't 'spose to tell."

He tried not to smile. "Secret's safe with me."

"Some people wait for their wedding." Becky swirled the wine in her glass and looked out at the water.

Tank geared up for a major deflection in case she started grilling him about his personal life. There was no way he was going there with her.

"Some people can do it," she said with surprising authority. "But not me." Her head went back and her eyes closed. Tank thought she looked very sad.

"How 'bout I get you to bed?"

Her eyes flew open, and she smiled seductively. "Really, Mr. Kimball?"

He swallowed. No wonder guys fell all over her. Becky was an open invitation, appealing even in this state.

She took a hold of his hand and swayed as she maneuvered out of her chair. Tank took her glass and put it on the table. "Give me your other hand."

She braced herself on the table and then slowly raised her hand up to his shoulder. "Please, I have to touch your trasp ..." she giggled and fell into his chest.

Tank rolled his eyes and scooped her up into his arms. "Where's your room?" He started toward the door while she made herself way too comfortable exploring his shoulders. He gave her a little shake. "Just hold on. Stop doing ... *that*." He tried to sound firm and intimidating, but she just giggled and snuggled into his chest.

He grabbed the door handle and somehow managed to get her inside. He stepped carefully around Burt, who was sleeping on his mat just inside the door.

"Your room?"

He shook her again, but she had fallen asleep.

***

Tank flipped a pancake and checked the sausages. The coffee had turned out well, thanks to his sister and her great little shop. He glanced at the clock, wondering when Becky's guests would wander in. He contemplated how he might discourage the jerk who'd propositioned the innkeeper.

He didn't have long to plan.

"Good morning. Oh! I was expecting Becky!" A sleepy female voice interrupted his thoughts.

He turned. "Morning."

An attractive brunette smiled tentatively at him. "Mind if I have some coffee?"

"Sure, help yourself," he replied, not sure what the morning routine was, since he'd never been a part of it. He regretted that momentarily. It would be nice to know what he should be doing for these people.

"I'm Dana Reynolds," she said, pouring coffee into the mug Tank handed her. "My husband will be down in a few minutes."

"I'm Tank," he replied. "Breakfast will be right up. Cream's in the fridge."

"Thanks," she said, sipping her coffee. "Where's Becky?"

Tank flipped the last pancake and started piling the finished ones onto a platter. "She was a little under the weather this morning."

"Oh, I'm sorry." Mrs. Reynolds seemed genuinely concerned. "Are you her husband?"

Tank dropped a pancake on the floor. "Nope. Just helping out."

"Where's Ms. Jacobs?" There was only one person to whom that voice could belong.

Tank turned slowly and regarded the loser who'd been so quick to dismiss his pretty wife and hit on Becky. Girls would consider him handsome, Tank supposed. Fit, but scrawny.

"She's not available this morning." He looked squarely at the guest. "Guess I kept her out too late last night." He wasn't necessarily trying to flex, but it seemed like a good time to reach up and grab another frying pan; not that he needed one.

"Oh," Mrs. Reynolds smiled at the thought.

Her husband bristled, but didn't appear ready to challenge Tank. Few people did.

Tank continued to glower as he picked up the plate of food and moved toward his guests. Mr. Reynolds quickly made room for him, but Tank made it a point to stop and stand very close. Sometimes it was useful to tower.

"I'll be getting you whatever you need this morning."

***

Becky yawned and stretched and cringed at the pounding in her head. She squinted at the obnoxious sunlight pouring through the curtains, then sat bolt upright. It wasn't supposed to be pouring, yet. She glanced at the clock in fear.

Eleven o'clock! Maddy was going to kill her! What were her new guests thinking? Were they furious? She wasn't so worried about Tank. She threw off the covers and froze. *Tank.*

Oh! Why did he have to come out to the porch and witness her stupidity? She put her head in her hands. What had she said to him? What had she done? Patchy memories fought for her groggy attention. Something about trapezoids haunted her, but she really didn't want to think about it.

She stood up slowly. She'd think about Tank later. She had more pressing concerns.

***

"We had a nice breakfast. Your boyfriend took care of everything."

Becky choked on her coffee, glad she didn't spit it right out in Mrs. Reynolds' face. She cleared her throat and pasted on a smile, trying to wrap her pounding head around the idea of Tank making breakfast for her guests. Who else could it possibly have been?

"What a guy. I'm sorry I wasn't available to take care of you myself."

Mrs. Reynolds flipped through the magazine in her lap. "He was very attentive. I enjoyed our breakfast very much."

Very attentive? Maybe they weren't talking about the same person. She couldn't imagine Tank in the kitchen, much less cooking and serving strangers with a smile. Becky tried to still the pounding in her head with her hand. She would never drink wine again.

"I don't think he cares much for my husband."

Becky's head snapped to attention and she regretted it immediately. "He wasn't rude, was he?" This, she could imagine.

"Oh no, nothing like that. It was just one of those things. You can tell when men don't like each other." Mrs. Reynolds fingered one of the buttons on her blouse. She seemed very taken with the magazine in her lap.

Becky would kill Tank if he was rude to Maddy's guests - right after she thanked him for completely bailing her out and cooking breakfast for them. She couldn't make any sense of it. Why would he help her like that? She ventured into the scary territory of the evening before. *They couldn't possibly have ...*

She shook her head. No way. *Done with men forever.* She repeated her mantra several times to regain her emotional footing.

Becky looked out over the water, willing Maddy's ocean to calm her. She'd have to go find Tank and thank him. Her stomach, already unsettled, rebelled at the prospect. The idea of running into Mr. Reynolds on the way was enough to make her run screaming down the beach, even with her headache.

She took a deep breath. Maddy was coming home tonight. She had to get this sorted out. She would be professional with her guests, and she'd thank Tank and send him packing. Then she would make every effort to insure that she never, ever saw him again.

six

Becky slowly climbed the stairs, considering how to knock on Tank's door *(tap, rap, pound?)* and dreading the brutally uncomfortable interaction that was sure to follow. What he must think of her, she didn't care to contemplate. She still hadn't processed the extent of her drunken rant. Had she really told him about sleeping with someone after Maddy's wedding? She desperately hoped she imagined that part. She'd agonized over it enough in her private thoughts.

Drawing a fortifying breath, she walked down the hall, slowing when she noted that his door stood ajar. Should she knock or call out?

Knocking was definitely less scary, so she tapped lightly on the door.

No response.

She tapped again. Nothing.

"Mr. Kimball?"

She pushed gently on the door. The room was empty.

Tank had cleared out with all of his stuff. Becky stood in the middle of the room, her hands planted on her hips. *Figures; coward.*

She walked to the window and looked out at the beach. Well, she got what she wanted. Tank was gone, and she didn't even have to apologize; *not yet, anyway.* She should be very relieved.

She crossed the room and yanked the sheets from the bed, wondering when she'd see him so she could put the whole mess behind her. She didn't like loose ends. What if he told Grace?

No doubt, he would. Becky sighed. So much for that friendship. She carried the sheets down to the laundry room, and heard Burt fussing at the front door.

Maybe Tank hadn't left, yet. There might still be a chance to get this all resolved before he moved out.

She started the load, smoothed her hair and made her way through the house. Burt was definitely waiting for someone to make an appearance. Whoever it was, was not coming in on their own.

No way it's Tank.

Her momentary disappointment was just that. Becky reached the door and hauled it open. The handsome guy from the coffee shop - Grace's guy - stood on the porch.

"Come on in," Becky said, seamlessly switching gears into charm mode. "Nice to see you again ..."

"Alex," he supplied.

"Right. Becky," she said, taking his hand. "Grace said you might be stopping by."

He stepped inside. "And this is?" He reached his hand out to Burt, who was desperately trying to get around Becky to say hello. She'd gotten pretty good at holding the one hundred plus pound dog at bay while greeting the guests.

"This is Burt. He's very gentle, but very big. Guess that's obvious."

Alex didn't seem concerned about the dog's size, and greeted the animal with the ease of a dog lover. "Grace said you might have a room available?"

"Sure. No problem. Come on over here and I'll get some information."

He followed her into the small office area, and in a few minutes Becky had everything she needed, including a credit card. *Nice dealing with a normal person.* She showed Alex to a room upstairs and asked if she could get him anything else.

"Thanks, I'm good."

"Heading out for coffee?" she smiled.

"Yeah, coffee sounds really good about now."

"Say 'hi' to Grace for me."

"Will do."

"And Alex, tell her ..."

"Yes?"

"Well, just tell her I'm really a nice person, no matter what her brother says."

He grinned. "There's a story there."

"There is, but I won't bore you with it."

"I'll deliver the message."

***

After Alex left, Becky trudged up the stairs again to clean Tank's room. At least he wasn't a pig. The only real evidence of his having stayed there was the bedding and towels, and they were already in the laundry. She glanced at a hat stand in the corner, and noticed Tank's sweatshirt draped over the top. He *would* use a hat stand for his dirty clothes. She pulled the sweatshirt down and held it up. It was enormous. She could fit into it several times and probably invite a friend. It smelled like Tank; not necessarily sweaty, but definitely lived in by him. *Enough of this*. Tossing it in the hall, she went back to work.

She wiped down the untouched dresser, smiling a little at Tank's having been trapped in this room with its delicate antique furniture. Had he attempted to sit in the chair by the desk? Judging by its ornate, spindly legs, she thought not. For a guy who'd shunned any kind of company, he'd picked an odd place to be alone with his thoughts. No wonder he was always out on the beach with Burt.

She ran the vacuum and gave the windows a once-over. No one else was currently scheduled to visit the inn until Thanksgiving. Of course, Alex might become a regular customer. She smiled at the thought. As much as she hoped for a kindred spirit in Grace, she couldn't deny the transformation that a good man had helped to bring about. Grace's new smile was nothing short of miraculous.

Becky sighed. Grace deserved to be happy. Maddy deserved to be happy. She'd be happy for them, and leave it at that.

***

Burt went wild with delight when Maddy, John and the boys stormed the inn just in time for dinner on Saturday.

Maddy absolutely radiated happiness; so did John. The group settled in the sunroom with Burt, who was content to rest at Maddy's feet once his energy was spent.

Becky smiled at the scene. For all that Maddy and John were clearly happy reuniting with the rest of their family, they were also very content just to be close to each other. They sat on the couch, John's arm draped around Maddy's shoulders, listening as the boys recounted their adventures with their aunt and cousin. John's hand gently stroked Maddy's arm.

For some reason, that one little gesture put a lump in Becky's throat, and she got up to get drinks. As happy as she was for them, she felt peripheral to their gathering. She got out lemonade for the boys and decided to brew some coffee for the adults.

Maddy joined her as she ground the beans. "Can I help?"

Becky directed her to the lemonade. "I'll be out in a minute with the coffee."

"Sounds good." Maddy slipped an arm around Becky's shoulder and gave her a squeeze. "Thanks so much for taking care of everything around here. The place looks great."

Becky smiled at her. "No problem. I enjoyed it, really."

She felt Maddy study her face for a moment. "But?"

"Well, it was fine, but we do have some debriefing to do." She blew her hair out of her eyes. "We had a few unexpected guests."

"Oh no! The mice?"

Becky laughed. "No, I mean real guests. We had a two-week single that ended today, and another single that just came today and will stay 'til tomorrow or Monday. The Reynolds are here, of course. They'll leave tomorrow."

"Right. Well, it's good to have some extra business this time of year. Everything go alright?"

"It was fine. Interesting. It's all okay now. I'll fill you in later."

Maddy eyed her with concern. "There's nothing I need to know?"

Becky thought for a brief moment. "No. Just watch yourself around Mr. Reynolds."

"Ew. Really? I'm so sorry. Do you want us to stay tonight?"

"No. It's nothing I can't handle."

"You're sure?"

"Of course. You need to go start your new life at John's house. You'll all be back here soon enough when the 'penthouse' is finished."

Maddy giggled. "I love it when you call it that."

Becky marveled at her sister's utter lack of anxiety about all of her recent life changes. *So not Maddy.* "You're lucky I'm here to run the show for a while. What would you do without me?"

Maddy hugged her again. "I don't ever want to find out."

***

Maddy, John and the boys left for the night, taking Burt with them. Soon afterward, Alex returned, planning to shower and head back out with Grace. The Reynolds had gone out for the evening. Becky was more than relieved.

Alex was getting ready to leave when a vehicle pulled into the drive. They'd been standing on the porch talking, when the headlights blinded them momentarily and then swung toward the shed on the side of the property. At first Becky thought the couple had returned, but then recognized the narrow set of the headlights. Only a Jeep had eyes like that.

Alex observed the size of the man getting out of the vehicle. "Is this Grace's brother?" he asked in a low voice.

Becky looked up in surprise. Apparently, they hadn't met yet. "Yes, indeed," she replied.

Tank approached the porch with his usual swagger-stomp. Becky couldn't help but grin a little, despite the fact that she dreaded dealing with their unfinished business.

"You left in a rush this morning," she said as he walked up the steps. "I found your sweatshirt." She'd planned to make eye contact, but got as far as his traps and froze. Color washed over her as a memory of exploring them with her hands, rather thoroughly, surfaced. She stepped back, mortified, and finally forced herself to look up into his eyes.

Tank simply stood regarding them both.

Alex stepped forward to shake his hand. "I'm Alex."

Tank nodded, took his hand. Becky, reeling from the memory of the night before, was glad she wasn't on the receiving end of that particular handshake.

"Where is it?"

She snapped to attention. He was right back to being awful, which made it easier for her to focus and answer his question. "Inside on the washing machine."

He moved to pass her. She almost grabbed his arm, but thought better of it. "Hang on, I'll get it."

"Don't bother."

He pushed past, and Becky shook her head at Alex's raised brows.

"So, that's Tank," she said quietly, watching him stride down the hall. She took a deep breath. "Charming, huh? I thought you might have met him, already."

"I can see the family resemblance, though I don't think you should tell Grace I said that."

Becky laughed. "I can see it in the coloring, that's about it. And the green eyes."

"You saw his eyes? His brows were so drawn it was hard to tell."

"I did see them once. He's been here two weeks, remember. It was one morning; I think it was too early for his scowl to be fully engaged."

Alex grinned but held his tongue. They could hear Tank returning.

Becky decided to thank him and get it over with. Maybe with Alex around, it wouldn't be as awkward. She wasn't sure she could handle another interaction with Tank, especially with that trap memory haunting her.

Taking another deep breath, she stepped into his path. For a moment, she didn't think he was going to stop.

She might just be Maddy's new welcome mat.

He paused inches away, clearly not worried about her personal space. He didn't say a word, just stared.

Becky reminded herself that no man made her nervous. First of all, she needed to see more than his Adam's apple, and she sure didn't need to be that close to any of his muscles. She took a step back and sought out his eyes; they were hooded, as always.

"I want to thank you for your help this morning. That was ... that was incredibly cool of you." Becky was not particularly good at eating humble pie, and this was a rather large piece. She felt like she might actually choke.

Tank simply stared at her.

She decided to move out of his way.

He trotted down the steps, sweatshirt in hand, and jogged to his vehicle. Becky watched, actually speechless.

Alex cleared his throat. "Well, that was ... interesting."

Becky shook herself. "He is ... well, there's just no describing him."

"I think I can understand some of what Grace has been dealing with."

Becky nodded, watching as Tank spun out of the small lot and onto the road.

"Okay, well, I'm heading out," Alex finally said. "You okay?"

"Oh, sure. I'm used to this. He's got his own place now, anyway, so I'm good."

Alex nodded. "Right. Well, take care."

"Breakfast is at nine. Coffee's on by seven."

"Sounds good."

***

She was exactly what she said she was. Tank shifted into third and tried not to speed through the narrow streets. He couldn't for the life of him figure out why it bothered him, but there it was. He'd suspected she was easy, he'd heard it from her own mouth that she was, and then not eight hours after he'd moved out, she already had someone to replace him.

Not that he was being replaced, of course. He wasn't *that* guy. But she already had someone else in her clutches, and it sure didn't look like she was fighting with *him*.

He pulled up in front of his little cottage and drummed his fingers on the steering wheel. He should never have bailed her out and made breakfast. He should have let her just wake up to angry guests and deal with it. Maybe Mr. Reynolds would have been a little less likely to ---

Who was he kidding? Tank got out of the Jeep and slammed the door. Becky was the type to attract any kind of guy, and as long as she made herself available, they'd keep coming. Why did he care?

He walked up the steps to his porch. He'd be happy if he never saw her again.

seven

Becky waved Maddy over to her table in the coffee shop. Her latte was half gone, and her sister's drink was getting cold.

"I ordered for you. Thought you'd be here on time and I'd save you waiting in line. Busy day?"

Her welcoming grin took the sting out of her 'Becky-direct' greeting. Maddy smiled apologetically. "You have no idea." She sat down at the table and exhaled dramatically. "I've spent a lot of time with Parker and Blake, but this is my first day waking up and being with them non-stop. They are full of energy," she said with feeling, reaching for her cup. "Thanks for this."

"Sure," Becky smiled. "Maybe if you focused more on sleeping at night, you'd be ready for the boys, come morning."

Maddy rolled her eyes.

"So, what are they doing now?"

"They dropped me off and they're heading to the house to play in the attic." She sipped her coffee. "I don't know how John's done it on his own for the last two years."

"He's had help - his sister, what's-his-name with his crew. And he knows everyone in town."

"Yeah, Karen and Frank have been great. People at church, too. Still, he's on *all* of the time. And he's so patient."

"Well, give yourself time to get used to being a mother. Most people don't do it overnight." Becky considered her sister over her mug. "And I hate to break it to you, but John's probably not always patient, perfect as he is."

Maddy grinned. "So tell me how everything went here. I know you're used to the routine, but was it okay on your own? Any problems?"

"Wait. No honeymoon details?"

"Haven't we had this conversation?"

"Sort of, but there was nothing to discuss last time, remember? That time you got married and had nothing to say the next morning? I think you have something to say now, and I want to hear it."

"Not happening," Maddy said with a smile.

"Fine," Becky replied. "That couple from Vermont showed up; had a great time. Missed their dog so they left early."

"Really?"

"Weird, huh?"

"People and their dogs ..." Maddy shook her head.

"I know, right? And I told you about our unexpected guests."

"How'd they find out about us?"

"Grace. She recommended us to her brother and to her new boyfriend. He's the one who's still there. Nice guy."

"That's great. I'll have to thank her," Maddy replied. "Is she here today?"

"Don't think so. Boyfriend, remember?"

"Oh, right. Well, what's her brother like?"

Becky sat back with a sigh. "Where do I begin? I thought he'd be okay, since he's Grace's family and all."

Maddy's brows creased as she sipped her cold coffee. "He left yesterday, right?"

"Yep. He's still in town, living in a cottage somewhere down the beach. I don't know if he's going to be staying in the area, or just hanging around for a bit."

"What does he do?"

"He played professional football."

"Really!" Maddy almost dropped her cup. "Cool! John will be excited. Did you say, 'played'?"

"Yeah, I think he's retired due to an injury. Not too happy about it, either, which made him *wonderful* company."

"Wow, not your typical guest, huh?"

"Please. I couldn't get him to give me his name, much less a credit card. He finally paid for the two weeks in cash - can you imagine? Just came in and dumped it in front of me, all in twenties." Becky bristled at the memory.

"That's crazy," Maddy replied, eyeing her with an all-too-familiar, expectant look.

"What? He was a jerk the whole time. *So rude*. Made cracks about me not being the real innkeeper, never thanked me for anything." She crossed her arms and lifted her chin.

Maddy considered her. "He never gave you his name?"

"Calls himself 'Tank.' "

"Tank, like 'fill up my tank' Tank?"

"Try 'my tank is empty' Tank. That's the only name he'd give me. Well, his last name is Kimball. Anyway, it's weird."

"And he was difficult the whole time - the whole two weeks? What's his deal?"

Becky knew she had to come clean about Friday night and Saturday morning, but she wanted to give Maddy a little more time to stew about how awful Tank was.

Maybe they needed more coffee.

"So, what does he look like?" Maddy asked, glancing over Becky's shoulder.

"Just like you'd expect a tank to look. Big, boxy, obnoxious." Becky's phone buzzed and she reached for her purse to check the text.

"Six feet four or so - wide, wide shoulders?"

Where is my stupid phone? "Yeah. Wide everything - neck, head, you name it."

"Hair?"

A job possibility near Boston? Cool! "What? Hair? No."

"No hair?"

Have to deal with this one later. "Well, it's so short, it might as well not be there. You can see his head," Becky wrinkled her nose in distaste.

"More like a crew cut, really."

"I guess," she conceded, finally processing the fact that Maddy's attention was elsewhere.

Oh no ...

"Maybe I should introduce myself; ask him how he liked Maddy's Inn."

Becky froze and slowly slid down in her seat. "Please, don't!"

"Are you slinking?"

"Oh, please," Becky replied, a whole different inflection on the word. She made an effort to appear comfortable where she'd landed. "I don't *slink*. There's just no need to engage with him." She refused to look over her shoulder, but she could sense that he was coming closer.

"I really think I should," Maddy replied with a grin. She stood and planted herself in the aisle.

***

She had big blue eyes and light brown, wavy hair. Somehow she looked familiar, but Tank was sure he'd never seen her before. He wished she'd move out of the aisle. He just wanted to beeline it to his sister's office without talking to anyone. If she didn't move he'd have to slow down or run her over. *Probably shouldn't run her over.*

"Hi, I'm Maddy Jac - oh - Fordham. Maddy Fordham." She smiled and blushed becomingly. "I think you stayed at my inn?"

That's why she looked familiar.

He shook the hand that she extended. Apparently, the sister had manners. "Tank Kimball. Nice to meet you."

"Thanks, you too. So, did you enjoy your stay? I'm pretty new to the B&B business; any advice you have to offer would be great."

He couldn't help himself. He glanced down to his left and into the brown eyes he'd tried to avoid for the last two weeks. Not even twenty-four hours, and here she was, again. Avoiding her was not going to be as easy as he'd thought.

He focused back on Maddy. "You have a nice place. I appreciate your making room for me on such short notice."

He could feel Becky's reaction, didn't have to look at her to know that she didn't buy his effort at polite conversation. He probably shouldn't enjoy irritating her so much.

"We're glad you stayed." Maddy glanced down at her sister, who was no doubt itching to disagree.

"Saturday morning's breakfast was especially good." Tank made a point to lock eyes with Becky, and she colored appropriately. He almost smiled; it was satisfying to see the tables turned and have Becky be the trapped, uncomfortable one. He liked the speechless part best.

"Oh, great. Nice to hear," Maddy replied, undoubtedly unaware of what had happened. "Well, we hope you'll recommend us if you get the chance."

***

"So, what's going on?"

Becky drained her drink and jumped up. "Let's get out of here. I'd rather not run into him again."

"Okay, we'll talk back at the house. But we *will* talk."

Becky shrugged and made her way through the coffee shop. She had never experienced the ridiculous, polite act that he'd just performed for Maddy. Apparently, he'd duped Otis, too, and probably the Reynolds couple, while he'd played chef for them.

She slowed as she left the building and started down the block toward her car. Tank seemed to be friendly with everyone, except her. *Is it me?* She racked her brain for memories of his interaction with anyone else. He avoided people like the plague, so she could hardly come up with any examples.

He'd been rude to Alex, that's for sure, and Grace seemed to expect him to behave badly. Becky breathed a little easier, though she really couldn't say why. It was still a matter of fact that she brought out the worst in a man, and she never brought out the worst in men. She wished it didn't bother her so much.

***

"Okay. What's up? He didn't seem so bad."

Becky pulled into the very limited flow of traffic. "That's because he was in public. He had to pretend to be human."

Maddy smiled. "Seriously, what is it between you two? I've never seen you back down with anyone."

"I did not back down! I just didn't want to deal with him. You don't know what a jerk he can be."

Becky could feel her sister's eyes on her, evaluating. She knew her next question before she asked it.

"What did you make for breakfast on Saturday morning?"

"Funny you should ask. I didn't make breakfast on Saturday morning." She kept her eyes on the road.

"What did our guests eat, Becky?"

"Pancakes and sausage, I think."

"I see. Was it a serve yourself kind of deal? I thought we'd make the breakfast, since it's in the name of our business."

As convicted as Becky felt, she liked that Maddy kept using the plural pronoun. She sighed. "Tank made breakfast on Saturday morning."

The sudden tension was palpable. Becky finally ventured a look at her sister, and crumbled a little inside.

They drove the remaining few minutes in silence. Pulling into the drive, Becky parked her car and turned to Maddy. "I'm really sorry. I drank the better part of a bottle of wine on Friday night, without having really eaten much of anything during the day. I didn't wake up until almost noon on Saturday. Tank knew, well, he figured out what happened, and I guess he made breakfast."

Maddy stared at her sister. "You got drunk and let one of the guests make breakfast? Becky, I trusted you to take care of things! How could you do that?"

The look on Maddy's face hurt far more than her words. Becky was used to being a disappointment, but it hit hard to let her sister down this way. She fought to speak past the lump in her throat, but there was really nothing she could say.

"When were you going to tell me?"

The lump dissipated a little. "I figured you had enough on your plate right now. I would have told you in a couple of days."

"Really?" Maddy's voice was laced with doubt.

"Yes, of course I would. It was stupid; I know that. It was a ridiculous, irresponsible thing to do."

Maddy sighed. "Why did you do it?"

Good ol' Maddy. Somehow, there was mercy mixed in with the disappointment in her eyes.

Becky leaned her head back against the seat. "You know how I told you to watch out for Mr. Reynolds?"

"The couple that left today?"

"Yeah." Becky ran her finger around the steering wheel. "Well, he hit on me after they checked in. Kind of suggested we meet later on Friday night."

Her comment was met with silence. Maddy was no doubt trying to figure out if she had invited or welcomed the suggestion.

Becky closed her eyes. "You have every right to think that I was asking for it, but, believe it or not, this time I wasn't." She opened her eyes and faced her sister. "It came out of the blue. I showed them to their room, and I thought they were all happy, so I went back downstairs." She sighed. "He followed me right back into the office. I figured he'd forgotten something."

She laughed without humor. "I guess I was right. He forgot that he was married." She shuddered. "He was just so nasty - made my skin crawl."

"I'm sorry, Becky."

"You don't have to be sorry. I still dealt with it stupidly."

There was no arguing that. Maddy held her tongue.

"I was just going to sit on the porch and have one glass of wine. Everyone had gone to bed. I figured - I hoped - the guy had been full of hot air and would leave me alone." Becky shook her head. "One glass became two, and then I started thinking about things I shouldn't have, and I just kept drinking."

Maddy processed this for a moment. "How did Tank know you needed help on Saturday morning?"

"Well, lucky for me, he came out to the porch in the middle of my little party."

Maddy's silence pulsated with unasked questions.

"He sat with me for a bit - I think he was actually kind of nice for a few minutes - and then he must have helped me to bed, 'cuz I sure don't remember getting there myself."

"Oh, Becky."

"That's how he figured out that I'd be good for nothing the next morning. He must have gotten up and just, I don't know, made breakfast, I guess. I still don't get it. We never really talked about it."

"You never thanked him?"

"I tried to - it didn't go over well."

"And that was all yesterday morning."

"Yeah. He left before I had a chance to talk to him. He stopped back last night to pick up a sweatshirt, and was as rude as ever. Didn't even respond when Alex introduced himself. Just glowered."

"Who's *Alex*?"

"Grace's boyfriend. He'd stopped back to change before going out again. We were talking on the porch when Tank showed up."

Maddy was quiet for a moment, then Becky thought she saw a bit of a sparkle begin to light her eyes. It was almost more unsettling than her disapproval.

"Don't even *think* it. He's an animal and he hates me."

"Right. Of course." A very tiny smile started to form.

"Besides, I'm done with men forever."

"Really?"

"Really." Becky ventured a look at her sister. "You wouldn't understand. Come on, let's go see your perfect husband and your perfect step-sons. Maybe Parker will tell me how ugly my sweater is."

eight

Tank walked from one end of his cottage to the other in about fifteen steps. How did his childhood vacation home get so tiny? He surveyed the kitchen, contemplating how his mother had cooked for four people in that little space. They must have eaten at the small table occasionally, but he remembered having most of their meals on the porch. Well, the porch wasn't going to be an option in the upcoming winter months. He wondered if this house was going to work for him after all.

Grace had been so excited to find it available for rent. He'd gone along with it, not caring where he ended up as long as he got out of the inn and away from the innkeeper's sister. Now that he was prowling the tiny cabin, he had his doubts. It had two small bedrooms, one bathroom with a tiny cubicle of a shower that he could barely turn around in, a kitchen, living room and the porch. Even the yard was minuscule, but all of that hadn't mattered when they were kids. They'd always run down to the beach, anyway.

Stepping out onto the porch, Tank looked down the street toward the water. He wanted something closer to the ocean. Rolling his shoulders, he jogged down the steps. He'd go for a run and look for rental signs. He had nothing better to do.

It felt good to stretch his legs, and he opened his stride when he hit the beach. He should be running sprints at practices right now. This time of year was always about football and nothing else. It was just as well that he didn't have any kind of television reception at the cottage. It was painful to follow his team and be helpless to do anything. They were supposedly having a "rebuilding year." He shook his head and picked up his pace. He should be on that field doing his job, not running aimlessly down the beach on the coast of Maine.

Tank ran north, the cold wind in his face. The weather had definitely changed. Good thing he couldn't really feel anything. He'd just keep running, and either things would start to make sense, or he'd fall over in exhaustion and not have to think anymore.

He lumbered on. He never fell over in exhaustion. Things had better start making sense.

The water was gray and menacing, but he loved how the waves pounded the sand. It fit his mood perfectly. He continued to run, forcing thoughts of football out of his head.

Looking up, he noted a variety of houses along the beach, many of them older homes. He scanned the small yards, looking for real estate signs. There had to be some winter rentals available.

The houses started to look familiar and Tank slowed his pace. He didn't want to run into anyone from the inn, but he wasn't particularly anxious to get back to his little cottage, either. What awaited him there? No TV, no distraction, no cool dog to play with, not even anyone to pick a fight with.

A vision of his blonde-haired, brown-eyed nemesis taunted him as he slowed to a walk along the shore. She was every bit the awful woman he'd predicted. There had been moments when he thought he saw a real person surface, but they were few and didn't last. He had almost started to believe that she was hurting on Friday night. What an idiot. *Done with men forever,* she'd said, and she had a new one, maybe two, right under her own - or her sister's - roof.

He was getting close to Otis' house and figured it was time to turn around. He glanced to the inn beyond, and noticed two people coming down the steps to the beach. *Great. Busted.* He didn't know which way they were going to walk, and didn't have time to adjust his course to go the opposite way. He sure wasn't likely to blend into the scenery. He slowed as the couple started toward him. There was no mistaking the guy from last night, and no explaining the urge he had to deck him.

They were holding hands. *That was fast.* Tank stood hunched against the cold with his hands in his pockets, waiting for them to look up and see him. They were only about twenty-five yards away; were they so enraptured that they didn't even realize they weren't alone on the beach?

That awful woman was ... he did a double take. That awful woman wasn't as tall as he remembered, and she was decidedly brunette. She was ... *Grace?*

"Tank! Hey - what are you doing here?"

She jogged up to him. "I've been trying to get a hold of you all week! Daphne said you stopped in at the shop? Did you get into the house okay? I planned to help, but you haven't answered your phone."

Tank looked at his sister, bewildered. "I'm in. No problem."

She looked at him like she didn't buy it, but was apparently too happy with her man to pursue it further. "I also wanted you to meet my old high school friend. Alex, this is my brother, Tank. Tank, this is Alex."

Alex extended his hand as he had the night before, and this time Tank shook it with a little less vigor. "Alex."

"Hi, Tank. Nice to officially meet you."

Tank grimaced. "You, too."

"What are you doing on this end of the beach?" Grace chattered on. Grace never chattered. "Were you coming to the inn?"

Tank looked up at the house he'd stayed in for two weeks, unable to explain why he was at the doorstep, again.

"No. Just out for a run; didn't realize how far I'd come until I saw you on the porch."

"Well, then we'll walk you back, unless you want to go in?" Her smile seemed genuine, though there was something in her voice that he didn't like.

"No, I'll walk with you."

"Burt! No! Come!"

The group turned as the Irish wolfhound came bounding off the porch toward them. Becky stood helplessly at the top of the steps, hands on her hips, apparently unwilling to chase the dog.

"Oh no, did we let him out?" Grace asked.

"He can push the door open," Tank explained, bracing himself and intercepting the dog as he ran up.

Alex laughed as Grace stepped behind him. "Becky mentioned you two had bonded," he said, tucking Grace into his side.

Tank considered the man who was moving into his sister-protection territory, even as he wondered what else Becky had said about him. Mostly, he just focused on the dog. He scratched Burt's ears, making a point to get a hold of his collar.

He looked up at Becky, who had taken a step or two toward them, but clearly wasn't in any hurry to get her sister's dog.

He sighed. "Come on, Burt."

The dog walked happily at his side while they made their way up to the porch. Becky met them on the sand.

"Thanks," she said, grabbing a hold of Burt's collar. Tank moved his hand quickly to make room for hers.

"No problem," he replied, starting back to the others.

"Tank?"

He turned slowly. She'd never said his name before; not that it mattered.

"I'm sorry about the other night. Really sorry you had to, ah, step in like you did."

He shrugged, looked out at the water. He didn't like it when she was vulnerable.

"I don't know why you would help me, after the way we've, well, we haven't exactly gotten along. Anyway, I owe you."

He turned back to her. "You don't owe me anything."

She looked at him, actually trying to make eye contact. Luckily, it was getting too dark to really see her eyes. Tank studied his shoes and kicked the sand.

"I made breakfast because I was hungry," he finally said.

"Oh, right, okay."

Was that confusion in her voice? He didn't like that either. Better to make her mad; that he could deal with.

"It had nothing to do with you."

"Got it. Sorry I brought it up."

Good. She's angry. Time to leave.

Doing what he did best, he turned without another word, and jogged back to his sister.

***

Becky watched Tank join Grace and Alex, and fought the urge to throw something at his big fat back. Okay, it wasn't exactly fat, but the target was large and tempting. She'd made an effort to thank him and apologize, and, of course, he was rude. What did she expect?

Well, there wasn't anything else she could do. It wasn't like they needed to be friends or anything. She just didn't want fighting with Tank to get in the way of her friendship with Grace.

She pulled Burt back into the house and finished straightening up the kitchen. Alex would leave tomorrow, and then John would come in and start renovating the third floor. How long would it take him to turn the attic into an apartment for the family? As soon as they were in the house, Becky would need to have a place to go.

She tried to feel the thrill of the freedom to live anywhere and do anything, but the open-endedness of her life felt more overwhelming than exciting. The Boston area job that she'd been texted about was in a middle school, and her certification was for high school. Grace had mentioned a long-term substitute position at the high school in Clairmont, but it was for French. Becky did have a minor in French, so she could probably make it work; she just didn't know if she wanted to commit to spending the rest of the school year in Maine. As fond as she had become of most of the people in town, she felt pretty sure that this rural area was not supposed to be home.

She turned the TV on and flipped through the channels. Leaning her head back on the pillow-covered couch, she let the colors on the screen flash meaninglessly before her. Why was Tank so rude? Was she really that offensive to him? She'd honestly made an effort - admitted she'd needed his help - and he just made her feel more stupid and worthless.

With luck, he'd get tired of life in Maine and move on. Not that *she* was staying, of course, and not that she cared where he ended up. He just needed to go away. Most likely he would. Why would a guy like him choose to live in a small town like Clairmont?

Becky stood up and turned off the television. She'd talk to Maddy about the high school job. Maybe it wouldn't be so bad to stay through spring. It was a sweet little town. It might be fun to refresh her language skills, and she could use the time to think about what she really wanted to do.

Feeling a renewed sense of purpose, she scanned the books on the shelves in the corner. She'd take one to bed and get lost in someone else's adventure for a while. Tomorrow, she'd take on her own.

***

Tank tried to make an office space on his small kitchen table. He opened his laptop and looked up the scores for the week. His guys had lost - again. He groaned to himself as he scanned the statistics. *So many turnovers.* He forced himself to look instead at some of his investment numbers. At least everything there looked good.

He searched real estate companies to see if he could find a listing of local rentals. He didn't have the heart to ask Grace about it just yet. She'd been so excited to find the spot he was in.

Waiting for a page to load, he considered Grace's new *friend*. Alex seemed like a nice guy, though he and his sister hadn't known each other long enough to be so cozy. Apparently, he'd gone to their high school, but it was after Tank's time. Grace had mentioned him last weekend, but he had no idea they were going to try to make a long-distance thing work. Maybe he should try harder to stay in touch with his little sister.

At least he got a good vibe from Alex. He'd pay closer attention in the weeks ahead, if the relationship lasted that long. For all that they weren't a very emotional family, his ties with Grace were strong. He wasn't going to let just anyone come in and steal her away.

The page loaded and he found half a dozen houses listed. Two of them were close to the water. Both had a lot more space; either one would probably do.

He wondered what kind of contract Grace had set up for him. Whatever it was, he'd pay his way out of it if he could get closer to the ocean. He needed room to move, both inside and out. He'd check into a new place tomorrow.

nine

Two weeks later, Becky walked into a room full of high school juniors and seniors. Her crash course in French review left her head swimming in dual languages, but she found herself ready for a new challenge. The idea of sitting around the inn, while John tore the attic apart and Maddy swooned and sighed over her happy marriage, had lost its appeal. She'd gotten busy and contacted the high school. Since long-term subs available to teach French were in short supply, she'd gotten the job fairly easily. She was relieved that the references from her prior job had been positive. Passing the brief series of tests necessary to qualify her to take over the position didn't prove to be overly taxing, but they didn't really prepare her for facing a classroom of teenagers.

Luckily, her last job had done that.

Setting her bag down by the desk, Becky draped her coat over the chair and turned to face the class. She didn't have her own room to decorate or nest in - she'd be moving around the building for the different classes - but she did have a job, and it wasn't cleaning toilets. It was a start.

"*Bonjour tout le monde. Je m'appele Mlle Jacobs.*" She wrote her name on the board. She turned and surveyed the class. "*Comment vous appelez-vous?*" she asked the girl in the front left corner of the room.

Surprised, the girl looked up and responded in decent French.

"*Bonjour, Kacey,*" Becky replied, checking the name on her attendance list and moving on to the next student. There were some snickers when a student or two stumbled through the introductions, but most of them remembered the simple formula.

In the back of the room she addressed a young man, likely an athlete, who easily had fifty pounds on her. He reminded her of a smaller version of a football player she knew. She fought the urge to be irritated just because.

She looked at him inquiringly. No one else had made her repeat the question.

He leaned back in his chair and looked her over. "I forgot the question." *Mr. Smooth - oh goodie.*

"*Vraiment?*" Becky replied. "*Mais, pourquoi? Vous n'etes pas tres intelligent?*"

Not everyone fully understood her question, which was sad, considering it was a third year class. A few did laugh quietly, and the boy's smirk faded as Becky moved past him to the next student. If he wasn't going to give her his name, she'd mark him absent. She knew from past experience that high school students, especially guys, were not prone to taking her seriously. If she didn't strike first, and effectively, she'd be scrambling for respect for the rest of the year.

"Ooh la la," said the jock with the attitude.

Becky stiffened slightly; she wasn't really surprised that the interaction wasn't over. She turned back to him. "*Vraiment? 'Ooh la la'? C'est votre nom? Interessant.*"

She turned and wrote on her clipboard. The kid just got himself a new name.

***

"So, how did it go? Did you like it? Did you find your way around okay?"

Maddy met her at the door and peppered her with questions. Tired as she was, Becky was happy to have someone care. She'd never had anyone to come home to after starting a new job.

"It was pretty much like I expected. I had two block classes - don't know how the kids sit still that long. Anyway, upperclassmen for the first class, freshmen for the second."

"Were they nice - respectful?"

Becky rolled her eyes. "They're teenagers, Maddy."

"Oh, well, how did it go, then?" Maddy opened a pot on the stove and Becky was happy to confirm what she'd thought was simmering apple cider. Maddy ladled out a mugful, sprinkled it with cinnamon and slid it across the counter to her.

"Thanks. This is perfect," Becky said, warming her hands on the ceramic mug. She took a moment to just breathe in the drink in her hands, then sipped it slowly.

"Well, the guys responded predictably. The older guys know too much, and they follow your every move with a predatory look. The underclassmen tend to stare and turn red. The girls are aloof until they figure out that you really do have something to teach them."

"Well, that's kind of sad. Wasn't anyone nice?"

"Sure, there were a few kids in each class who warmed up to me and answered questions - tried to get involved. The rest will come along eventually." She sipped her cider again and started to relax, glad that Maddy and John were still working in the house. She appreciated the company.

"I'm sure they will," Maddy agreed.

"But why do I always bring out that side of men and *boys*?" Becky grumbled. "Why can't they just take me seriously? Look at the way I dressed. This is, like, my accountant outfit."

She stood and modeled her rumpled suit. Simple straight skirt, jacket and blouse. Didn't get more boring than that.

"Well, honestly, Becky, you might have chosen something a little less form-fitting ..."

The door to the back stairway opened and a whistle interrupted their conversation. Frank Davidson, John's contracting partner, followed his greeting into the kitchen.

"That's what you wore to school today? Those poor boys." He grinned and walked over to the fridge.

Becky ignored Maddy's apologetic look and glared at Frank. She had grown to like Frank, but now he was one of them. *Stupid men.*

"Which is why I'm done with men forever."

"Oops! Did I say the wrong thing?" Frank asked, unscrewing the cap to a water bottle. "You look great, Becky. Very ... professional." His eyes glinted mischievously, and Becky's efforts to silence him with her stare proved pointless.

"I didn't dress to impress the *boys* today," she said with a scowl. Since when did she ever explain herself to anyone?

"I'm sure they were impressed, anyway. Did you see my dad?"

"No, my classes aren't near the shop wing."

"Well, I'm sure you'll meet him sooner or later. You won't be able to miss him; very social guy." Frank smiled at what was undoubtedly an understatement.

"What a shocker."

"He'll look out for you, though. If your classroom ever needs anything fixed - a.c., electrical, whatever, he's your man."

"Thanks," Becky replied. "I won't really have my own room, though. I'll be moving around for my classes."

Frank nodded. "The perks of being a long-term sub."

He finished his drink and said his good-byes. A moment later, Blake and Parker came tromping down the stairs, their father close behind.

"Hey, Miss Becky! You look pretty!" Parker exclaimed.

Becky blinked, stunned by the rare compliment. "Well, thank you, Parker."

"We only had to go to school in the morning today. Can I have some cider Maddy-mom?"

Maddy grinned at Parker's new name for her. "Sure thing. How about you, Blake?"

"Yes, please," Blake replied as he carefully situated himself on a stool next to Parker. The three years that separated the brothers showed less in their size than in their temperament. Blake smiled a greeting at Becky, but didn't comment on her wardrobe.

"Hi, Becky," John greeted her as he circled the counter to give Maddy a kiss on the cheek. "How was school today?"

Becky smiled at the question, and at the fact that John had to greet Maddy with a kiss when they'd already spent the day together.

"So, how long have you two been apart? Twenty, thirty minutes?" she asked.

John grinned and pulled Maddy into his arms. "Fifteen, and it's killing me."

Parker giggled. "Dad, you're always kissing her! She probably doesn't like it so much."

Maddy raised a brow at John. Deciding the gesture was more invitation than censure, he dipped her in a dramatic embrace. Shaking her head at the display, Becky couldn't help but note that Blake and Parker were both smiling. They were all impossibly happy.

Maddy wriggled out of John's arms to get more mugs. "Actually, Becky, John's been upstairs working all day. I only saw him at lunch."

"And when you brought us cookies," Parker reminded her.

"And when we ran errands," Blake observed.

"And Dad was gone for a really long time after Uncle Frank came and ..."

"Okay, guys," John said. "Let's hear about Aunt Becky's day."

Becky grinned. "Well, mine wasn't nearly so interesting. I taught French to a bunch of teenagers who don't really want to learn it."

"Then why did you do it?" Parker asked, licking around the side of his mug.

"Good question, Parker," Becky replied. "I'm not really sure. But I'm going to try it again tomorrow and see if I can get them to like it any better."

"Let them draw pictures," he offered. "That's fun."

"They don't draw in high school," Blake reminded his brother.

"Sure they do," Becky chimed in. "I had fun teaching them to draw in my other school. Maybe it's not such a bad idea."

Parker beamed, while Blake remained thoughtful, as always.

"How's the apartment coming?" Becky asked John.

"Slow going getting started," he replied. His look conveyed more concern than his simple statement did. "I wish I had my crew; could really use the manpower."

"Well, maybe I'll hear about someone looking for extra work at the high school."

"That'd be great," John replied. "Frank's dad is keeping an eye out for us, too."

Becky nodded. "We'll find you some help. There's gotta be someone around."

***

"I'm going to lose my mind if he doesn't find something to do."

Becky jogged along as Grace vented about her horrible brother, remaining as obtuse as she possibly could about the information being unloaded on her.

"I mean, he's not just good at sports. He's super handy. And he's an amazing carpenter. You should see some of the things he built for my parents."

Becky nodded politely.

"He's already fixed a bunch of stuff in the little cottage he's renting. If he's there long enough, he'll probably gut the place and renovate the entire thing."

"That sounds like a good project for him," Becky said enthusiastically.

"Yeah, but he doesn't own it. There's only so much he can do. Seriously, I need to find him something."

"He's a grown man. He should be able to find his own work."

"That's part of the problem, he doesn't really need the money. He just needs to be useful."

Becky groaned inside. "How about the shop? Don't you need some things done there?"

"Yeah, I'm sure he'd be willing to help me out. I just don't want it to keep coming from me, you know? I mean, I'd do anything for him, but he's got his pride."

Becky sighed.

"You okay?" Grace asked. "I'm sorry, I've done nothing but complain about Tank. How's it going at the high school?"

Becky looked at her friend, trying to stifle the words that were about to come out of her mouth. "John and Frank really need help on the apartment at the inn. John just asked the other day if I knew of anyone who might be interested."

Grace's eyes lit up and she slowed her pace. "Are you kidding? That would be perfect! And it wouldn't be my project or my idea!"

"Well, you can't tell him it was mine," Becky countered, slowing with her friend.

Grace laughed. "Yeah, I'm guessing Tank isn't your first choice for the job."

Becky rolled her eyes.

"But can't you see how perfect this is?" Grace continued, adding a happy little hop to her jog. "John will be amazed at what Tank can do."

"I'm sure he will," Becky replied without enthusiasm.

Grace grinned. "I'll talk to him about it tonight. Tell him that I heard about it at the shop." They were just walking up to the door after their run. "See? I won't even be lying!" Her eyes sparkled as she said good-bye. "You're a life-saver, Becky. Thanks so much for letting me know!"

Becky waved and walked back to her car. How she ended up in the middle of that mess was beyond her. Now she'd have to let Maddy know so she could let John know and there was no doubt in her mind what would come of the whole business. She just hoped that the guys worked days while she was in school. The less she saw of Tank, the better.

***

"No way. I don't need the money and I don't need anyone's pity."

Tank heard Grace sigh in frustration as he shifted his weight on the same couch that they'd sat on as kids. How could the owners not have updated the furniture?

"No one's pitying you, Tank. They just need help right now, and you're a big, strong guy with time on your hands."

"You didn't suggest it?" He looked up at her accusingly.

"I'm just letting you know about the opportunity."

Tank grunted. "I thought Maddy's husband had a crew."

"During the summer, yes. It's just John and Frank in the slow season."

"And what is the project they're working on?" He shouldn't be asking. He would regret letting this conversation go any further.

"They're turning the third floor of Maddy's B&B into an apartment for the family."

"Their family? I thought they just got married."

"John has two kids from his first marriage."

"Really."

"Yes, really. So anyway, the attic is huge, I guess, and they're transforming it into living quarters."

"Why do they need me?"

His sister sighed again. "They just need manpower. They want to get it done as quickly as possible so that they can get settled in before the next season starts."

"Which is?"

"Well, next summer, I guess."

"So they have plenty of time."

"No, not really. They have other jobs - people still need work done in the off-season - so I guess this has to be on the side. Plus, they will have some guests throughout the winter, so their opportunities to work will be limited."

"You sound way too invested." Tank shifted and crossed his leg. He'd already hauled the coffee table into the spare bedroom so he could move around in his tiny living room. "And I don't know how long I'm going to be around here. I don't really want to get involved with anyone in town."

"I'm not asking you to get married, Tank."

His head shot up and he eyed her warily. "Why would you say something like that?"

She shrugged, acting all nonchalant. "I don't know; you just seemed freaked out about getting to know anyone. They're good people Tank. This is a great little town."

His shoulders relaxed a little. "What kind of commitment are they looking for?"

"I think they'll take you any time you're available. My guess is that they'll be working mostly in the evenings, but I'm not sure."

He sighed heavily. So much for being left alone. He looked out the window and could see what his neighbor across the street was watching on TV. The truth was, this place was way too small and he was losing his mind. Maybe it wouldn't be such a bad thing to get out of the house and be productive. He could help them out for a week or two and see how it went.

"Okay, I'll look into it, under one condition."

"I can't guarantee that you won't see Becky. She started teaching at the high school, so I suppose she'll be gone days, but I don't know what she does with her evenings."

Tank eyed his sister quizzically. "I don't care what the innkeeper's sister does or where she does it."

He hated that Grace was fighting a smile.

"Oh, sorry. What's your condition?"

"I need more space than I have here. I appreciate that you found this house for me, and I know you like the idea of my living here, but it's just too small. I can't move."

"Oh, well, it's just a monthly contract, so it won't be hard to get out of."

"You're not mad?"

"Why would I be mad?" Grace asked. "I just want you to be happy."

Tank nodded. Why couldn't more women be like his sister? Alex was a lucky man.

"Do you want me to try to find something else for you?"

"No thanks," he replied. "I found the place I want. It's closer to the water. I've already spoken to the real estate agent and made arrangements."

Her face lit up. "Really? Good for you!" She considered him for a moment. "I thought you weren't going to commit to staying around here." She crossed her arms and grinned at him.

"I'm not committing to anything. I just need more space."

"I see. Well, what's the condition, then?"

He shifted uncomfortably. "I just want you to be okay with it."

"But you're already doing it."

"I'm already doing it."

She smiled. "Well, I'm okay with it. Should I give John your number or tell him you'll be in touch?"

"I'll stop over there tomorrow."

ten

Tank eyed the inn warily. He'd decided to walk rather than drive his Jeep. Parking in their driveway meant commitment. Strolling past the house and stopping in was something else.

He reached up and rubbed the back of his neck. He was probably crazy for doing this. He didn't even know these guys or the scope of the project. He'd stop and see what Otis had to say.

He had just started up the steps to Otis' house, when the screen door slammed next door. If Maddy's husband was so handy, why didn't he fix that stupid door? Tank watched as Maddy walked out on the porch with Burt, who recognized him immediately and trotted over to say hello.

"Oh hey, Tank, right? How are you?" Maddy called out.

She was beaming, and all she was doing was letting her dog out. Why was everyone around him so happy? Tank intercepted Burt's sloppy greeting, and couldn't help his own small smile. "Hey buddy, how're you doing?"

"So, I guess you two got to know each other?" Maddy asked with a laugh. "He really likes you."

"Yeah, we hung out a bit. I miss this guy." Tank scratched Burt's ears and the dog leaned heavily into his side.

"I think Otis may have gone downtown, but he'll probably be back soon. You're welcome to wait over at our place, if you'd like."

Tank glanced up. *Might as well.* "Thanks."

"My husband would love to meet you," Maddy said as they walked back to the house. "Mind if I tell him you're here?"

"That's fine," Tank replied.

Maddy opened the door and Tank followed her into the kitchen, looking around at the familiar space. If her husband was responsible for the renovation, he was impressed. He found himself increasingly curious about the project underway on the third floor. "My sister says you're renovating the attic?"

"Yeah, it's pretty exciting," Maddy replied. "They've already framed the bedrooms. Want to go up and take a look?"

Tank shrugged. "Sure. Don't want to get in the way."

"Oh, no, that won't be a problem."

Maddy led the way to the second floor and continued on to the unfamiliar territory of the third. She opened the door into the attic, and the sound of power tools filled the air. They stepped carefully across bright orange cords and made their way to the area that was clearly going to be a small kitchen. Tank looked around, impressed. These guys knew what they were doing.

A man, undoubtedly the husband, looked up from the table saw. He flipped his safety glasses up and walked over to them. Tank was familiar with the assessment he was receiving and figured it would be a good time to make a friendly impression. He extended his hand, but Maddy's husband beat him to the introduction.

"Hi - John Fordham." He grinned as he slipped his ear protectors off. "Sorry for yelling."

Tank shook his hand. "Good to meet you. Tank Kimball. I heard you might be looking for another set of hands."

Another man walked over with his framing gun. He had the biggest grin Tank had ever seen.

"You're hired! Frank Davidson." He gave Tank's hand a hardy shake. Tank couldn't help but smile in return.

"Well, you may not want me up here. You don't know if I can tell the difference between a dry wall screw and a roofing nail."

John and Frank exchanged a look.

"Busted!" Frank crowed.

Tank felt himself grinning again. He probably should have thought to use a less savvy example. "Is this a good time?"

John clapped him on the back. "It's perfect." He walked Tank over to the far side of the room. The minute the tour began, Tank knew he was sold. It would be good to build something again.

***

"He's here, in the house." Becky slowed her step like she might not stay, although she didn't know where else she'd go.

"He's in the attic with John and Frank. They've been up there for over an hour; don't think they're coming down any time soon."

Becky dropped her bag on the kitchen stool. "I didn't think he'd do it. Are they getting along okay?"

"As far as I know," Maddy replied. "John looked so happy - so relieved." She grabbed her jacket. "I've got to pick up the boys from school. Wanna come?"

Becky sighed and rolled her shoulders. "No, I just need to chill. I don't think I'm up to their energy level right now."

Maddy smiled. "I get that. I'm still working on being ready for them after school."

"Getting better sleep at night?" Becky purred innocently.

"Let's just say my nights are well spent," Maddy grinned. "I'll be back in a few, then you can tell me all about day four."

"Not a whole lot different from day one," Becky yawned, reaching for the fridge. "But I survived."

"Okay, well, relax. Be back soon."

Becky waved her off and took a diet soda into the sun room. The sun shone brightly on the water, but the air outside was cold. She shuddered, not sure she was really up for a Maine winter.

Sitting down on the couch, she crossed her ankles on the coffee table, knowing full well she'd get after anyone else who did it. Closing her eyes, she reminded herself not to relax too much. The last thing she wanted was to run into Tank when he finally tired of playing carpenter with the boys.

***

"Miss Becky, look what I made at school!" Parker giggled. "Look at your head!"

Becky pulled herself from the cavern of pillows she'd sunk into, apparently having napped after all. She righted herself and pushed her hair out of her face.

"Guess I lost a battle with this comfy couch," she said, shaking herself awake.

"Look at my picture." Parker stuck a drawing of a horse in front of her face. "My teacher says I'm going to be an artist, just like you are!"

Becky tried to focus on the picture. How long had she been asleep? It couldn't have been long if Maddy had just returned with the kids. She felt like she'd been out for hours.

Teaching was taking a bigger toll than she'd expected.

She considered the horse that Parker had drawn. "This is really good, Parker. I like how you showed motion with his legs here."

"Yeah. He's running." Parker looked up over her shoulder. "Dad's coming!" He jumped up and ran toward the kitchen.

Becky groaned; just her luck. Why didn't she go to her room when she had the chance? She didn't even have her bag close by so she could pull out some books and pretend to be busy. She jumped up from the couch; there was one other way to escape.

∗∗

"So, what do you think?" Maddy asked as the men filed into the kitchen.

Tank noted that John immediately walked over to his wife and slipped his arm around her. She looked up at him with a smile that would stop any man's heart. Tank wasn't sure she even remembered asking a question, but he answered it anyway.

"It's impressive. They're doing great work."

"You should see this guy with a sabre saw," Frank joined in with enthusiasm. "We were hoping for someone to do the heavy lifting, but he knows all about carpentry. We hit the jackpot."

Tank shook his head. It had been a long time since anyone praised his carpentry - a long time since anyone knew he had any of those skills. "Just following your lead."

"Can you stay for dinner?" Maddy asked, then added, "Why is Becky outside without a coat on? It's so cold!"

"She said Burt needed to go out," a young voice supplied.

Tank turned to see the boys his sister had mentioned approaching uncertainly from the sun room. He squatted so that he was closer to their level. Kids, he could handle. "Hey there. I'm Tank," he said, extending his hand.

The older boy, with blond curly hair and green eyes, shook it. "Hi, I'm Blake. This is Parker."

Parker, brown-eyed with brown hair, grinned as he came along side his brother. "You're so big! Dad, look at his arms!"

John walked up and laid his hand on Parker's shoulder. "How about you just say 'hello' to our guest?"

Parker giggled and put his hand out to Tank. "I'm Parker."

"Nice to meet you, Parker," Tank replied with a grin. He straightened up and Parker's eyes went wide, following the ascent.

"Can you eat supper with us?" he asked.

"No, buddy, I'm sorry." He turned to Maddy. "Thanks for the offer, but I think I'll head home and clean up."

"Hope you'll stay another time," Maddy replied distractedly, still apparently puzzling over why her sister was outside freezing with the dog.

Tank knew perfectly well why she was out there. He just wondered where she'd go when it came time for him to leave.

"Thanks again for your help," John extended his hand and Tank shook it. "We're doing this all day tomorrow and Saturday if you'd like to join us; next week is a little uncertain with the holiday."

"Oh, Thanksgiving!" Maddy exclaimed. "I need to talk to Otis." She made a note on her pad. "Tank, you and your sister are more than welcome. Or maybe you have family close by?"

"Family's in Connecticut. Not really sure what I'm, or we're doing."

"Well, it'll be informal here, but we'd love to have you."

"Thanks. I'll talk to Grace and see what her plans are," he replied, a little unnerved by Maddy's kindness.

"Meanwhile, there's an apartment to frame," Frank reminded him. "Feel free to stop by here anytime. We'll find something for you to do."

"I will," Tank grinned.

***

She was absolutely frozen, but wasn't about to go back inside until she was sure Tank had left. Since he wasn't very sociable, she figured she shouldn't have to wait long, but something kept her from walking back into the house.

'Something' walked out onto the porch a moment later. *Great.* Why couldn't he have left through the front door like a normal person? Apparently, he'd walked, and now she had to talk to him. It had been almost three weeks since they'd stood in just about the same place, only she'd been on the porch and he'd been on the beach with Burt. Weird role reversal, *that means absolutely nothing.* She crossed her arms, trying not to look cold. Her heels kept sinking into the sand. She hoped she didn't tip over.

Burt, the traitor, ran right up to Tank, who sauntered down the steps to greet him. He would saunter, *Mr. 'I'm just as comfortable here as you are.'* Becky pulled her heels loose and eased around the two of them while they had their little reunion. If she could get up a few of the stairs, he wouldn't look so big.

Tank turned as she got to the second step. "Cold enough for you?"

She swallowed a shudder. "Yep."

"You're teaching at the high school?"

Oh, it was Conversation Tank. How did she get so lucky? "Yes."

"Teaching ..."

"French."

He looked up in surprise. "Thought you were an artist."

"I am." It was kind of fun responding in 'Tank speak' - minimal information, with absolutely no encouragement.

"Huh. You want him?"

"Want who?"

"Whom."

"What?"

"Never mind." He pushed Burt toward her. "Go on, boy."

Becky took a hold of Burt's collar, while Tank, without another word, turned and jogged down the beach. *Naturally.* She could learn a host of valuable social skills from the bum. She walked into the house, relieved and unaccountably irritated at the same time.

eleven

The coffee shop was warm and welcoming after the long day at school. Becky greeted one of her favorite baristas and ordered hot chocolate with whipped cream. It was cold, it was Friday, and it seemed appropriate.

"How's it going at the high school?" Daphne asked, sliding the mug across the counter.

"Word gets around fast," Becky replied. "Why don't you tell me?"

Daphne grinned. "Well, my little sister's a senior, so she gives me the details. She's taking Spanish, so she doesn't have you, but she definitely knows you're in the building."

"That sounds ominous," Becky said, lifting her mug carefully and tasting the whipped cream.

"Actually, the girls are mad 'cuz the boys are all talking about you. That's pretty much it."

"Terrific." Becky sighed, blowing some of her whipped cream across the counter. "Oh, sorry," she said, wiping it up. "Well, *I* will tell you that I actually have those kids speaking French, which is more than they were doing at the beginning of the week. At least the upperclassmen are."

"I'm sure you'll be great," Daphne replied. "The kids will settle down. It's just a big deal to have a new teacher."

"Well, it'll be a much bigger deal if they get the replacement they want for P.E."

"Another teacher's out? I can't believe my sister didn't tell me."

"Well, this just happened today, or maybe last night. Anyway, I'm not really sure what the story is, but they're talking about asking Grace's brother."

"The football player?"

"Yeah. Apparently, one of the teachers is related to the real estate agent who set him up with his rental." Becky grimaced. "Guess that means he could be around a while."

Daphne smiled. "Well, that should make Grace happy. As if she's not happy enough already."

"I know, right? What happened to my serious, reasonable friend?" Becky pined.

"Well, whatever it is, I hope it happens to me," Daphne said with a laugh. "I'd better get back to work. Good luck at the high school. And don't worry about those boys. They'll shape up."

Becky smiled and walked to her booth in the back of the store. If Grace was around, she'd make a point to stop and say hello. Becky thought she should know about the rumor at the high school. Let her tell Tank if she wanted to.

***

"So, that's all I heard. I'm pretty sure you need some sort of certification to be a long-term sub, so it's not like he'd be qualified, but I just thought I'd give you the heads-up."

Grace sat back in the booth, a thoughtful look on her face. "Well, he has his B.S. in science - secondary education - but I doubt he's kept his credentials, or whatever it is you need, current."

Becky swallowed. "He was an education major?"

"Well, he never actually did the educating, besides student teaching, I guess. He got drafted and went straight to football. I wonder if he'd want to teach again after all these years?"

"Probably not," replied Becky, wishing more than knowing it to be so. "He doesn't really like people."

Grace laughed. "I know you say that, but he wasn't always that way. He used to be more sociable - maybe not the life of the party - but definitely comfortable with people." She sipped her tea. "I think the whole major life change has just left him out of his element. Once you get to know him ..."

"Well, we don't have to worry about that, do we?" Becky asked brightly. "Anyway, I just thought you should know, in case you want to pass the information along. That way he won't be caught off guard and take someone's head off when they approach him."

Grace laughed again. "I really have to thank you, Becky. This is the second job you've found for my brother."

"Please. I'm not looking for these things. I just keep being an unwilling courier. Tell him about it if you want to."

"Why don't you tell him yourself, see if you guys can come to some kind of truce?" Grace suggested, still smiling.

"No, I never see him."

"He works at the inn where you live."

Becky gave her a dark look. "We make it a point to avoid each other."

"Really? He said he talked to you last night."

"Why would he do that?"

"Talk to you or tell me?"

"Pick one."

Grace grinned. "I don't know. Maybe he was enthralled with your conversation."

Her eyes sparkled and Becky wished, once again, for her formerly quiet, serious friend to reappear.

"Not likely. Tell him if you want, but I'm staying out of it."

***

"It was probably just a rumor." Fuming, Becky hiked her school bag higher on her shoulder and glared up at Tank. No matter how she timed her entrance into the house, she always seemed to run into him. She'd thought she was safe, with the holiday just days away, yet here he was, and he had the nerve to approach her about the news that no one was supposed to know. She wasn't going to last in this small town.

Tank shrugged, and Becky's eyes were drawn to his stupid traps. She could see their outline under his heavy sweatshirt. She fought the memory of having had her hands all over them. Was he remembering that little episode, too? She sincerely hoped not.

"Grace told me to ask you."

Becky refocused on the conversation. "Well, I don't know much. One of the P.E. teachers left suddenly and they're looking for a replacement."

Tank's brows drew low over his eyes. "What does that have to do with me?"

She sighed. "Your name came up because one of the teachers is related to your real estate agent. So now they know there's a former pro athlete in town, and they were going to send someone to talk to you about helping out."

Tank snorted. "Helping out?"

"Well, I imagine they'd pay you for your services."

He eyed her suspiciously. "Why are you involved?"

"Believe me, I wish I weren't." Becky danced a little, trying to warm her feet. "I just told Grace as a courtesy to you. Didn't think you'd want to be blindsided when someone approached you."

Tank's expression softened the slightest bit. "Oh."

"I'm not trying to find you a different job, much as I'd rather not have you working under my roof." She glanced at the house longingly.

"Your sister's roof."

She narrowed her eyes. "You know what I mean."

He stepped aside so she could go in. She hurried past him, anxious to get warm. She almost didn't hear him in her rush to get away.

She turned in surprise. "What did you say?"

He considered her for a moment. "I said 'thanks.' "

"Really."

Tank shook his head and jogged down the steps and out to his Jeep.

***

"To celebrate the upcoming holiday, we're going to have a quiz."

A universal groan reverberated throughout the room as Becky handed out the papers. "It'll be fun! It's all about Thanksgiving - we discussed this vocab on Friday. I told you to study."

The freshman class was not impressed. They grumbled as she chattered on about turkeys and sweet potatoes, and then the room quieted as they all tried to remember their vocabulary words.

She walked around the classroom, observing their progress. When they finished, she would divide them into groups and get a little competition going. Boys verses girls, perhaps. That was always a good motivator.

She glanced out at the grey skies. John was replacing the attic windows today; she hoped they'd get the job done before the rain came. Her mind wandered over the conversations she'd heard among the three men while she hid - *rested* - in her room in the evenings. Tank sounded like a different person with them - laughing and discussing their boring carpentry topics with more knowledge than she would have expected.

"Ms. Jacobs?"

She jumped out of her reverie and looked over at the student who'd called out to her.

"*Mademoiselle, s'il vous plait.*"

"Oh, right, *Mademoiselle* Jacobs, are we correcting these, or do you want me to hand this in?"

The girl who asked was sweet and earnest; adjectives that had never landed on Becky for any measurable time. Still, for some reason, she was drawn to this particular student.

"*Nous allons regarder ensemble.*"

The girl stared at her blankly.

"We'll look at them together," Becky said quietly, and the girl smiled, apparently finding a way to equate the two sentences.

Becky smiled back and continued her circuit around the room. There were definitely things about teaching that she enjoyed.

***

Arriving back at the inn, she was relieved to see that Tank's Jeep wasn't parked in the drive. There was still a chance that he'd walked, but even he wouldn't be so foolish on this cold, rainy day.

Then again, maybe he would.

Becky walked right into the group in the kitchen, apparently catching the tail end of a conversation that immediately roused her suspicions.

"Thanks, Maddy," Tank was saying, with an unfamiliar-to-Becky, friendly air. "I'll let Grace know." He looked up as Becky entered the room, and a cloud seemed to come over his face.

The others turned to greet her with a little more enthusiasm.

"Tough day?" Maddy asked.

Great. Apparently, she looked as bad as she felt.

"It was okay. Hey, everybody." She glanced around at Frank and John with a smile, then turned back to Maddy. "Are you going to get the boys? I'll go with you."

"Well, I'm going to pick them up and go back to the house. You're more than welcome to come with us, but we weren't planning to hang out here this evening."

"Oh." So much for her escape plan. "I guess I'll stay here and get ready for the weekend. What's up for tomorrow?"

"Well, I think these guys are going to put in one more long day before Thanksgiving," Maddy looked apologetically at Tank. "And I'm planning to come over and get a jump on the cooking."

Even Becky could find a reason to smile at that. Maddy wasn't very comfortable in the kitchen and this would be her first Thanksgiving meal.

"Have you found a good turkey recipe?"

"I think so." Maddy looked half anxious and half excited. "I was going to try Mom's, but I found one online that seems a little more foolproof."

The men started filing back upstairs after their coffee break, and Becky let the kitchen clear before demanding answers to a few other questions that she had.

"What was Tank thanking you for?"

Maddy looked taken aback at the sudden change in topic. "Thanking me? Oh, just now? Well, we were talking about Thanksgiving, and ..."

"What could Tank possibly have to do with our Thanksgiving?"

"*Our* Thanksgiving is going to include John's mother, sister and niece, Otis, Tank and Grace."

"You're kidding!" Becky wanted to throw a tantrum like her freshmen class did. "Grace is great, but Tank?"

"I could hardly invite one without the other, and really, Becky, we know Tank better than Grace."

"But it's going to be so awkward - we can't stand each other!"

"Well, you can survive for one day. Think about it, Becky. He's been playing football right through the Thanksgiving holiday for years. This year will probably be tough for him. I'm actually really glad that he accepted. I didn't think he would."

"I can't believe he did, either."

"I think he's starting to bond with John and Frank. He's an amazing carpenter, so they're thrilled, and I think they're getting him to talk about football." Maddy smiled a little. "I think there's a lot of cool stuff going on upstairs."

Becky didn't really want to think about Tank's healing process. She tried a different approach. "Why would you want to invite so many people when you've never cooked a turkey before?"

Maddy sat down on a bar stool. "Well, I didn't really think about that when I started inviting everyone." She sighed. "It just seemed like having Thanksgiving here in our beautiful dining room was a nice thing to offer after everything people did for us on our wedding."

Becky sat down next to her. "Are they bringing food to help?"

"Well, John's mom makes pies, so she's got desert covered."

"That's a relief."

"I know. And Otis has his special rolls he makes, and says he's going to try his hand at sweet potatoes."

"Okay. Who's got the cranberry salad and mashed potatoes?"

"Well, Tank said they'd do a fruit salad. Oh, and he'll bring the wine." Maddy pulled her list from the counter closer to check her notes. "That leaves the turkey and stuffing, which I figured I could do. And you make great potatoes, so you can keep that job."

She turned to Becky with a bright smile, as though promising her the mashed potato gig would make the whole Thanksgiving mess more palatable.

Becky shook her head with a grudging smile. "I hope you know what you're doing. And you'd better go get those boys."

Maddy looked at her watch. "Oh, right." She tucked her list into her purse. "I'll stop at the store and grab a few things. It'll probably be crazy tomorrow." She stood and pulled her coat from the back of one of the kitchen chairs.

"You take Parker and Blake grocery shopping with you?"

"Yeah. They're usually good sports about it. Parker will sneak something into the cart every once in a while, but Blake polices it pretty closely for me." She grinned. "He takes care of most of the discipline issues."

Becky smiled at the thought. "Well, good luck."

She pulled herself off her own bar stool and contemplated her options for the rest of the day. If the guys were going to work into the evening, she'd get her run in and then make herself scarce. She'd already be spending far more of this weekend with Tank than she'd ever dreamed possible. No need to rub salt in the wound.

twelve

The alarm clock sounded - alarming. Becky rolled over and slapped it repeatedly. The shrill whistle kept blaring. She sat up groggily.

The smoke alarm?

She all but fell out of her bed, trying to wake up enough to land feet-first. She could definitely smell smoke.

The turkey.

Maddy had wanted to try a roast-all-night-in-foil recipe which would leave the turkey thoroughly done for their noon meal. She'd been ridiculously worried about undercooked turkey. Apparently, that was no longer a concern.

Becky hurried into the kitchen, the smoke burning her eyes as she made her way to the oven. Burt trotted up to her, sneezing and whining, and she ran to the door to let him out. Turning back, she tried to make out the damage. Smoke was pouring out of every conceivable crevice of the stovetop, but at least the fire was contained in the oven. By the time she'd loosed the fire extinguisher and pulled the pin, John came flying through the stairwell door, Maddy and the boys close on his heels.

"Becky! Are you okay?" Maddy cried. "Where's Burt?"

"He's out," Becky assured her, holding her fire, so to speak, while John approached the oven to assess the damage.

He had the good sense to turn the oven off, and Becky applauded his quick thinking. He remained calm, crouching down to look through the oven window.

Maddy urged the boys, already wrapped in blankets, onto the porch to get fresh air, while John put the fire out. She walked back into the kitchen, rubbing her arms. "My alarm didn't go off - I was supposed to check this two hours ago!"

"Windows," Becky suggested, and she and Maddy got busy airing out the house.

After opening the last window in the sunroom, they returned to the kitchen, shivering.

"What did I do wrong?" Maddy wondered. "This was supposed to be a fool-proof method."

"The pan must have leaked," Becky replied. "And once that grease gets burning ..." she shook her head.

"And I invited so many people."

Becky tried not to appear too glad that their Thanksgiving party was canceled. "Everyone will be fine. John's sister or mom can host their family and we can work on cleaning up here. Grace and Tank can take care of each other. People will understand."

"I hope so." Maddy sighed. "I'm going to have to scrub these cupboards and walls and probably wash curtains to get rid of the smell." She wrinkled her nose and sat down on a bar stool. "And we have guests coming tomorrow!"

Becky tracked down their coats and wrapped Maddy's around her shoulders. "We'll get this cleaned up, Maddy. We'll crank some music and make it a party."

The boys brought Burt back inside and snuggled on one of the couches. "What will we have for dinner?" Blake asked, concerned.

Maddy made an effort to rally. "We'll think of something. We might have dinner at your Grandma's or Aunt Karen's."

"I'll give Karen a call," John offered.

"Okay, everyone get dressed," Becky directed. "We've got a house to clean."

***

Several hours later, Maddy and Becky finished re-hanging the curtains in the sunroom. They'd spent the morning wiping down the walls on the first floor and airing out the rooms on the second. The next job would be to wipe down all of the kitchen cabinets and wash everything that had been affected by the smoke. *Happy Thanksgiving.*

"Do you want more coffee?" Becky asked, rolling her shoulders. She'd been reaching overhead for the last thirty minutes and was ready for a different job.

"Sounds good. I'm going to run upstairs and check on the boys. Be right back."

"Take your time!" Becky called after her. Relieved as she was to avoid certain company, the price she had to pay was pretty steep. They'd be cleaning all day.

A knock on the kitchen door made her jump. Maybe Otis was stopping by? A shadow crossed the window next to the door and the body that cast it was no eighty-year-old man. *Tank.* Becky had called Grace earlier, and though her friend wasn't feeling well, she assured Becky that she'd let her brother know that dinner was canceled.

Becky opened the door slowly and tried not to scowl. Tank sported nice slacks and a sweater, and carried a bowl and a bottle of wine. He looked less than thrilled that she was the one to greet him.

"Come on in," she said, standing out of his way and then shutting the door behind him.

"Everything alright?" he asked, obviously smelling the residual smoke.

"Well, we had a turkey issue. I called Grace and she said she'd let you know." Hopefully that un-invite was fairly clear.

Tank nodded, looking as uncertain as a man his size could look. He finally set the bowl and bottle down on the counter. "I don't always have my phone with me. She probably left me a message."

"Well, she probably also let you know that she isn't feeling well." *Run along. Go check on her.*

He actually made eye contact. "Is she okay? What's wrong?"

The concern in his eyes was almost touching. Becky fought to stay irritated with him.

"I'm not really sure. Some kind of head cold, I think. I was going to run some soup over later this afternoon." *Or at least I'm planning to now.*

He nodded. "I'll give her a call and check in."

"So you do have your phone."

He looked at her darkly. Becky stood her ground, her arms crossed, not entirely sure why she was picking a fight with him when he'd just found out his sister was sick.

"She's probably sleeping now," Becky conceded, "but if you want to use Maddy's phone, it's over there on the counter."

"Thanks."

They stood there awkwardly, not knowing how not to fight. The stairwell door rattled, then opened, and Parker spilled out into the kitchen.

"Mr. Tank! Aw, cool! You're here!" He boldly approached the football player and received a fist bump for his bravery. Becky marveled at the difference in the size of their hands.

"How you doin', Parker?" Tank crouched down, still dwarfing his new friend.

"Good! Our turkey blew up, so we're having samwiches for dinner. Isn't that funny?"

Tank grinned - a rare sight. "Hilarious."

"Are you going to help us clean?" Parker asked, as though he'd had anything to do with the cleaning so far.

"Oh, well ..."

"No, Parker," Becky quickly interjected. "Mr. Kimball is busy."

"Who?" Parker looked confused.

"Mr. Kimball - him," Becky pointed.

Parker's face fell. "We have to wash cupboards," he grumbled.

"Bummer," Tank replied, ruffling Parker's hair as he stood.

"I'll ask if you can stay and eat with us," Parker offered, his eyes lighting up, again.

Becky groaned inwardly. Why had Parker come down before she could get rid of Tank? As she tried to think of another way to call Parker off, John came through the door.

"Hey, Tank. Good to see you."

"John." They shook hands. "Happy Thanksgiving."

"It's definitely one for the memory books," John grinned. "I'm sorry we can't have the meal like we planned, but we're going to put something together after the clean-up."

"I haven't had a normal Thanksgiving in almost ten years. Wouldn't know what one looks like."

"I invited Mr. Tank to help," Parker jumped in.

John smiled. "Well, we could also ask Mr. Tank to come back a little closer to eating time." He looked up from his son. "Sorry Grace is sick. You're still more than welcome - I'd enjoy watching football with you."

He looked so hopeful, Becky knew her day was doomed.

"I could stick around and help out."

"Are you sure? This isn't really what we had in mind," John replied.

"I'll check in with Grace. If she's okay, I'll stay." Tank cleared his throat. "Gotta warn you. I'm not much good at watching football."

John smiled. "I'll take my chances."

***

How Tank ended up with Parker as a cleaning partner, Becky could hardly imagine. He'd offered to wipe down the highest shelves and surfaces, and had made his way from the front of the house into the dining room, with Parker in tow. She tried not to listen to their conversation, but since they were working around the corner, it was hard to ignore them. Becky almost asked them to close the door, but they needed everything open for ventilation.

The kitchen was just about done; all that remained was to wash the floor. Becky refilled her bucket with warm water and soap and retrieved the mop from the cupboard. Maddy was upstairs closing windows and checking the bedrooms. John was probably building another addition on the house.

"... and I like to draw like Miss Becky, only now she's my aunt. I used to call her Betty, 'cuz I didn't know."

Becky stilled. Why couldn't Parker find someone else to talk about? She wasn't surprised that Tank had no response. She clearly wasn't one of his favorite subjects.

"She showed me how to draw animals. She draws so good! And paints. She likes butterflies. Did you ever see her tattoo?"

Becky dumped half of her bucket's contents on the floor. Scrambling to contain the water, she swallowed the expletives warring for expression and called out to Parker.

"Hey Parker, can you give me a hand?" She grabbed some towels from the laundry room and returned to the mess.

Parker strolled around the corner. "Hi, Aunt Miss Becky! Why are you on the floor?"

"Well, I was going to wash it anyway, but I spilled some of my water. Can you help me wipe it up?"

"Sure," he agreed readily, getting down on all fours with her.

Tank appeared at the door of the dining room. "Everything okay?"

Becky refused to look up at him. She wiped at the floor like she was saving lives. "We're fine."

She could feel him watching her, probably imagining where her tattoo was. She quickly sat back on her heels, hoping her flushed face could be blamed on the cleaning. "Are you done in the dining room?"

He was fighting a grin. "Yes, ma'am."

She scowled at him. "Don't call me 'ma'am.' " She looked back at Parker who was sliding all over the floor with his towel. "I think I've got it, Parker. Why don't you help Mr. Kimball, again?"

"Why do you call him that?" Parker asked.

Becky got back to work, wiping up the rest of the water. "Because that's his name."

"His name is Tank. Like an army tank!" Parker said, his eyes lighting up at the connection. This time, Tank did grin, and Becky quickly looked away. Those two were a dangerous combination.

"Well, why don't you go show him some of your cars and trucks?"

"I don't have my toys here, but, hey! I can show him our hide-out! Come on!"

Parker grabbed Tank's hand and pulled him toward the kitchen stairwell. "You gotta see this! You won't fit, but you can look. It's so cool!"

Becky bit back a smile as the giant followed the little elf up to the secret hide-out that the boys played in whenever they came to the house. Maddy had discovered a tiny room off one of the clos-ets, accessible through a sliding door under the shelf. How she ever found it was beyond Becky, but the boys were enthralled with the space. Maddy had gone in herself the first time she showed it to them. Becky shuddered at the thought.

At least they were out of her hair for a while. If Parker decided to share any more secrets, she didn't have to hear him do it.

***

"What are those big chunks in the red stuff?" Parker asked as the cleaning crew finally stopped and gathered around to eat.

John leaned down and said something quietly in his ear, and Parker rephrased his question.

"What kind of fruit salad is this, Mr. Tank?"

Tank smiled. The kid was growing on him. "It has strawberries and pineapples and cranberries and some jello and nuts. That about covers it," he answered.

"Oh, nuts!" Parker wrinkled his nose, and John cleared his throat. "I'll just pick 'em out!" Parker decided, trying to maneuver the serving spoon from his less than ideal angle at the island in the kitchen.

Maddy reached over to help him load his plate, and Blake and Otis followed. Becky tailed Otis, and John, the polite host, waited for Tank to jump in line. He had no choice but to stand next to Becky and her tattoo, which had taken much more of his mental energy than it should have throughout the day.

They helped themselves to a simple meal of sandwiches on Otis's homemade rolls, Becky's potatoes, and Tank's mystery fruit dish. No one seemed bothered by the fact that it was a rather un-typical Thanksgiving meal. Even Maddy, who was initially apolo-getic, seemed to accept the fact that this was not a meal that would grace a magazine cover.

The football game was about to begin, and the plan was to eat in the large and comfortable sunroom. It was Tank's favorite part of the house - very contemporary compared to the Victorian decor that decked out the rest of the inn. He wasn't comfortable in any of those rooms; always felt like he was going to knock something over and break it. This room, with its view of the ocean, big fire-place and comfortable furniture was a place he could relax in.

The mood was upbeat and casual. Tank liked casual. Tank liked food. It was the football part that concerned him. Why had he agreed to share this day with virtual strangers?

He had checked in on Grace, who was happy to stay at home and get over her cold. She insisted that she didn't want company, but he did notice that Becky had put a plate together for her and was planning to deliver it. Apparently, John's mother, sister, and niece had decided to have a small celebration at his mother's house, saving their family gathering for the following day. That suited Tank just fine. He wasn't crazy about crowds, at least the ones he had to share a room with. Otis was good company, and Tank was glad when he arrived toward the end of the cleaning-fest. He was now comfortably settled in a recliner with his food.

Tank pulled a chair next to Otis, leaving the large, comfortable couches for the family. He knew he'd end up prowling during the game, and didn't want to disturb people by jumping up every few minutes. He watched the pre-game show, all the while imagining what was going on in the locker room. He knew just where he'd be sitting, fully padded, arms resting on his knees and head down, fo-cusing his mind on the job that lay before him.

The players started running onto the field and Tank's heart twisted into a painful knot. He thought he could handle this; even thought the company might help, but he wanted nothing more than to clear the room and throw a fit. He took a deep breath. If he walked out now, everyone would feel sorry for him; then he'd really be angry. He forced down another bite of Becky's stupid potatoes. Maybe if he focused on his present source of irritation, he'd be distracted from the past.

The present source was snuggled next to Blake on the couch. She whispered something to him and he grinned. Now there was a kid Tank understood. He got a kick out of Parker, but he *got* Blake; the older, responsible brother, who took everything a bit too seri-ously while his brother had all the fun. He remembered being seri-ous as a kid, and Grace was always his lighthearted counterpart. He'd wanted to be more like her, but just didn't know how. Then she married that jerk, who pretty much wiped out her joy. Tank found himself clenching his fists. He'd never liked Jim, and while he was sorry to see his sister go through a divorce, he was glad that Jim was out of her life. Tank would make certain he stayed out.

He took another bite of the potatoes and tried not to like them, but they were really pretty good. He noticed that he was cleaning his plate a lot faster than everyone else. He'd have to slow down. No point in scaring these folks.

Looking back up at the screen, he watched the kick-off, and the game began. After that, there was no thought of potatoes or food or Grace and her love life. Football was everything, playing or not. He put his plate on the floor, leaned his elbows on his knees, and helplessly watched the game.

***

Becky finished her food, fighting the urge to ask Tank for his fruit salad recipe. It's not like they needed to make small talk; she'd just find it online. Besides, he was so focused on the game, he wouldn't notice her if she sat in his lap and slapped him. Not that *that* was an image taking shape in her mind.

She turned toward the game. She liked football well enough, she just didn't have the opportunity to watch it very often. Following the general flow of the game was no problem, but she usually got distracted comparing the body types of the players, and trying to figure out how they were really built under all those pads. Now that she had a real life example in the same room with her, her perspective on the players changed dramatically.

She knew football players were big, just not *that* big. She tried to imagine a whole line of Tanks, further enlarged by all of their pads, charging at another line of Tanks in pads. How did they survive the carnage? She peeked at him from behind the pillow she was holding. He was riveted, of course, his foot tapping madly as he watched each play unfold. She tried to imagine him out there, doing what the guys on TV were doing.

It wasn't a stretch. He'd fit right in. The mind-blowing part was just how much weight was being thrown around that field, just so someone could move a bit of pigskin from one end to the other.

Silly game.

Maddy got up and started gathering the plates, and Becky followed.

"Please, relax. I'm happy to clean up," Maddy said.

"Thanks. I think I'll run this meal over to Grace and check on her," Becky replied.

"Sounds good. Say 'hello' for us."

Becky contemplated asking Tank if he had any kind of message for his sister, but one look at him convinced her that Grace didn't exist in his world, and wouldn't, at least until half-time. She threw on her coat and left.

***

Half-time had come and gone and Tank finally settled down a bit as he watched the end of the game. Slowly, but surely, the world around him came back into focus: Otis nodding off in his chair, Parker and Blake playing a game of checkers on the floor, Maddy curled up in a corner of the couch next to John, her computer open on her lap. John was the only one really watching the game with Tank, but he occasionally leaned over and whispered something to Maddy. She'd smile and nudge him with her knee.

Tank looked away. He didn't need the world to come into that sharp a focus. At least he didn't want to flip the tables, anymore; that much was good. He'd paced a bit and threw his hands up in disgust on occasion, but for the most part, he'd behaved. It was probably a good thing that he had an audience for his first Thanksgiving game on the other side of the television screen. There was no telling what he might have done on his own.

He got up to get a water bottle, and realized that Becky had disappeared. More accurately, he realized that she hadn't yet reappeared. He'd been uncomfortably aware of the fact that she was no longer in the room.

A moment later she walked through the dining room door. Her cheeks were flushed from the cold and her normally precisely arranged hair had a wind-blown look that he'd have found attractive on anyone else's head.

She stopped short when she saw him, then brushed a hand over her hair and walked in with her 'Becky-air' regained. She slipped out of her jacket and draped it over a barstool. Nodding at him - the bare-minimum acknowledgment - she walked into her room.

Tank decided to take advantage of her absence to get back to the safety of the game. As he turned, Maddy met him on her way into the kitchen.

"Oh, your wine," she said, noticing the bottle. "Would you like a glass?"

"No, I'm good," he replied, anxious to put what little distance he could between himself and Becky.

"Well, I think it sounds like fun. Maybe Becky will have glass with me. Did I hear her come in?"

"Yeah, she just went into her room."

"Oh, good," Maddy looked at him for a moment. "I don't suppose I could get you to open it for me? I'm not a master with the cork-screw."

Tank swallowed a disappointed sigh. "Of course."

Maddy wound around to the other side of the island. "Here's the - oh, wait. Hold on."

She dug in the drawer for a while and Tank fought the urge to drum his fingers on the counter.

"Got it!" Maddy pulled the cork screw out with a smile and handed it to him.

"Got what?" Becky asked, walking back out of her room with her hair fixed and big fluffy slippers on her feet.

Tank thought about the bare feet he'd seen a few weeks before, propped up on the railing in the evening breeze. Why he was contemplating those feet in the big fluffy slippers was beyond him. He attacked the wine bottle with renewed energy.

"Tank's opening the wine he brought. Have a glass with me?"

Tank glanced up; he couldn't help himself. Becky was looking at him and had lost some of the rosy color from her cheeks. He could almost sense her inner battle. She clearly didn't want the wine, but she didn't want to acknowledge any kind of issue with it. He almost smiled, watching her squirm.

"I think I'll wait," she finally replied. "I just had a cup of tea with Grace. Palate's in a different place right now."

Of course, she'd just gone to visit Grace. In his obsession with football and the innkeeper's sister, he'd forgotten all about his own sister; his sick sister. *What a jerk.*

"How's she doing?" he asked, hoping his apparent indifference wasn't obvious to his hosts.

"She's doing better," Becky replied, not really directing her answer at him. "She's mostly nervous about not being up for tomorrow."

Tank nodded. It would be a busy day at the shop, especially if the Black Friday shoppers from the outlet mall found their way into Clairmont for some small town shopping. It would drive Grace crazy to miss a day like that.

"I reminded her that she's got a great staff, and to just concentrate on feeling better," Becky finished. "She says to say 'hello' to everyone."

At this she glanced up at Tank. He nodded, and they shared a non-combative moment. "Thanks for checking on her," he said.

Becky shrugged. "She's my friend."

The bottle opened, Tank offered to pour and Maddy set out the wine glasses. He finished his job and then hustled back into the living room. Five minutes left in the game.

Becky walked in and curled up in the corner of one of the couches. What was it with women and curling up on furniture like cats? Tank couldn't remember the last time his calves were tucked under any other part of his body; probably the last time he was tackled.

He tried to concentrate on football, but his team's 'rebuilding' had continued throughout the game and it was difficult to watch. He studied the line and the plays they were calling, and the whole thing became painful all over again.

Maybe he should have had the wine.

Parker and Blake finished their checkers game, and from the look on Parker's face, it had not ended well for him. He and his long face went over and climbed into John's lap. Without skipping a beat or a play, John folded him in his arms, wordlessly comforting his son while watching the game.

Tank wondered if he'd ever be holding a son in his lap and watching football. He'd put off thoughts about settling down and raising a family because he always figured there'd be time for that when he was done playing. He considered John and Parker, and acknowledged that starting that chapter of his life might be one upside to the whole injury business.

He turned to see how Blake was handling his victory. He was sitting on the other couch, quietly talking to Becky about something. She was attentive, but not overbearing. She probably made a cool aunt, Tank conceded.

He turned back to the game. He did not like the direction his thoughts were taking.

thirteen

The weeks leading up to Christmas were a blur of teaching on the weekdays and taking care of guests on the weekends. Apparently, Claimont and the surrounding towns were popular for Christmas shopping and pre-holiday getaways.

Becky had been asked to take on several sections of a health class the following semester, which she was happy to do. Maybe there was something else she could pick up. She'd keep her ears open. She liked teaching, for the most part, and staying out of the inn during construction was the best part.

Maddy tried to involve her in the selection of paint and window treatments for the apartment, insisting she needed Becky's eye for color. Her input was disinterested. It seemed like the penthouse was now Tank's place. He'd had so much to do with the construction of the rooms that decorating no longer held the same appeal for her. Let them ask Tank what color he thought the walls should be, and then enjoy decorating the army green or slate gray he would likely choose. Becky just didn't care anymore.

She spent the occasional afternoon at the coffee shop after school, but for the most part, she lived at the library or in her room, preparing for the next semester. While she made a science of avoiding Tank at the house, it generally meant avoiding John and the boys, as well. It didn't surprise her that a virtual stranger had become a favorite with the family over her. Her dislike of him increased by the day.

She turned her energy on her classes. She'd always been pretty smart, but never particularly studious, so Serious Student Becky was a whole new person to get to know. It was good for her to be doing something other than art, which came much more easily for her. Re-learning French was challenging, but fun.

The course materials for the health class didn't look too complicated, although talking to teenagers about sex might prove intimidating. On the other hand, nothing they had to say could shock her. She'd find out soon enough.

***

A week before Christmas, Becky had finished her shopping and was on her way home to wrap presents. She had four guests checking in during the evening, which seemed a little close to the holiday, but she didn't mind. It meant no construction in the attic. Besides, the guests tended to enjoy shopping and eating out in the area, and generally kept to themselves.

Becky was counting on it. She needed peace and quiet, and time to prepare for flying back to Illinois to spend Christmas with her parents. John and Maddy and the boys would join the family for a few days between Christmas and the New Year, but, for the first time in a long time, Becky was planning on some serious alone time with her folks. The closer the time came to leaving, the more uncertain she became. Why had she finally agreed to spend more than the minimal time at home? She supposed she was a little interested in finding out, herself.

Meanwhile, there were papers to be graded, breakfast menus to plan, and big, dumb football players to avoid. Pulling into the drive, she was relieved to find it empty. She liked having the place to herself, pretending it was her own beautiful home on the water. The ocean was beginning to grow on her, and for all that she griped about not having the freedom to move out, it was going to be a huge adjustment when she did. She'd never be able to afford a place with a view like the inn.

Lucky Maddy, well, *smart* Maddy had sold her home in Seattle at just the right time, and had sold her shares in her computer company for a pretty penny, too. Then, with the right combination of grants for women starting new businesses and low interest loans, she'd purchased the mess of a house that her B&B was before John got his hands on it. Somehow, she'd made the money last until the renovations were almost complete. It probably didn't hurt that she'd seduced the renovator.

Becky shook her head with a wry smile as she climbed the steps to the porch. Maddy would never have tried to seduce John. They had fallen in love, navigated the inevitable problems, and gotten married. *Storybook stuff.* She sighed as she let herself into the house. She would have seduced the renovator and anyone else who served her purpose. How had she and Maddy grown up so differently?

She was sure her parents had often wondered the same thing. How could one daughter make all the right choices and one daughter be determined to make all the wrong ones? Becky supposed there was still time to make a few good ones, but there was no undoing the poor choices she'd already made. Maybe that's why she was determined to be done with men forever. They were clearly her undoing; always had been.

It was time to show some restraint. What better place to practice, than this small town on the coast of Maine, where all the good men were married and there was virtually no one to tempt her? Maybe that wasn't really practicing, but Becky needed all the help she could get.

Heavy steps pounded down the stairwell and Becky dropped almost every bag that she'd carefully maneuvered through the house and into the kitchen. She barely had time to contemplate the source when Tank came bursting through the door. What grown man made an entrance like that? And what was he doing in the house, anyhow?

He stopped and looked at her, as surprised as she was. "Thought you'd be gone for a while, yet."

"What are you doing here?" Becky demanded, stooping to pick up the bags she dropped.

"Hanging cupboards."

She ground her teeth; she wasn't really looking for details. "Well, I have guests coming, so you need to go."

Tank didn't move, just stood there staring at her. "Sorry about your packages; didn't mean to scare you."

Her eyes narrowed. "Don't try to be nice, now. The damage is done."

He looked a little surprised, but she didn't care. Nasty Tank was probably softening up under John's influence. She wasn't interested in this version of him, either.

He cleared his throat. "I came down for a drink. I was planning to finish the section I'm working on, then get out of your way."

Becky stopped and stared at him in his sawdust-covered T-shirt. His huge forearms were covered with dust but she refused to look at them any longer than was necessary to determine that they were ... dusty. "I thought there was no working while there are guests in the house."

He walked to the sink. "Are they here, yet?"

"Due any minute," she lied. She was counting on this time before people showed up. She needed him to go away.

He washed his hands and forearms, and then turned to her. "I won't make a sound. They won't even know I'm here."

She regarded him suspiciously. Unfortunately, she knew he was perfectly capable of doing just what he said, his most recent entrance notwithstanding. It was creepy how quiet he could be when he wanted to. She also knew that she could hardly go against John's wishes for whatever Tank was doing upstairs.

"Fine," she finally sighed. "Just keep quiet."

He grabbed one water bottle and put another in his tool belt. In true Tank style and just like she requested, he disappeared without a word.

***

Tank finished the cupboards by mid-evening. The kitchen was coming along well; John and Frank would be pleased. He packed up his things and tried not to think about how important this project had become to him. The relationship with John and his family was even more important. It had been a long time since he'd felt connected like this.

It was different with guys on the team. This was a real family kind of thing. At times he felt like he should work harder at keeping his distance, but then some project would come up, necessitating his working extra hours with John, and the relationship continued to grow.

Frank was a lot of fun, too. There was never a dull moment when he was around. He and John had endless questions about Tank's life playing ball, and it felt good to talk about it. While he'd hesitated in the beginning, it wasn't long before he was telling stories and filling them in on all of the ups and downs of his professional career.

While they made it clear that he was a big help to them, getting to know them and investing in a project had proven incredibly valuable to him. He needed them - and the job - much more than they needed him.

While he was ready to keep at it until the apartment was done, he knew that he needed to start thinking about his next step. He liked the house he'd moved into - it was much bigger than the cottage, and if he were honest, he could see himself settling in there, at least for the next few years. It would make sense to invest with the current market, but he didn't know if the owners had any intention of selling.

He'd been there the better part of a month, and he was starting to imagine the house filled with his own things. He missed his stuff. He missed the money he was spending storing his stuff halfway across the country. It was time to start making some decisions.

He also needed to get out into the community, and stop living in fear of being recognized. The area didn't seem to be heavily invested in pro-football, and that suited him just fine. It might be a good place to make a new start. No one had approached him about the P.E. job, but maybe it was time he looked into doing something with all of the energy he'd stored up over the last months.

***

True to his word, Tank made his way soundlessly down the back stairway. His stealth was apparently for nothing; he could hear Becky's guests talking and laughing in the kitchen. So much for sneaking out unnoticed.

He considered circling around to the main staircase and heading out the front, but his jacket was still in the kitchen. Even if he wanted to brave the cold, and he had no problem doing that to avoid Becky, his house keys were in his coat pocket.

Tank slowed as he reached the door to the kitchen, which was slightly ajar. Something about the conversation was unusual; the group was speaking in French, or at least he thought it was French. He didn't need a translator to understand that there were no men in the room. This was a group of women, talking fluently in another language, and Becky was with them.

He listened a moment more; it wasn't like he was eaves-dropping, he couldn't understand a word they were saying. It was interesting, and, he grudgingly conceded, impressive that Becky was keeping up. She even said something that made the other women laugh. He almost smiled. It was kind of an accomplishment to be funny in another language.

The angle of the slightly open door faced away from the table, and Tank contemplated how to enter the room without alarming the women. He'd really startled Becky when he'd come down earlier. He wasn't making the same kind of careless entrance now, but suddenly appearing at the door when they weren't expecting him might be just as alarming. He had no problem being quiet, but once he was in a room, he rarely went unnoticed. He could just imagine Becky's look when he entered this time.

He slowly pushed the door open and walked into the kitchen. One woman squealed, another gasped, and another said something in frantic French. There were five women, including Becky, the others in their late thirties, early forties. They were gathered around the table, sharing a bottle of wine, though he noted that there was no glass in front of Becky. He couldn't imagine what brought a group of French-speaking women to the coast of Maine just days before Christmas.

Standing uncertainly, something he was not accustomed to doing, he waited for Becky to explain who he was. She'd had her back to him initially, but had quickly gotten to her feet and composed herself, sort of. Her flashing eyes didn't surprise him. As much as he enjoyed baiting her, it seemed he didn't even have to make an effort to make her angry. It was getting a little old.

"Sorry to interrupt, just getting my jacket."

Becky's glare simmered to a glower and she turned to face the women. She said something, in French, of course, and the women settled down and began to regard him with interest. She said something else, and there was a giggle or two and one of the women blushed.

He didn't like not knowing what was being said, and he wasn't going to hang out and be the target of Becky's French humor. The conversation continued as he picked up his jacket and started toward the door.

Becky's voice was cool and collected when she finally spoke to him. "Mr. Kimball, come meet my new friends."

He slid his jacket on and eyed her warily. This wasn't a polite invitation, he could hear it in her voice.

"They're from Nova Scotia. They came for a wedding down the coast and decided to stay here in Clairmont to do some Christmas shopping."

Tank nodded, glanced at the women, then back at Becky.

"I told them that you were a guest, too, just for fun. They'd love to know what it's like to dance for the Boston Ballet. I can translate, if you like."

It was Tank's turn to glower. Becky's innocent smile incensed him further, because it would have been really attractive under any other circumstances. He looked back at the women, who were eyeing him with more than polite interest. He shook his head and made for the door.

He knew one French word, but he refrained from saying it as he stepped into the cold. He hoped that Becky's visit with her parents happened soon and lasted a long time. The idea of living in the same town with her took some of the steam out of his resolve to settle down in the area. The idea of pursuing a job that would have him working at the same high school was idiocy.

He started walking down the beach, hunching his shoulders against the cold. His frustration started to wear off as he walked along the water and listened to the winter waves brushing the shore. *The Boston Ballet.* He shook his head with an almost grin.

He planned on getting back at the innkeeper's sister, and he'd have fun doing it.

fourteen

It was good to be back at the inn. Becky dropped her suitcase in her bedroom and walked through the first floor, turning up the heat and giving the rooms a once-over. Everything looked as she'd left it before Christmas. She turned on the indoor and outdoor holiday lights and smiled. They were very festive, and she was in no hurry to take them down.

No guests were scheduled during the month of January, which was no surprise. A less hectic pace would be nice as she started the coming semester. Maddy's family would be a day or two behind in their return, and as far as Becky knew, no work would be done on the house while John was gone. She truly had the place to herself for a couple of days.

Plenty of wood remained stacked by the fireplace in the sunroom. She'd settle in for the evening with a book or a movie. The last week and a half with her parents had gone well, but it had left her with a lot to think about. She wasn't ready to do that, yet.

Half an hour and most of a box of matches later, a fire roared in the fireplace. Becky wrapped herself in a blanket and curled up with a book she'd found in Maddy's little library on the corner shelf. Three days remained until classes started, and Becky was determined to enjoy the time before taking on the kids again.

She opened her thriller and hoped it didn't get too intense. She didn't usually scare easily, but she did feel a little isolated, alone in Maddy's big house. She glanced out the window, hoping to see Otis' lights on next door. He was either away visiting family or friends, or maybe he'd just gone to bed early. She hoped it was the latter. She liked the idea of having someone close by.

***

At ten-thirty, she was still reading, riveted by the story unfolding in her hands. The woman in her book was also alone, not in a big old house, but in a deserted bus station. She'd figured out 'whodunit' and had missed the last bus out. The woman huddled in the bathroom, hiding and hoping the 'who' wouldn't do it again.

Becky put the book down to get her bearings. Her heart rate was up a bit, and she had to give the author credit. It had been a long time since a book had done that to her. She looked around; everything was as it should be, though she needed to stoke the fire. She considered the dwindling pile of wood. A trip outside would be necessary to replenish the stack.

No way I'm doing that tonight.

She snuggled into her blanket. She should probably go to bed, but she wanted to stay by the fire while it had a little life left in it. Besides, she wasn't about to leave her friend alone in the bus station until morning. She'd read until everyone was safe and sound.

***

"So, how was your Christmas?"

Grace yawned. "Becky? What time is it?"

Becky tried to sound casual. "Oh, around midnight, I guess. Sorry to call so late. I just got in a little while ago and I thought I'd check in and see how you were doing."

Grace yawned again. "Well, I'm fine, but I was sleeping. I have to get up early to open the shop."

"Oh, right, of course. I'm sorry, I lost track of time."

There was a momentary silence on the other end of the line. "Becky, are you okay?"

She tried not to look out the oversized windows onto the porch. Why had they decided against shades? Any serial killer could be looking in at her and she'd never know it.

"Becky?"

"I'm sorry, I'm fine." She pulled one of the pillows on top of her. "Okay, well, honestly, I've been reading kind of a scary book, and I got myself a little freaked out."

She could hear Grace's sigh. "Put the book down and go to bed."

"Well, that's the plan."

"But?" Grace's voice took on a different level of concern. Becky felt bad, but she was just so happy to be speaking to a live person. Maddy hadn't answered her phone.

"Well, I'm sitting in the sun room with all these windows, and, I don't know, I could swear I heard someone out on the porch."

"Oh. That is creepy."

Becky would much rather be told she was crazy.

"Well, what's Burt doing?" Grace asked. "He'd bark if there were anyone out there, right?"

"Sure, he would, but he's not here right now. I'm supposed to pick him up at Frank's in the morning." *If I live through the night.*

"Oh, shoot."

"Yeah, I really wish he were here. I wouldn't think twice about the noises - I never have before."

"Well, maybe you should call the police. They won't mind coming and checking the place out."

"I really don't want to make a big deal out of it. It's probably nothing."

"You don't sound like it's nothing, and you usually don't get scared like this."

"Well, yeah, not usually."

"Seriously, Becky, that's what they get paid for. Just call them."

"I don't know. I think it's just the book. I swore off romances, so I tried a thriller."

Another audible sigh. "Well, that's what you get for swearing off romance."

Becky rolled her eyes.

"Want me to send Tank over? He's not that far down the beach."

Becky could hear her friend's grin. "I'd rather have a S.W.A.T. team storm the place."

"He wouldn't mind stopping by and making sure you're safe."

"Are you kidding me? He'd mind like crazy. And I'd never live it down. Hold on ..." Becky was sure she'd seen a shadow moving across the porch. She swallowed a little squeal.

"Are you okay?"

"Yes," she whispered. "But I think I saw something out there."

"This is ridiculous. I'm calling the police."

"What if it's the officer who always comes to the shop whenever I'm there? He's relentless. He'll think I'm making some creepy move on him."

There was silence as Grace conceded her point. "Well, there are, like, half a dozen guys on the force. And that one woman."

"She's terrifying."

"I know. Probably just what you need."

"Well, then I'd feel really stupid. I just need to deal with this by myself."

"Which is why you've kept me on the phone for the last ten minutes."

"I just wanted a witness."

"Right. I'll explain everything I saw to the police."

Becky smiled a little. Then she heard another unwelcome sound. "Oh no. My phone is dying. I have to plug in."

"Well, call me back when you do."

"I will. Thanks, Grace."

***

"Just go check on her. Please. And Tank?"

"Yeah?"

"Don't scare her."

"Okay. "

"I mean it. I've been on the receiving end of your pranks. Don't do it. Not tonight. She's really freaked out."

"Got it. I'll just go make sure the house is secure."

"Tank ..."

"What?" His tone oozed innocence.

"You never talk like that."

"I'm a changed man, Grace. Just a good deed doer out to do a good deed."

"If you scare her, I'll ... Just don't do it, Tank," she warned him.

He grinned again. "Good night, Grace."

***

Tank traded sweats for jeans and threw on a pair of boots. He hadn't been asleep when Grace called, so it wasn't a big deal to go on her little errand. He'd been watching some sports re-caps and then an old movie while he worked on replacing the kitchen faucet. The owners of the house had given him carte blanche on any repairs he felt like doing. *So kind of them.*

There were a dozen or so houses between his and Maddy's Inn and though the air was cold, it was a fairly easy jog down the beach. He'd actually sort of missed fighting with Becky over the holidays and was looking forward to sparring with her again, after he taught her a lesson about reading scary books in the middle of the night. He grinned again at the thought. He'd made a science out of scaring his little sister when they were young. It wouldn't be too difficult to recall some of those well-honed skills.

Becky would be furious. Tank could hardly wait to have her angry with him again. He kind of liked her flashing eyes.

His breath caught a little as his body processed the cold. What kind of an idiot would be out terrorizing women on a night like this? He slowed his jog as he approached the house.

Okay, he was that idiot. He hoped he was the only one.

The inn was lit up like a jack-o-lantern. Didn't Becky know that anyone could look in and watch every move she made? The thought was disconcerting, and he picked up his pace again, jogging up to the house. He still doubted that anyone was prowling around, not in this little town, but if someone was out there, Becky was giving him a show.

It was the middle of winter. Did the woman ever wear pants?

***

Becky drummed her fingers on the kitchen counter, cursing her old phone battery. She'd forgotten that if she let it completely run out, it was a while before the phone would charge enough for her to turn it back on. She could use Maddy's house phone, but she didn't have Grace's number memorized. The phone book was ... somewhere. She wasn't about to go looking for it.

She pulled the rather small blanket around her shoulders. It really hung more like a cape and didn't offer a whole lot of warmth. Her pajama shorts and T-shirt weren't cutting it like they had when the fire was blazing. She'd have to put warmer pajamas on when she went to bed - if she went to bed.

She shivered. That stupid book had turned her into a jittery mess. She was furious with herself, but she just couldn't seem to tap into her rational mind. Every time she started to calm down there was a new shadowed movement outside, or the wind blew a branch against a window, or the stupid old house would creak in some terrifying new way. Becky was about to jump out of her skin. She really needed to get Grace back on the line and get some perspective.

She tried turning the phone on again. Nothing. She took a deep breath. It was time to put on some jeans and a sweatshirt and face her fears. She couldn't go on like this. Facing the windows, she backed up toward the door to her room. She reached back for the countertop she knew was there, missing it with her hand, but hitting it with her hip. The jolt made her jump again. She turned and sped into her room.

Turning on the overhead light, she spun around, trying to face every possible danger at once. Nothing seemed out of place. Her heart pounding, she slowly walked to the door that led out to the side porch. There was no reason it should be unlocked; no one had used the door in two weeks. Still, she had to check.

The lock was secure, and she was breathing a sigh of relief when she heard a creak overhead. She froze and waited for a painfully long moment. *Nothing.* If there was something upstairs, it stopped moving. She slowly let out the gasp that had been her last breath. She looked at the window and then overhead again. *Pants.* She needed pants and something for her feet. Then she'd face whatever was out there or above her.

***

Tank circled the house and found no recent tracks in the snow. All of the first floor lights on the beach side were on, including the Christmas lights. The ones in the front of the house were off, the Christmas lights excepted. All in all, it looked very festive. He circled Otis' house for good measure and then the house on the other side of the inn. He was relieved to find no one lurking around.

He looked up at the second floor of the inn. He supposed it was possible that someone was up there, but he hadn't seen more than Becky's prints leading from her car to the porch. If someone were inside, they'd been there for a while. Tank didn't think that was likely.

He walked back to the beach side of the house and contemplated his next step. He could call Grace and tell her that things looked secure. She could tell Becky, and, though she'd be irritated that he'd been creeping around the place, she might rest easier. On the other hand, on the off-chance that someone was inside the house, he should probably walk through and make sure.

He patted his phone pocket; *empty, of course*. He'd have to go for option two.

He stepped up onto the porch. Scaring Becky had seemed like fun a half hour ago. *Now, not so much*. She'd be furious with him for getting in her business, and most likely there'd be no reason for him to be there at all. He walked to the door. Should he knock? What would scare her least?

***

Fully dressed, and her hair brushed for good measure, Becky felt more confident. Reason was starting to return. The book had put ideas into her head that were simply not rational. She was out in the middle of nowhere, not in a crime-ridden section of a big city. The house was old and creaky and the wind was howling more than usual. That was it. She was a big girl, and she wasn't going to hide from her fears anymore. She'd turn every light on and search every room. She'd even check the porch for any sign of a disturbance out there. Then she'd throw her book into a snowdrift and go to sleep. She almost smiled at how silly she'd been acting. She and Grace would have a good laugh about it in the morning.

Walking into the kitchen, she considered the windows that normally offered a breathtaking view of the ocean. She tried to recall the happy association, and not just see a row of black voids, separated by flimsy little curtains. She took a deep breath.

I can do this.

A big gust of wind howled through, and Becky jumped as the remaining logs clunked and settled in the fireplace. Her heart pounding, she walked into the sunroom and confirmed the source of the racket. She took the fireplace poker and pushed the wood toward the back, deciding to hold onto the handy metal stick as she checked the porch. That's where she'd heard the most alarming sounds earlier. She'd peek out and make sure there were no foot-prints, and then search the rest of the house.

The inner door opened with more creaking than Becky had ever recalled hearing before. She flipped on the porch light and slowly opened the outer door. A little bit of snow had blown up onto the porch; a nice even layer that would clearly show ...

A scream caught in Becky's throat as she noted the huge prints in the snow. All of her fears flooded back over her like a tidal wave and she barely had the presence of mind to raise the fireplace pok-er when the hulking figure advanced.

***

She was going to try to kill him. Tank looked on in disbelief as Becky raised her weapon with both hands and prepared to bring it down on his head. This is how she answered the door?

Apparently, knocking was not a good idea.

He did the only thing that would keep both of them from seri-ous injury. He caught her hands, taking control of the poker, and spun her around. He applied gentle but decisive pressure until the metal rod dropped at her feet. Then he pulled her back into his chest, giving the poker a kick across the porch for good measure.

It was not exactly the rescue mission he had planned.

***

Becky had never felt anything like the raw panic that took over when she came up against a real intruder. The adrenaline surge was an unparalleled sensation. She truly felt like she could do serious damage with the fireplace poker, and wasn't the least bit hesitant to try. It never occurred to her that the intruder in the dark, hooded jacket was someone she knew and loathed.

It did finally occur to her when the beast had her in some sort of body lock. She'd fought against the supposedly unknown villain, unleashing all of the fear that her book and too much time in an empty house had inspired. Of course, it was Tank, there to witness and even inspire another round of indignity on Maddy's porch. She needed to find a new place to humiliate herself.

First, she needed to find a way out of his vise grip. She could barely breathe. With an effort, she let her body relax, and in the moment before Tank let her loose she could feel his own adrenaline pumping. So maybe she'd scared him a little, too. There was some satisfaction in that.

Satisfaction, she could handle. The other emotions beginning to surface as she remained wrapped in his admittedly very strong arms were not emotions she cared to explore. She began to tense up again and Tank lowered her gently to the porch. He loosened his grip but didn't let go.

"You okay?"

"I'll be okay when you let - me - go," she replied, twisting her limbs free.

She rounded on him immediately. "What are you doing out here?" She shoved him for good measure.

Now that she knew she was safe, relatively speaking, a whole new kind of adrenaline kicked in. She was furious. She wanted to shove him and punch him and pound him for all of the fear and anxiety and the host of new and unexpected emotions she'd experienced in the last few minutes.

So she did.

***

Tank focused on catching his breath. It didn't help that Becky was in full-on attack mode again, but at least she didn't have the fireplace poker this round. He stood with his fists clenched at his sides and let her shove and punch. If she reached for his face, he'd stop her. For now, she needed to vent. She must have been really scared. He felt kind of bad.

So he let her punch.

About a minute or so in, he decided he'd had enough, and pulled her into his arms. He was the last person she'd want comfort from, but he was the only one around.

So he held her.

She was too shocked to resist at first. Her arms, caught in mid swing against his chest, finally relaxed. She stood for a moment, trying to catch her breath. She wasn't exactly cuddling, but she wasn't fighting it, either.

His hand accidentally brushed her silky hair, and he paused. There was a very real possibility that holding Becky was almost as much fun as fighting with her. *Dangerous territory.*

She must have sensed it, too, because a moment later she shoved away from him. "What are you doing out here?" she asked again, her voice calmer, but only because she was exhausted.

He shoved his hands in his pockets, making a small effort to control the limbs that had just betrayed him. "Grace asked me to come over and make sure there was no one prowling around."

Becky breathed a moment more, confusion warring with her recent fury. "Well, turns out it was you." She shivered, apparently realizing that she was wearing only a sweatshirt. "I need to go in," she said, turning back into the kitchen.

It would have been an ideal time to leave, but Tank felt like he should finish the job and walk through the house. Not that she was likely to let him at this point, but he thought he should offer.

Becky, still pretty jumpy, paced in the kitchen, rubbing her arms. She watched him follow her in and rolled her eyes. "Great." She walked over to heat up some water for tea or something.

She finally turned back to him. "Why didn't you at least knock? Why were you just lurking out there?"

Tank had a feeling it would be a while before he was properly thanked for coming out in the middle of the night to make sure she was safe. He should have figured it would end this way.

"I did knock, and you came out at me with a fireplace poker."

She looked at him warily. "I didn't hear a knock."

"I wouldn't have just stood out there waiting," *for long,* he qualified to himself. He had hesitated a bit, wondering if he should even knock on the door at all. Turns out, it was a legitimate concern.

"All I heard was a big gust of wind and the logs crashing in the fireplace," Becky replied, trying to sort out what had happened. "I opened the door to check for footprints, and then," she shuddered.

Tank had to admit that it wouldn't be fun to run into himself unexpectedly in the dark. He'd really frightened her. When he thought about wanting to do it intentionally, it made him a little sick. Then he thought about Grace and sighed. She'd never believe what had happened out here wasn't premeditated.

"I'm sorry I scared you." Hadn't he said that to Becky the last time they talked, before Christmas? What kind of a stupid relationship was this?

Becky looked up at him, clearly wanting to stay angry, but struggling in the face of his apology. "I'm sorry I sort of attacked you."

Sort of? Tank tried not to grin. Her qualification admittedly sucked some of the steam from her apology, but he understood why she'd done it.

"It's okay, it didn't really ..." He stopped, but not soon enough.

She eyed him with renewed irritation. "Hurt, right? That's what you were going to say? It didn't really hurt?"

He shrugged. What could he say? It had been uncomfortable but it hadn't hurt. Hadn't budged him, either. That probably made her mad, too.

"Well, you can go, now. I don't think anything could scare me more than you already have."

He shifted. "I walked around the house and checked the neighbors' yards. Do you want me to check upstairs?"

She drew breath to lay into him and tell him how much she didn't need him - it was all there in her eyes - but then she seemed to change her mind.

"No, just go. Thanks for coming over here in the middle of the night. This was silly. I'm sorry Grace involved you."

He might be hearing it from Grace, but Grace was sure going to be hearing it from Becky. She was not happy.

"Okay, if you're sure."

"I'm sure."

Tank walked out onto the porch, jogged down the steps, and continued down the beach. He would rather have checked through the inn, but he was not about to cross her anymore than he already had. If there was anyone in that house, they'd meet more than their match in Becky. She was no one to mess with tonight.

fifteen

"Ecoutez bien," Becky directed the class, though getting them to 'listen well' on the first day back after Christmas break bordered on impossible. To make matters worse, she'd been assigned a new room, with a row of windows that looked out into the cafeteria, which also served as the study hall area. Apparently, there were blinds, but they didn't work. Her students were constantly looking out to see who was misbehaving or walking by or doing anything that would excuse them from listening in French class.

With a sigh, she walked over and stood in front of the window. "Okay, enough with the study hall." She caught herself and continued, *"Regardez moi, s'il vous plait."*

Half of the class, the girl half, craned their necks to look around her.

"Who's that?"

"The new P.E. teacher."

"Wow."

"I know, right?"

Becky's blood slowly went cold. *No way.* She turned and looked out the window. Across the cafeteria, strolling toward the gymnasium like he owned the place, was the porch villain from just a few nights ago. She marked his path with a small group of teachers and one of the administrators. He was a head taller than most of them.

Her momentary distraction was not lost on her students.

"Hey, Ms. Jacobs, have you met Mr. Kimball?" More than one girl snickered.

"En Francais, s'il vous plait."

"Est-ce-que vous..." Several attempts followed as the students tried to remember how to ask their question in French.

"C'est suffit." Becky walked back to the front of the room. Let them speculate all they wanted about whether or not she knew the gym teacher, but they'd better do it in French. Her own speculation about the situation would have to wait until after school.

***

"Why didn't you tell me you took the P.E. job?"

"Why would I?"

Tank and Becky picked up their bickering in the parking lot after school. He *would* park his Jeep close to her car.

"It would have been nice to have a heads-up."

"Didn't think you'd care."

She narrowed her eyes at him. "I didn't think you'd do it."

Tank shrugged. "No point in trying to hide anymore. People pretty much know I'm here and don't really care."

Becky raised her eyebrows at this surprising admission.

"I figured I'd try the teaching thing and help the school out 'til the end of the year," he finished.

She was trying to be angry at him and he was wrecking it. That had happened more than once, lately. It really threw her off.

"Well, you interrupted my French class. They saw you walk by, and that was the end of it. The girls were all in a ..." She stopped, wishing she hadn't taken her complaining that far.

He showed no emotion, of course; just ran a hand over his jaw; his stupid, prickly jaw. The man needed to shave. "Kids were wound up all day. I figured they'd be tired out after their break."

"Yeah, so did I. I was hoping for a nice, quiet start to the semester." She eyed him again. "I can't believe you're doing it. What about the penthouse?"

"The penthouse?"

She rolled her eyes. "The apartment at the inn?"

"Oh." His eyes crinkled a little as he fought a smile. "I'll help finish it on the weekends." He must have read the look on her face, because he added, "Don't worry, you won't have reason to be alone and afraid for a good long while."

He was still perfectly capable of making her want to scream. "Nice. How long before I live that down?"

"Long time," he replied, his mouth quirking as he walked to his Jeep.

***

"Seriously, can you believe it?"

"What, that he's teaching at the high school? Makes sense to me." Maddy tossed the salad and set it on the island.

"No, it doesn't. We're mortal enemies. I don't want to work with him."

"You sound like a fifth grader."

"You sound like my mother."

Maddy laughed. "Honestly, what's the big deal?"

Becky picked up one of the sliced peppers and broke it in half.

"You gonna eat that or play with it?" Maddy asked, moving her salad bowl out of Becky's reach.

"It's just that, I don't know, the high school was my space, you know? I was just getting comfortable, and it was kind of cool having my own connections over there. He's there one day and everyone's in an uproar." She sighed and took a bite out of the pepper. "I have to be neutral about him, and believe me, that's not easy."

"I don't think I ever really got why you disliked him so much, except for the whole bailing you out and making breakfast and serving the guests thing."

Becky rolled her eyes. "That's because you've fallen under his evil spell. You're celebrity-smitten."

"Oh please, I never watched football until this fall, and that was just to spend time with John."

"Whatever. You're still smitten."

"True. But not with Tank," Maddy grinned. "And you're determined to make a villain out of him. He's a good guy."

"You didn't see him lurking out on your porch in the middle of the night for no reason."

"He was trying to look out for you. Seriously, Becky! Did you even thank him?"

"Of course, sort of," she qualified. "I didn't ask him to come prowling around."

Maddy shook her head. "I think John's home with the boys. Better table the Tank discussion. You won't get much sympathy here."

"I know! Have you seen Parker and him together? It's definitely not cool."

Maddy smiled. "I think it's great. And Blake has really opened up around him too. You know, I think he'd make a great uncle ..."

She timed her exit perfectly, hustling out to greet her family, and leaving Becky to stare after her in disbelief.

***

Becky walked through the high school looking for yet another new room. This was the first day of her health class, and she was anxious to get a take on her students. If she had mellow kids, it would be so much easier. The outspoken, self-proclaimed entertainers would be a tough crowd for the sex ed portion of the class.

At least this class was first period. Most of the kids would likely be too tired to give her a hard time. She could hope.

She found the room and tried the knob; already unlocked. She was running a little late - the wrong turn by the library had cost her - so someone must have let the kids in. She took a deep breath and pulled the door open.

A quick scan of the room revealed mixed results. She recognized a few of the kids from her French class; that was mostly okay except for one girl with a particularly nasty attitude. Maybe she just didn't like languages. Becky finished her quick appraisal of the students and stopped cold when her eyes rested on a figure at the front of the room; the large, hulking figure perched on her desk.

She pulled air into her lungs and tried not to panic. "Excuse me, Mr. Kimball, may I speak with you?"

He stood and walked to the door. "Yes, Ms. Jacobs?"

Their formality was absurd. She stepped outside and he followed.

"What are you doing in there?" she hissed.

"Taking attendance."

Her eyes flashed unspoken invective as she slowly said, "Yes, I know that. Why are you in this room?"

"This is my class," he enunciated just as slowly.

"This is *my* class," she whispered frantically, doubt beginning to trump anger. "What are you teaching?"

"Health."

She choked back an unteacherlike response. "*I'm* teaching this health class."

"We're both teaching this health class."

"You're a P.E. teacher. What do you have to do with health?"

His raised brow acknowledged the silliness of her question.

"Not a chance. I'm doing it alone," she insisted.

"You sure?"

Of course, she wasn't. It never occurred to her that they intended her to team teach the class. Why hadn't they said anything to her? More importantly, "How long have you known about this?"

He looked over his shoulder. They could both hear the class getting restless. "The syllabus said it was team-taught. I didn't know who my partner was until you walked in the room."

Doubt radiated from her in waves.

"Believe what you want. I signed on pretty late so I'm just trying to roll with whatever they need me to do."

"Well, I don't need your help."

"Too bad. I'm already making friends in there." He smirked at her. "I'm going back in to teach this class. You wanna bail, go ahead."

"I'm not bailing!"

"Sounds like you are to me."

"Well, you're just a football player, what do you know?"

He lifted the folder of class materials he was holding. "I know all about this - all about ..." he leaned in close, "... health."

She backed up a step and lifted her chin. "Well, I'll bet I know way more than you do about ... *health.*"

Their eyes held for a long, interesting moment.

"Prove it," he said, and walked back through the door.

***

Tank entered the room and held the door for a surprised Becky. *Nice touch*, he thought. If he was going to keep the tactical advantage he'd gained by being with the kids first, he had to appear gracious and welcoming to the new teacher. He would process the irony and, if he was honest, the intriguing aspects of the predicament, later. For now, it was time to be professional.

"Class, Ms. Jacobs will be teaching health with me."

He could have been reciting the alphabet in Hindi for all that they were paying attention to him. Every eye, especially the male variety, was glued to Becky as she made a very well-rehearsed entrance. Tank had counted on her being more flustered; he'd forgotten that she'd been teaching for years.

She was going to charm those students right out from under him.

Two could play at that game. If she was going to cash in on her 'presence,' then he would, too. Presence he had in abundance; let her try to compete. He strode to the front of the room.

"Alright, settle down. Let's finish attendance and talk about what we'll be covering."

***

Becky made the most of her entrance, working every angle she'd spent the last few months trying to downplay. Leaning against the teacher's desk, she carefully schooled her seething features while Tank launched into the course overview.

She looked on politely while considering his presentation. He had a natural command of the class, which, she supposed, wasn't entirely surprising. If you're accustomed to performing in front of thousands of people and a television audience, you probably didn't have a lot of problems with nerves. Still, this was her arena. His weakness would show sooner or later, and she'd be ready.

She searched her memory for any clue that she would share this class with another teacher. Nothing came to mind. Had she known she was sharing the course, she would have connected with the teacher and made a plan. She certainly would never have signed on to teach with Tank. What a joke! She felt her face grow warm at the idea of discussing these issues with *that* man.

Focus on the class, she reminded herself, and then noted that they were definitely focused on her. What had she missed? They were all looking at her expectantly, and to her dismay, Tank turned with a raised brow.

She straightened and donned her most distracting smile. "I'm sorry, I was looking at the syllabus. Did you ask me something?"

Tank glanced at the unopened folder on the desk. She dared him with her eyes to challenge her. He looked at her a long moment and then said, "Just wanted to know if you needed to add anything at this point."

She exhaled slowly. Point for him. "You're doing fine," she assured him sweetly. "Why don't I take over for the self-evaluation?"

He considered her offer a beat too long for Becky's comfort. Uncertainty gave way to relief when he finally nodded. "Sounds good."

Becky smiled her ever confident, 'I knew you'd come around' smile, and he seemed to look right through it before turning back to the class.

She would dissect that uncomfortable interlude later, after she took whatever steps necessary to change teaching partners. Even if it meant losing the money and giving the job to someone else, she was getting out. There was no way she was going to subject herself to the constant confusion of battling with Tank in front of a teenage audience.

***

Tank had to admit, she knew her stuff. Becky was prepared for the class and appeared thoroughly familiar with the self-evaluation tool they were using. He was accustomed to thinking and acting under pressure, so he'd done well enough for the first half of the class. He'd have some homework to do before they met again.

He observed how she walked through the room confidently, quietly interacting with students, answering the appropriate questions and effectively silencing the others. He settled into his seat to watch. It had been a long time since he'd been in the classroom. He might as well see if there was anything he could learn from her.

Apparently, some of the male students forgot he was in the room, because it wasn't long before they began to mark her progress as avidly as he did. Their interest didn't appear to be entirely professional. When Becky leaned over to listen to a girl's question in the corner of the room, most of the boys in the rather large class simply turned and watched. Some were making gestures, others were grinning, and they were all ogling.

Tank felt a ridiculous urge to hurl himself into the mix and see how many of the kids he could flatten with one leap. He did his best to squelch this less than professional inclination as he stood, heart rate accelerating, to get their attention.

Before he could speak, Becky turned, quickly but smoothly, and caught most of the boys in open-mouthed stares. As though she'd dealt with the problem a hundred times before, and she probably had, she crossed her arms and seared the room with her flashing eyes.

"Problems with your *self*-evaluation, boys?" she asked.

It was quiet for a moment, and Tank started to cool down. *Good for her.* She dealt with them herself, which was probably best. Using the term 'boys' was a nice touch; kept the kids in their place.

A voice from the corner of the room, just a little too loud for his intended private audience, said, "But I'd rather evaluate ..."

He never finished. Somewhere between 'rather' and 'evaluate,' Tank launched himself from the desk. The whole process of crossing the room, picking up the desk with the kid in it and turning it to face the wall took seconds. He spun and glared at the rest of the class, but only one person had the nerve to return his stare. The students instantly became absorbed with the papers on their desks; no one even dared to laugh at the kid who'd been silenced.

Becky reined in her reaction, glanced at the clock, and then walked to the front of the room. She picked up her materials, put them in her bag, then addressed the class.

"Time is just about up. Be sure to finish the evaluations and be ready to discuss them next class."

Papers rustled and chairs scraped the floor as the students prepared to leave. Tank stood in the corner, arms crossed, trying to figure out what had come over him. He thought through his reaction: he hadn't touched the kid or threatened him. He'd just redirected him, figuratively and literally.

He took a deep breath and walked to the front of the room. Becky looked out at the class, completely ignoring him. She was packed and ready to go. He had a pretty good idea where she was headed, and she looked ready to book it as soon as the bell rang.

He'd have to talk to her before she got herself removed from teaching the class. Whatever their differences, they could do it. It would be good for the kids and it would probably be good for them. He didn't even know for sure why, but there was no way he was going to let her run away.

***

Becky could feel him in the hall behind her. How did he do that? She'd left the room with the kids, and even Tank would have understood the need to see the rest of the students out before leaving the room locked on his way to his next ... whatever. Apparently, his whatever included stalking her path to the office.

She quickened her pace as much as she reasonably could with a hallway full of kids. Sensing that Tank was gaining on her, she fought an unreasonable urge to panic. She had a head start and a long stride, she should easily have lost him in the crowd of teenagers filling the halls.

She rounded the corner; one more long stretch to go. It wasn't necessary to look behind to see if he was still following. The looks on the faces of the girls walking past said it all. Wide-eyed and whispering, they looked right past her to the spectacle further down the hall. She scowled in frustration. He wasn't even good-looking; he was just big, and he'd played professional football. So what? She smiled distractedly at the physics teacher - *oh, big mistake.* Now he'd stop by her room after school again.

Becky finally reached the door to the registrar's office. Relieved and determined, she reached for the handle, and the usually heavy door swung open with ease. She followed the edge of the door up to a large hand connected to an all-too-familiar oversized forearm. Without looking further, she sighed and walked into the office.

"Ms. Jacobs, Mr. Kimball. How was your first day with the health class?" The registrar happened to be in the outer office and greeted them warmly.

"Actually, if you have a minute, I'd like to talk to you about that," Becky replied, trying hard to ignore the overwhelming presence behind her.

"Ms. Jacobs, may I have a word with you first?"

She'd never heard him use that tone of voice. It was bordering on ... courteous. She turned slowly, formulating her unequivocal denial. When she made eye contact, her heart almost stopped, he was looking back at her so earnestly.

She eyed him suspiciously. First he leaps across the room to defend her honor, then follows her across the school, and then asks politely to speak with her? She'd never been more alarmed.

She dated the guys who made the obnoxious comments, not the rescuers. She led carefully chosen men on a merry chase and expected them to follow on *her* terms. Guys who were courteous? Not even on her radar. How had her enemy become all three in the space of half an hour?

"What is it?"

He looked over her head. "We'll just be a minute."

Becky groaned quietly as she passed back through the door he held open. The halls were almost clear as the second hour class had begun.

"Well, you have me, Mr. Kimball. What do you want me for?" She let her voice drip with innuendo, looking him right in the eye.

He ignored the overtones, but not her eyes. "You need to stick it out. We should teach this class together."

"Why? And what made you think I wasn't going to stick it out?"

He gave her the single raised eyebrow, again.

"I think this is a really bad idea," she argued.

"Why?"

"We can hardly stand each other." She lowered her voice as another teacher rounded the corner.

"We're professionals. We can do this."

This time she gave him the look.

"We're good for the kids," he stated matter-of-factly. "These are important issues. They'll listen to us."

She looked at him for a long moment. "So Mr. Hermit becomes Mr. Socially Aware. Very touching. You do understand what we'll be teaching, don't you?"

"I get the basic idea."

"Come on, Tank, this is serious."

He looked at her oddly.

"What?" she asked impatiently.

"Nothing." He shook his head, then rubbed the back of his neck.

Becky ignored his enormous bicep for as long as she could. "Oh please, put your arm down. I've seen the muscles."

He lowered his arm. "I was rubbing my neck. It's an old injury that gets irritated when I'm ... *irritated*."

Irritated Tank was much easier to deal with than Earnest Tank. "Well, you see the problem. We can't even spend two minutes together without fighting. That's not 'good for the kids.' "

"We're not fighting, we're talking."

"Same thing where we're concerned."

She looked away from him and out the window toward the football field. Why didn't he get it? Teaching this class with him was such a bad idea. What subject matter could possibly be more awkward? She turned back, and he was watching her as though he'd heard the thoughts bouncing through her head. It was disconcerting, to say the least.

Of course, she felt like she had to refute any mind-reading he may have done. "I'm not afraid of you."

His lip quirked. "Good."

"We're probably going to make fools of ourselves, fighting in front of the kids."

"Well, maybe they'll learn what not to do."

Becky's own mouth quirked at that. Then she frowned. "Why? Why me? You could do this with anyone."

Tank slowly shook his head. "Don't want to teach this class with anyone else."

She eyed him warily. What did that even mean?

Then it dawned on her. "Oh, that's right. People. You'd have to get to know another living being and work with her. It would be too overwhelming."

He shrugged. "Something like that."

She searched his eyes. *Bad idea.* She cleared her throat and looked away. "Fine."

Tank seemed to relax a bit.

"But we prepare independently. No *studying* together." She glanced past his eyes and over his shoulder. "We'll divide and conquer, so to speak."

"If that works."

"It will. And another thing. No more tossing kids around in their desks. That was scary."

"I didn't toss him, I redirected him."

"Seriously, you can't do that." She crossed her arms, and finally gave in to a little grin. "Did you see his face when he left the room? He was not happy. I'd look out for him."

"I can handle him."

"I don't doubt that, but he's the type that could cost you your job."

"Don't really need it."

"Oh, please. Fine. Just ... behave."

This time Tank actually grinned. "I'll try."

sixteen

"I'm so sorry, you must have been terrified," Grace shrugged out of her coat as she followed Becky into the kitchen.

Surprised by this unusual greeting, Becky was quick to assure her friend. "Terrified is a little strong. Uncomfortable, maybe. Cabernet okay?"

"Sure, sounds great."

Becky poured them both a glass of wine and led the way into the sunroom, where she had snacks on the table and a fire roaring in the fireplace.

Grace sat down next to her and started to sip her wine. "Oh, cheers!" She lifted her glass to Becky's and they clinked.

"Cheers," she replied, happy that Grace was able to break away for a girls' night out, even if 'out' was at the inn.

"Uncomfortable?" Grace resumed their conversation. "Tank said you put up quite a fight."

Becky furrowed her brow. "Well, it wasn't that big a deal, really. We worked it out in the end. I just can't figure out why he'd want to do it."

"I'm sure you know that I asked him to, but I begged him not to scare you."

"Scare me? I was unprepared for him, but he didn't scare me," Becky replied.

"He said you screamed and attacked him with a fireplace poker."

Becky sat stunned for a moment, then burst out laughing. "You're talking about his coming to the house the other night."

"Of course. What are you talking about?"

Becky sipped her wine and laughed again. "I just found out today that Tank and I are team-teaching a health course at the high school."

Grace looked confused, then smiled, then giggled a little herself. "Wow, we should probably start over."

"Okay, I'll summarize," Becky said with a grin. "Yes, Tank came out the other night, and yes, I attacked him with a fireplace poker. And thank you for not even scowling."

Grace laughed. "I warned him."

"Well, I guess he knocked, but I never heard him." Becky sat back with her glass. "Anyway, when I opened the door and saw someone outside - as big as he is - and of course he had his hood pulled up - anyway, I lost it and started swinging."

"Yikes. And no one got hurt?"

Becky recalled pummeling Tank's chest. "No one got hurt. Just my dignity. And hey, I tried calling you the next day. Where were you?"

"Working. And my phone died for good this time. Had to get a new one yesterday. So, what's with team teaching?" Grace's speculative look was not lost on Becky.

"Well, somehow we were matched up to teach the health class, which includes a significant unit on sex ed."

Grace sipped her wine and grinned, big. "That's really, just, something."

Becky rolled her eyes. "Yeah, and it was really nice finding out about it in front of the kids when I walked into the classroom this morning." She put some crackers and cheese on a napkin.

"Did Tank know?"

"Not about me, but at least he knew he had a partner. I didn't get that memo."

"Wow. So what did you do?"

"Oh, we behaved alright in front of the kids. Then, before I had a chance to beg my way out of it, Tank convinced me to stick with it and teach the class with him."

"Convinced you?"

"Yeah, I still don't know how." Becky sipped her drink.

Grace took a bite out of a piece of celery and considered her friend with interest.

"Or why," Becky shook her head. "I know I kid around about it, but we seriously don't get along." She swirled her wine. "You'd think he'd want out as much as I do."

She could have sworn her friend was biting the insides of her cheeks to keep from smiling.

"What?" she asked with a scowl.

"You're trying to figure out why a healthy, single, thirty-year-old man wants to team teach a sex class with a beautiful, single woman?"

Becky's scowl deepened. "It's not a sex class, exactly. Please." She took a hefty swallow. "And anyway, it's not like that with us. He's made it very clear that he doesn't find me attractive, and, well, same here." She looked around the room, refusing to meet her friend's eyes.

"Do you remember the boys on the playground who used to chase you and pull your hair?"

Becky was not going to ask Grace to clarify. She was only going to get so much understanding from the man's sister.

Twenty minutes and another glass of wine later, they jumped at the sound of Maddy's voice as she entered the kitchen. Neither one of them had heard her come in the front door.

Becky stood quickly to greet her sister.

"Why do you always look at me like that?" Maddy glanced past her to the evidence of their little party. "I have things to drink about, too."

"We were just, ah, talking, and ..."

"Well, do you have enough for me, or should we open this?" Maddy pulled a bottle out of her bag. "I got this from John's mom for Christmas. It looked a little terrifying; John won't touch it. Not sure what that means."

Becky laughed. "I'll grab you a glass. We'll figure it out."

***

"Did you make the copies for tomorrow's class?"

Becky looked up from the desk where she was packing up her materials for the day. She seemed a little startled, but answered evenly. "Of course, I did. I said I would."

Two weeks into their teaching adventure, and she was as removed and snippy as ever. They hadn't even started the interesting stuff, yet.

"Just thought I'd check. I have to make some copies for another class, and the copy room gets backed up."

"Yeah. They need a better system."

Tank nodded. "You remember that I won't be around on Friday - my P.E. class is going cross country skiing."

"Yep. Got it on my calendar." She looked up briefly. "Guess you'll miss my power point on black tar heroin."

He shifted, getting comfortable against the door frame. "Well, I'll be taking a few of the trouble-makers with me. You should be grateful."

Becky shrugged. "I'm sure you'll cover it on your trip. Just make sure they're ready for the test next week."

"Yes, ma'am."

She glared at him. "Anything else?"

"That's it."

"Good." She slipped her coat on and pulled her gloves out of her bag.

For some reason, Tank stayed and watched her prepare to leave. Becky didn't make eye contact as she walked to the door, slipped past him into the hall, and then skidded to a halt. She turned around, and a look of panic, so brief Tank wasn't sure he'd even seen it, gave way to an abruptly cheerful smile.

"So, where are you parked?" she asked brightly.

He eyed her for a moment and then glanced toward the hall. He was just inside the room so he couldn't see what - or whom - she saw.

She followed the direction of his gaze, and then, feigning surprise, called, "Oh, hey Bernie."

Tank heard a greeting from somewhere down the corridor, and Becky turned back to him.

"I really appreciate the ride home today. Don't know what's up with my car."

He noted the subtle look of pleading in her eyes. Someone didn't want to be left alone with Bernie.

"Hey, Becky, I'd be happy to give you a ride," Bernie, apparently, called out.

Becky glanced at him and then back to Tank. The panic resurfaced.

"Okay," Tank said slowly.

She thanked him with her expressive brown eyes. Tank found himself staring as she dipped her head back toward Bernie.

"I'm all set, thanks," she called back.

"Any time."

It sounded as though Bernie was doing something in the hallway, so Becky kept up her act.

"I just have to run down to the office. I'll meet you - where did you say your car was?"

"I didn't."

Her eyes quickly lost their gratitude and found exasperation, but she kept the cheerful expression on her face. "So?"

"The lot by the football field."

"Okay, I'll meet you out there in five?"

"I have copies to make," he reminded her.

"Okay, well, no rush," she replied with waning enthusiasm.

"And I have to stop at the hardware store on the way home." He wasn't sure why he added that. He didn't think she really planned on riding with him.

"No problem," she said with the last vestiges of her fake smile.

Tank looked at her a moment more, and left the room.

***

"Get in the Jeep."

"I told you I don't really need a ride."

"You do now."

Becky glanced over her shoulder and saw Bernie about twenty yards behind them. There was no way she could get into her own car now.

"You're not really going to the hardware store, are you?"

Tank looked at her across the hood of his vehicle. "Of course, I am."

"Oh," she ground out, rolling her eyes.

"You want a ride, or not?"

Becky pulled the door open without answering. She dropped her bag on the seat and climbed in after it. "How long is this going to take?"

"Long time," he replied cheerfully.

Becky sighed and looked out the window, staring longingly at her vehicle. "Maybe you could just pretend to fix my car for a few minutes?"

"No, thanks."

She tossed him a decidedly ungrateful look. He shifted the Jeep into gear and backed out of the parking space. "Buck up, sweetheart. This wasn't my idea."

She looked ready to snap back and then sighed again. "I know. I'm sorry I involved you."

That was surprising. She was probably not so much sorry for inconveniencing him as she was sorry that she had to ride with him. Still, she apologized.

Tank didn't know how to respond, so he didn't.

After a few minutes, he asked, "Who's Bernie?"

"Physics teacher."

"Seems attentive."

"He is. He stops by after class, whenever I'm in that room, which is every other day." She pulled her coat closer around herself and shivered.

"You cold?" he asked, turning up the heat.

"I'm fine, just irritated."

"Why don't you tell him you're not interested?"

He caught the end of an eye-roll when he glanced over at her. "It's not that easy." She paused for a moment. "I don't have the tools I used to have to deal with guys like that."

Becky's tools. Interesting thought. "What tools?"

"I'm accustomed to being very direct," she replied, a hint of challenge in her voice.

Tank's mouth quirked. That was not news to him.

"But I feel like ... this is Maddy's town," she continued, "her territory, and I want to be careful that I don't do or say something stupid that will reflect on her."

Tank considered this rather vulnerable statement. He nodded.

"Anyway, I keep saying no to coffee or whatever he suggests, and he just keeps coming back."

After a moment, Tank decided to open up a little, himself. "I'm dealing with the same kind of thing."

"Really? Who's after you?" Becky seemed to perk up at this turn in the conversation.

"P.E. teacher."

"Which one?"

He could almost see the wheels turning in her head as she considered the two women who taught in the P.E. department.

He shrugged. "They're both very friendly."

She waited for him to give details, then prodded for more. "So, what, do they ask you out? Hang out by your locker room?"

She was way too interested. He regretted bringing it up. "Let's just say a woman has a way of making her interest evident."

Tank turned into the lot of the hardware store and pulled to a stop. Before he put the Jeep in park, Becky had opened the door and hopped out. Tank followed, contemplating how to stretch his quick errand into an irritatingly long field trip. Becky would think twice the next time she wanted him to rescue her.

***

Becky wandered around the hardware store for a few minutes before finding Tank again. He was crouched by a bin of screws.

"You almost done?"

He looked up, not really seeing her as he did some mental calculation. "Almost."

She considered the dozens of bins of different sized screws. She couldn't imagine anything more boring.

"But I need to go check out the drain pipes after this."

Becky rolled her eyes.

Tank looked past her to the end of the aisle. "Your friend's here."

She didn't even look. "You're kidding."

"Nope." The monster grinned.

"Well, I'd pretty much rather be hanging with him at this point, anyway."

"Knock yourself out."

Becky looked down at him - a rare opportunity - and considered all of that weight balanced on the toes of his boots. She was tempted to give him a little kick to see if she could topple him over. He'd probably dent the floor where he landed.

She turned on her heel and left the aisle, peeking around the corner and then heading in the opposite direction of the physics teacher. She wandered through the snow shovels and bags of salt. *Winter.* She was sick of it already, and it had just begun.

"Ms. Jacobs?"

Becky spun around to see one of the math teachers approaching. Had they called a faculty meeting?

"Hi," she mustered a smile. "Please call me Becky."

"Hi, Becky. I'm Laura - Algebra teacher? We met a few weeks ago."

"Of course. How are you?"

"Good, thanks. Picking up some salt for my driveway."

Becky nodded; she certainly wasn't going to say what she was doing at the hardware store.

Laura's eyes lifted and widened. "The new P.E. teacher's here," she whispered.

"Oh, really." Becky turned and tried to make eye contact with Tank to keep him from approaching. He was engrossed with his phone, and didn't look up until he was a few feet away. He stopped and looked from one to the other of them and said nothing.

Becky sighed. "Mr. Kimball, have you met Ms. Callahan?"

He extended a hand. "Good to meet you."

Laura blushed. "You too. Welcome to Clairmont."

He nodded. "You all set?" he asked Becky, as though she'd been the one to keep him waiting.

Laura looked from one to the other. "You're together?"

"Oh no, Mr. Kimball is just giving me a ride home," Becky quickly explained.

Laura gave her a long look. "Oh, of course."

"Okay, well, we'll see you tomorrow," Becky replied, hustling to catch up with Tank, and leaving Laura to make what she would of the encounter.

***

She'd brooded the whole way home, but by the time Tank pulled into her driveway, Becky was fuming.

"I hate it when people treat us like they know something we don't know," she vented as they walked into the house. "They keep giving us that, 'oh, what a cute couple' look. Have you noticed?"

Tank shrugged as he set the bags down on the kitchen counter. "They're being stupid."

"Exactly," Becky agreed. "No one gets that I'm done with men forever. And you - you don't even like people."

He gave her a side-long glance.

"Every time we leave our classroom," Becky continued, ignoring him, "we get that speculative look from students and the other teachers. I don't know why they assume we're together."

"Gives them something to talk about."

"Well, we should give them a real scandal and shut them up."

Tank walked to the fridge and helped himself to a bottle of water. "Suggestions?"

Becky pulled off her jacket and gloves. "Well, the most expedient thing would be to start dating and then break up. Then they'd have to give it a rest."

"Long as I do the breaking up."

"Please. No one has ever broken up with me. Why would they?" She offered her devastating smile.

Tank glanced at her and shook his head. "Who would be dumb enough to sign on in the first place?"

"Really, Mr. Kimball, you positively ooze charm," she simpered. "There's no way I'd ever convince Maddy I've fallen for you," she added flatly. "She'd never buy it."

"If I ever decided to do this," he said, walking over to the window and looking out at the water, "there would be no doubt."

"Oh really? You're that good of an actor?"

Tank casually pivoted and looked at her. "Yes."

Becky eyed him warily. "What could you possibly do to make yourself likable?"

He rubbed the back of his neck and then stretched; she could imagine every muscle in his body rippling and settling slowly back into place. While she enjoyed her imagination's little journey, she remained purposefully blank as Tank walked over to where she perched on the bar stool.

She absolutely refused to get all flustered just because the big football player was standing within touching distance. She sucked in a breath and held it when he settled his hands on the counter on either side of her and moved in very close. Though she would have sworn that he never wore aftershave, she smelled something interesting that made her want to lean in just a bit and nuzzle his jaw.

She didn't, of course.

He stayed perfectly still, and Becky slowly started to unravel. He was close enough that the little brown flecks in his green eyes, previously undetected, were now evident. Any effort at speech would come out like a bleating lamb so she held her tongue and waited.

Tank's eyes drifted over her face and back to her eyes. "I like your eyes, Becky."

She nodded, sure they were as wide as saucers, not only because of the unexpected compliment, but because he'd used her name. She'd never heard him call her anything but Ms. Jacobs, maybe the innkeeper's sister - usually nothing at all.

With that, he slowly withdrew and walked out of the kitchen and out of the house.

She watched the door, dumbfounded.

Several moments later, she remembered to breathe.

seventeen

"I'll bet she does. She has that look."

"Well, I'd like to find out."

The guys sitting around the table laughed.

"Yeah, well, let me know," chimed in another.

Tank pulled his lunch from the refrigerator and tried not to listen to their conversation. He rarely ate in the teachers' lounge; this was one of the reasons.

"Maybe I can dig up some of my high school French. I remember a few key phrases."

Another laugh. "Not the kind of stuff she's teaching."

"Yeah, well, what she's teaching in the classroom is not what I'm interested in communicating."

Their laughs were interrupted by the *thunk!* of Tank's thermos on the table.

"Who's the lucky teacher today?"

"Same one as last week."

"And the week before."

He stared at them.

"Jacobs. Teaches French. Came just before you did."

Tank's jaw clenched. *No surprise there.*

"You know her?" another at the table asked.

Tank eyed the group, and the chatter stopped. "Yeah."

"So? What do you know?" one of the more vocal men asked.

He taught some sort of sociology class, if Tank remembered correctly. He didn't remember having a particularly good impression of the guy.

"She's a nice, decent woman."

There was a ripple of quiet laughter.

"Decent, huh? In what way?" the same guy snickered.

"You're not likely to find out, are you?" Tank asked, itching to make his point more obvious, ideally with his fist.

His target narrowed his eyes, but hesitated only briefly before saying, "She's only *decent* with football players?"

Tank planted both hands on the table and leaned in. "We're going out. If you need a filter for that mouth of yours, I'd be glad to arrange it."

The amped up tension in the room didn't bother Tank a bit. He thrived on amped up tension. He looked around at the faces staring back at him. He didn't like how these guys talked about women, especially their own co-workers. It served them right to have their little discussion shut down. He'd deal with the repercussions later.

"Hey Kimball, did I hear you say you were dating Becky Jacobs?"

His blood still boiling, Tank turned to a new voice in the room. Ed Davidson, the shop teacher and Frank's father, had walked in and apparently heard 'the news.' Their paths hadn't crossed much in the few weeks that Tank had been at the school, but Ed had made a point to introduce himself early on. Tank liked him immediately; he was a comically similar, older version of Frank. Under the circumstances, he was about the last person Tank wanted to see.

"We've just gone out a few times. Nothing official." His head reeled. He didn't want this thing getting any bigger.

"That's great!" Ed boomed. "My wife will be thrilled. You know she has a few of Becky's paintings? Don't know why she's not teaching art here."

Tank left the table and joined Ed near the door, hoping to give his friend incentive to lower his voice.

"She's a great painter," Tank agreed, marveling at how easily he could bend his opinion to suit his purposes. He hadn't been particularly fond of the seascapes she'd painted, but he'd talk about her art all day if it kept the discussion away from her new relationship status.

"Yeah, I need to talk to her about a portrait of Emily's horse." Ed scratched his head. "Do you call it a portrait if you're painting a horse?"

"Not really sure." Tank clapped him on the back. "Listen, I have to run." He could hear the guys picking up their conversation at the table behind him. At least that hadn't escalated any further. He really needed to watch his temper.

"Oh, there she is. I'll ask her."

Tank swung his head, following Ed's gaze with dismay. Sure enough, Becky was not only in the cafeteria, she was headed straight for the teacher's lounge. His gut clenched as she returned Davidson's greeting with a typical Becky smile. Her expression changed slightly when she saw him.

"Just the girl I wanted to see!" Davidson said cheerily as she entered the lounge.

Tank noted that all conversation ceased as the other men in the room stopped to stare at Becky. *Animals.*

"Hey, what's up?" she asked, seeming to take in the room and the attention focused on her without losing her cool.

She's probably used to it, Tank thought, though she had no idea what was about to hit her. He could hardly hope that Davidson wouldn't bring it up. He moved into a better position to make eye contact. She was sharp. Maybe she'd pick up on it and play along.

"Well, Emily's looking to have you do a portrait, or whatever you artists call it, of her horse. I thought I'd see if you could get it done by her birthday - middle of March."

"Sure. If you have any photos that I could use for reference, that would help," Becky replied, her attention torn between him and Tank. She seemed to sense that Tank was moving in for a reason.

"Ah, that's great. She'll be thrilled." Ed smiled and looked at the two of them.

Tank knew what was coming and boldly took a hold of Becky's hand. Hopefully, she'd make the connection with the offer he was about to make. "So, you up for another trip to the hardware store today?"

She looked up in surprise, her eyes searching his, something neither of them often allowed. He held his ground and tried not to focus on the almost gold ring in the center of hers.

"That's my idea of a date," Davidson grinned. "So, how long have you two been going out?"

***

All she wanted was the cake for the baby shower. Becky never went into the teachers' lounge otherwise, and it was clear why. It was usually male-dominated, and right now, half a dozen men awaited her response to the last question she'd ever expected to be asked.

She didn't think Tank had taken her seriously when she joked about pretending to date. Apparently, putting on this little show was now useful to him. She tried to make sense of it while deciding whether or not to play along. He'd better have a good explanation.

"How long *have* we been going out," she asked, her eyes finding Tank's again. Her fingers twitched as he gripped her hand.

Tank cleared his throat. "Couple of weeks, anyway."

He continued to look at her earnestly, and Becky could feel her face warming. A couple of weeks ago was the last time they'd spoken directly to each other, and he'd told her that he liked her eyes. Since then, they'd taught their class, talking to the students and avoiding each other like the plague. It was kind of like going out - junior high style.

Becky turned back to Ed. "Yep, couple of weeks."

He grinned. "Well, that's great. You both seem really happy."

Becky could only nod at this very strange observation. "Okay, well, I just need to get a cake from the fridge."

"And I have to head back to class." Tank let go of her hand.

Becky was not about to let him leave before she did. She hesitated only briefly before tucking into his side, trying to make the contact look natural as she reached around his waist. She grabbed a fistful of shirt, grazing his rock-hard obliques in the process. She'd have a hard time pinching him if it became necessary.

"I'm heading your way," she told him, all smiles.

It was his turn to look surprised, maybe because she suddenly needed to head to the athletic wing with her cake, or else because she'd made such bold bodily contact. They stood for a moment, aware that they had the attention of the entire room.

"So, let me grab that cake," Becky said, disengaging.

Tank seemed to know better than to take off after what she'd just done. He watched her as she picked up the cake and walked out of the teachers' lounge. Once outside the door, she left him and his buddies and headed back to her party. They had class together later; she'd be sure to get some answers then.

***

Becky watched from the back of the room as Tank walked in. She'd spent the last period puzzling over what his explanation might be, certain she felt nothing but curiosity as the time approached for their class to begin.

Seeing him walk through the door was another matter.

What if she were actually going out with him? She felt a strange and unexpected tingling down her spine. She sat up straighter, willing her body not to send stupid, faulty signals, and reminded herself that they were playing a game, a game he had yet to explain. She breathed in, willing away the ridiculous 'what-ifs.'

He ignored her, of course, walking to the front of the room and laying his materials on the desk. She watched his back, its sheer size was always impressive. Her gaze swung down the length of him and back to those huge shoulders. Her perusal didn't help calm her. She crossed her legs and waited for him to acknowledge her.

As if on cue, he turned, making brief eye contact before focusing on her legs. "Don't sit like that when the boys get in here."

"Excuse me?"

"They have enough trouble concentrating. I shouldn't have to explain that to you."

His tone was patronizing and infuriating.

All the more reason to stay calm.

"Jealous?" She swung her top leg, her momentary nerves predictably subdued by his rude behavior.

He scowled at her. "Hardly. Your skirt's too short. I need their attention today."

She bit back a very rude reply and swung her leg as provocatively as she could. He'd come in with guns blazing, but she was not about to get side-tracked. He'd pay for it eventually, but not before she found out why they were suddenly attracted to each other.

What a joke.

"Well, they'll all be facing you, so they'll hardly care. You'll be the only one staring at my legs, Mr. Kimball. Will that be a problem?"

The color rose in his cheeks and his eyes narrowed ominously. Becky smiled and kicked her leg a little, arching her brow as the students began to file in.

***

Tank felt Becky's eyes on him as he dismissed the class. He'd hardly stopped to draw breath for the whole lesson, which was not his typical style. His approach was usually much simpler, *Don't be stupid - don't do drugs.* For the last ninety minutes he'd pounded them with facts during his drug and alcohol wrap-up. Maybe his teaching partner had even learned a thing or two. Maybe she'd forgotten that he publicly announced that they were dating. Maybe he'd join the Boston ballet after all.

He heard Becky slide off the desk in the back of the room and walk slowly toward him. He could picture it - the legs and the black skirt which wasn't exactly short until she sat on the desk. She wasn't marching up to him, demanding answers. She'd chosen a much deadlier approach.

Tank focused on tucking his notes back into his binder. She'd never buy that he'd started the whole mess to protect her. She would, however, be expecting an explanation, and he had no other to give. He'd hoped that making her good and angry would buy him some time, but she hadn't taken the bait. She'd just watched him teach, smiling and swinging whichever long, very fit leg of hers happened to be on top of the other. He'd made every effort to ignore her, but failed miserably.

He turned and prepared for battle. "This doesn't have to be a big deal."

"Well, turns out it kind of is."

She stopped on the other side of the desk and hitched her hip on the corner. Great - the leg again.

"Do I get to know why you decided to start this little game?" she asked, far more gently than he expected or deserved. "P.E. teachers harassing you?"

"No." He picked up his bag and started around the desk. There was no way out except past the legs. He hesitated. She nudged his knee with her ridiculously pointy shoe.

"Not cool, Tank."

He stopped and looked at her. She rarely used his name; that and her subtle flirting would be his undoing. He'd so hoped she'd be spitting fire, and ideally leaving the room in a huff. He had no idea how to field this Becky.

"Let's just say it was necessary. A few days and we can just let it fade. No one will care."

Becky considered his lame explanation. "You're a hot-shot athlete. People will care."

"I doubt it. I'm not that big a deal."

She almost looked as though she might argue.

"Well, maybe *I* am."

He couldn't help but grin. Good for her.

She tilted her head. "You know, if you smiled like that more often, women might actually find you attractive."

"Women love me."

"Ha! Name one."

"Well, besides you ..."

"No, seriously. Name one."

Tank shook his head, trying to lose the grin. "Let's give it a week. I promise we don't even have to spend time together."

Becky considered the offer. She still hadn't insisted on a real explanation. Tank couldn't believe his luck. It couldn't possibly last.

"Okay, I got involved in a conversation that I shouldn't have during lunch. The most expedient thing was to say that we'd dated a few times." Tank sighed and looked out the window. "If we could avoid a noisy breakup in the next week or two, I think it'll be fine."

"Well, you'll have to treat me right."

He turned and she gave him a teasing smile that did strange things to his gut. He shifted his bag, adjusted the strap.

"We'll keep a safe distance from each other. No one will ever know that we're not ..."

"Close?" she asked, nudging his leg again.

Tank drew a deep breath. She was swinging her leg and looking remarkably innocent. He swallowed. He'd rather face a group of large, angry linemen.

"Not close," he repeated.

"Well, I'll need something to tell the girls," she countered, as though she'd given the whole matter a lot of thought.

"Don't need to tell the girls anything."

"Not even the P.E. teachers?"

He wanted to give her a shake. She was having too much fun. "They'll hear the rumor. That's enough."

"You'll have to get rid of this." She stood and gently cuffed his day's worth of stubble with her fingertips. "I would never date anyone with facial hair."

He exhaled slowly. "Don't worry. My facial hair will never get near yours."

"*What?*"

Becky tried to withdraw her hand, but Tank caught it against his cheek before she could reconnect with a little more force.

With his other hand he ran a finger along her jaw. "It's not too bad," he grinned.

She yanked her hand free and involuntarily ran a hand across her very smooth cheek. He found himself tracking the movement.

"You know this will end badly," she said.

"Probably," he agreed.

"Well, you started it. Whatever happens, it's on you."

Tank looked at her thoughtfully. "Fair enough."

eighteen

"Do you even own pants?"

"Do you have anywhere else to go but here?"

"I thought you'd want to see this." Tank handed Becky a newspaper, then stood in the entryway, hands on his hips.

She looked down at the paper in her hands. "What happened?"

"A reporter caught me on my way out of school on Friday."

She looked up in surprise. "Really? What did they want?"

"Kind of a long story. Do you mind if we ..." he gestured inside.

"Alright, come on in," she grumbled, leading him into the kitchen. He was dressed like he would be for school. What was he doing up so early on a Sunday morning?

"What are you doing up so early on a Sunday morning?"

"It's not early. It's eleven o'clock," Tank replied, settling onto a barstool. "I went to church," he added.

Becky eyed him warily. "Do you go to Maddy's church?"

"Yep."

"Does Grace go?"

"Sometimes. More now than she used to."

"Oh goodie. Everybody's finding Jesus."

Tank eyed her thoughtfully. "I wasn't the one doing the finding." He tapped his hands in a quick rhythm on the counter. "Mind if I have some coffee?"

Becky shook her head. "Whatever. Fine." She sat down on the other side of the counter with the paper.

"You gonna get dressed?" he asked, helping himself to a mug.

She looked down at the fluffy bathrobe that sort of covered her T-shirt and shorts. "Why should I?"

"Just thought you might want to."

"Well, I don't. You want to make sure I'm dressed appropriately, call ahead, or rent a room." She glared at him and sipped her coffee, trying not to care what she looked like.

Tank shrugged and filled his mug. He gestured at the paper. "Sports section," he directed. "Front page."

She flipped through the regional Sunday paper, which served several of the area's coastal towns. The sports section was generally dominated by high school sports, but Tank took that honor this week. "Tank Kimball Holds the Line at Clairmont Regional High School." *Cute.*

"So this kid caught me after school; said he'd been trying to track me down."

Becky started to skim the article.

"Someone," Tank continued, "I have a feeling I know who, though I can't really figure out why - gave him your name." Tank pointed to a spot in the article. "I'm sorry. The timing of all of this is unbelievable."

Becky brushed in annoyance at his hand. She read silently for a few moments, trying to figure out how to feel about being named in the paper in connection with Tank. There was a time - well most of her life, really - when she would have welcomed the attention; now, for some reason, not so much.

"So, what do we do?" She looked up at him again. The article stated that Tank, filling in at the high school to, "help out the community," was also in a relationship with Becky Jacobs, long-term French sub, also new to the high school. It went on to highlight Tank's career, which Becky was not about to read in front of him. She hoped he left the paper so she could do it later. If he didn't, she'd Google him.

He shook his head. "I don't know. Ride it out, I guess. I had hoped he'd focus on what I'm doing with the kids, but of course, he had to work the relationship angle in."

Becky sighed. "What do I tell Maddy? She'll never believe it. Neither will Grace, for that matter."

Tank looked at her speculatively. "I think Grace might."

Becky rolled her eyes. "You're her brother. I'm her friend. I actually confide in her. She knows it couldn't happen."

Tank sat back with his coffee. "You talk about me?"

Becky refused to be cornered. "Complain about you mostly. She's very sympathetic."

Tank's mouth quirked. "Well, she's always hinting that she thinks we'd be great together, so I think she'd buy it."

"*What?*" Becky jumped up. She ran a hand through her already messy hair and scowled at his grin.

"Not saying I agree. Just that she might not be a hard sell."

"Oh, please. If she's feeding you that kind of bull, then she's delusional and it doesn't matter what she thinks." Becky marched over to the coffee maker and refilled her cup. She turned around and glared.

Tank rubbed a hand across his jaw. "So, what should we tell them?"

"Stop grinning. This is all your fault." She crossed her arms. "You tell me."

He thought for a minute, the grin fading as directed. Becky felt its loss despite her pique.

"Well, I think it would be best to try to sell it to everyone, even the family. Tell them we started going out a couple of weeks ago. Kept it quiet. In another week or so, we'll tell them it didn't work out."

"Maddy won't believe it."

"That it didn't work out?"

"Hardly. That we ever tried."

"Do you have to talk to her about it?"

"Please. As soon as she reads the paper she's going to call me."

"She reads the Sports Section?"

Becky wanted to throttle him. "John does. Maybe she does, too. I don't know. They'll find out one way or another."

"So tell Maddy and ask her to play along until we get this figured out."

Becky considered this. "What about Grace?"

"Okay if we wait with her? I'm concerned that ..." Tank hesitated. "I don't want her implicated if something goes wrong."

"That sounds serious."

"I don't think anything will happen, I'd just rather ... wait with her."

"Well, that's fine for you; you never talk to her. What am I supposed to say when I see her?"

He grinned. "Tell her you finally saw the light."

Becky sputtered, fighting her own grin. "Oh please. I'm not that good of an actor."

"Well, can you make an excuse not to be around her for a week or so? Tell her you're not feeling well?"

"This is getting so complicated." Becky stood. "You should go. And you owe me big time."

Tank nodded and drained his coffee. "It'll be over soon enough."

***

Becky arranged her smile carefully as she approached the classroom the following morning. For some reason, her normal confidence completely eluded her. She willed her heart rate to slow down.

The room was unlocked - he was already there, of course. Did he have to be early for everything? Why couldn't she be the one waiting in the classroom, all cool and under control? She threw her shoulders back and opened the door.

There were several students in the room and they greeted her with more interest than usual. They marked her progress toward the other teacher, no doubt waiting for the first bit of evidence that the rumor was true. She could almost feel their phones humming.

Becky walked up to him and set her bag down on top of the papers Tank was pretending to read. She sat on the edge of the desk, waiting for him to look up from his interrupted work. It took longer than strictly necessary. She was not about to look like a fool playing his game, so she leaned down and whispered 'hello,' making sure their cheeks had a brush of contact.

She kept it very simple, letting the tone of her whisper speak for itself. When he finally looked up, it was with the startlingly direct look that had taken her breath away in the kitchen weeks ago. His eyes, in all their glorious greens and browns, were fixed on hers.

"Morning, Ms. Jacobs," he said, with much more warmth than she'd ever seen, felt, or heard from him.

It took a concentrated effort to close her mouth and rearrange her lips into a convincing smile. Every instinct begged her to slide into his lap and get a closer look at those eyes. She rarely saw them in full color, much less with any kind of invitation in them.

The invitation was palpable. He was messing with her - daring her to respond in front of the kids.

Oh, he is good.

The fact that he played the game so well was intriguing, enticing, and just a little heart-breaking.

A hint of a smile touched Tank's lips as Becky fought to regroup. It was all she needed to regain her focus.

"Good morning, Mr. Kimball." She kept her voice quiet, husky. "Ready for contraceptives?"

Her greeting had the necessary effect. Tank jumped out of his seat, almost toppling the desk in his haste to get away from her. She smiled and stood, breathing deeply before turning to face the class. Today's lesson on protection was going to be very interesting. She could hardly wait to hear what Tank had prepared.

***

Tank walked into the kitchen with Frank on his heels. Becky glanced at the clock. *Almost ten.* Didn't they know she had to get up early? They'd made an effort not to use power tools too late into the evening, but still, she could never relax while *he* was in the house. She forced a smile as Frank offered an apology.

"Sorry to keep you up, Becky. Been hard to coordinate with this guy, but we got our project done. Won't be here so late next time." His grin stole some of the sincerity from his apology.

"No problem. Glad you got it done."

Her heart beat irrationally as Tank approached her and slid his stupid, heavy arm around her. It was completely unnecessary. Frank didn't need any convincing; he probably didn't even care about their 'relationship.' Becky shifted to bear the weight better, and ended up tucked neatly into Tank's side. She wanted to stomp on his foot, but instead she slid her arm around his waist and dug her nails in.

"How's it going up there?" she asked sweetly.

Tank also shifted and grabbed the hand with the claws. He pulled her fingers around and flattened them against his stomach, patting them lovingly. "It's going well. Wanna come take a look?"

She faked a yawn. "I think I need to get to bed. You too, right? Class bright and early."

Frank cleared his throat while he loosened his tool belt and set it on the counter. "I'm just going to grab a bottle of water and take off. Tank, you want one?"

"Sure," he replied, catching the bottle that Frank tossed him, while keeping Becky tucked firmly into his side. She took the opportunity to remove her hand from his ridiculous abs. Like she needed a reminder of how fit he was.

"Okay, well, thanks again for your help, Tank," Frank said, walking to the dining room door. "I'm sure John will be in touch about the ceiling fans."

"Sounds good," Tank replied.

The minute the door closed, Becky turned uncomfortably under the weight of his arm and pushed on his chest.

"Okay, show's over. Get off me."

Tank closed her into his arms as the door re-opened and Frank stepped back in.

"Sorry - tool belt."

She heard muffled sounds as Frank made quick business of grabbing his belt and beating a hasty retreat. Tank had turned her toward the sink, his back to the door. For all Frank could tell, they were locked in a passionate embrace; *just couldn't wait for him to leave the room.*

Tank could tell that they weren't locked in a passionate embrace. Becky had no problem using her nails on his chest to keep him from getting too comfortable. Apparently immune to pain,

Tank simply held her close and whispered into her ear. "I'm going to cut those nails myself."

"I - dare - you," she growled, unnerved by his closeness and his stupid whispering.

He let her go, but only so he could get a hold of her hands. He pulled them out to her sides, and they stood, her nose only reaching his chest. She slowly looked up. He was way too close.

"Don't ever dare me," he said in a low voice.

Becky tried to look bored. "Quit being a bully."

"Quit sticking me with your talons."

"You're overdoing it with the physical contact."

Tank grinned down at her. She'd seen more of that grin than she cared to lately.

"Told you I'd leave no room for doubt." He brought her arms down to her side, still holding her hands.

She cleared her throat. "Well there's no one left to impress here, so why don't you just let me go and run along?"

He loosened his grip on her fingers slowly, as though he wasn't sure if she'd attack when he finally let go. She was sorely tempted, but she simply crossed her arms. She really needed some space. This game they were playing was getting dangerous.

She took a step back. "I'm going to bed." With that, she pulled a Tank and walked away.

***

The third year French class was restless. Becky tried to prepare them for their upcoming test, but the kids were not engaged. They had one thing on their minds; the status of her relationship with the former pro football player.

"Are you and Mr. Kimball ..."

"En Francais, s'il vous plait."

"Si vous sont datant M. Kimball?"

Becky swung her head around. Someone had been doing her homework. She considered the girl who asked the question, and finally answered, *"Oui."*

Like a subdued reaction at a fireworks display, the room vibrated with a quiet round of, "Oohs" and "Aahs." Becky shook her head. So much for Tank's plan of quietly breaking up in a week. The kids were invested, already. She could see the battle lines forming as sides were chosen.

She could hardly imagine what their health class would do. They'd barely survived day two of contraceptives. The kids had been fairly bristling with curiosity about their relationship, which had only been contained by Tank's snarling looks and new bulldozer approach to teaching. He'd insisted on leading the contraceptive charge and Becky was more than happy to let him do it.

"Oh, Mlle Jacobs can I please ask you something in English? Please?" a girl named Bailey piped up from the other side of the room.

"Apres la classe, s'il vous plait."

"Class is practically over. Pleeeease?"

Becky rolled her eyes. "Okay, fine. But I'm not answering any questions about my ... friendship with Mr. Kimball."

Bailey's face fell a little, but she pressed on. "Okay, well, it's about Mr. Kimball, sort of, but not really about your relationship."

Becky's eyes narrowed. "Talk to me after class."

The girl's face lit up again, and Becky sighed. "The rest of you can go. Please take the time to go through your review test before Friday."

Knowing that very few of them registered her request, Becky turned to Bailey and her 'sort of' question about Mr. Kimball. She raised a brow as the student approached and placed her books on Becky's desk.

"So, here's my question," Bailey began with a nervous giggle. "You know we're having our Valentine's Day dance, not this Friday, but next, right? It's a semi-formal dance, almost as big as prom."

Becky nodded. She'd seen signs up around the school, but hadn't given it much thought.

"Well, Mr. and Mrs. Halloway are supposed to chaperone, but her baby's due at the end of the month and she's *huge*."

Becky nodded. She'd attended her shower, and Mrs. Halloway didn't look like she'd make it through the day. *And that was almost a week ago ...*

"Well, we need some backup chaperones - ideally a couple - or I have to figure out two more teachers who won't mind giving up their Friday night and spending it at the dance. It would be perfect if you and Mr. Kimball would fill in. Wouldn't it be romantic? You can dress up and everything!"

The girl's eyes lit up with the possibilities, and Becky fought the energy emanating from her. It's not like she didn't remember how it felt to get all dressed up for a dance. This would be very different, however. She didn't want to spend an evening on display with Tank; not when everyone would be watching for their every potential PDA.

Becky fought an unwelcome shiver as she recalled standing in the kitchen with him the night before, locked in a fake embrace. Tank's pretend affection was incredibly unnerving. He was as good an actor as he claimed. *Dumb athlete.*

Bailey cleared her throat and Becky came back from what must have looked like a silly daydream about boyfriends and romance and dances.

"I don't know," she hedged, "I'm not really sure what Mr. Kimball is doing."

The girl tilted her head. "Really? Wouldn't you be going out on a Friday? Oh," she sighed, "he's just so ..." she sighed again and then blushed. "Sorry, I just ..." she shrugged and blushed some more.

Becky decided to have a little mercy. "I'll see what I can do."

"Oh, you're the best! Thank you!"

"But just for backup. We're going to hope that Mr. and Mrs. Halloway are still able to come and dance the night away, right?"

Bailey smiled a very satisfied and knowing smile. Becky didn't like it one bit. She'd used that smile plenty of times.

"Backup," Becky said, again. "And I can't speak for Mr. Kimball. This is all very tentative."

Too late. Bailey nodded and all but hugged her before grabbing her books and running from the room.

Becky sat on the edge of her desk. What had she gotten herself into?

***

"Somebody's got some explaining to do." Grace handed Becky her cafe mocha with a huge grin. "Have a seat. I'll just be a sec."

Becky nodded and sipped her mocha. She knew Tank wouldn't have talked to his sister about their whole relationship debacle, but it still irritated her. Didn't they talk at all? Why wasn't Grace demanding this information from her own brother?

Sighing, Becky put a tip in the jar and walked to the back of the cafe. Being in a fake relationship with Tank was stressful enough. Who would survive a real one?

A woman who was done with men forever shouldn't have to worry about such things.

She slid into their booth, trying to think how she'd act if she were really going out with Tank. She couldn't possibly generate Grace's ever-present smile and dreamy-eyed demeanor. Sipping her drink, Becky hoped the caffeine and sugar rush would spark the enthusiasm she sorely needed.

Grace slid into the booth with too much energy. "Okay, I've only got, like, five minutes, so you're doing all the talking."

"Not until you tell me what's up with Alex," Becky hedged. "I haven't seen him in months."

She hoped the deflection wouldn't bring up anything painful. Judging by the sparkle in Grace's eyes, everything was just fine with her lover-boy. Still, Becky had been meaning to ask; she'd been so busy at the school and Alex hadn't stayed at the inn.

"Oh, he's fine - we're fine," Grace gestured dismissively with her hand, but her eyes danced with all kinds of extra meaning for the word, 'fine.' "He's been staying out at Tank's when he visits. Those two are getting along, which is pretty cool."

"Really?" Becky replied, sipping her drink. Tank had become quite the social butterfly. She hadn't even seen Tank's beach house - not that she should have - but it still rankled, somehow. Then it occurred to her that people like Grace would expect that she was familiar with Tank's space. *Better to avoid that conversation.*

Grace smiled and leaned forward. "So tell me!"

Becky couldn't help but smile in response. Grace was so excited, and so crazy about her own man, maybe her energy would carry the conversation.

"Well, first of all, you need to know that the reporter made it sound like a bigger deal than it is. We just went out a couple of times. He had no business calling us a couple."

Ignoring all of the back-pedaling, Grace continued to beam as though Becky had announced their engagement. "I just knew it! I knew you, if anyone, could handle him. And I knew he'd come out of his shell with the right motivation!" She sipped her tea and continued to regard Becky with an open, hopeful smile.

Becky cringed a little inside. Tank was right; Grace was an easy sell. *And so happy!* Too many people were caring too much about this fake relationship. There would be a lot of heartbreak when they broke up that didn't even involve the major players.

She tried, again, to downplay the whole thing. "Seriously, we're taking it very slowly."

"Well, that's always smart," said the woman who had jumped into a serious relationship with a high school friend after a week's re-acquaintance. "And I just know you'll be good for each other." She grabbed Becky's hand. "He's a good man, Becky. He really takes care of the people he loves."

Becky pulled her hand back at that, but Grace hardly seemed to notice as she went on about her wonderful brother.

"He absolutely saved me when I got divorced. Flew across the country to help me move out, gave me money to start this business, actually listened to me when I asked him not to beat Jim to a pulp." She smiled as she paused to draw breath. "I know I've complained about him; he's not the best communicator, but he's fiercely protective, and he's so much fun when he starts to relax. He's not nearly so scary as he looks."

She slid from the booth, having dumped a hefty load of Tank rhetoric in Becky's lap. "I hate that I have to go! I'm sorry I didn't give you time to explain anything. I'm just so excited! Next time, I want to hear all the details - your first date - what changed your mind - all the good stuff!"

With that, Grace spun away and hustled behind the counter to deal with the long line of customers.

Becky shivered and sipped her mocha. The fact that her friend was so very happy for her under such false pretenses was a little hard to take. The sooner she and Tank got back to normal, whatever that was, the better.

nineteen

Becky spread the sex ed materials across the table with a sigh. How was she going to sell the kids on a course of action - or inaction, as the case may be - that she'd never bought into, herself? She didn't have to dig too deeply to acknowledge that her approach to sex hadn't left her terribly satisfied, but *abstinence?* How would she ever convince the kids to take it seriously?

She picked up the resource book and flipped through the chapter. Apparently, in the past the school had taken the approach, "Kids are going to have sex anyway, so just make sure they're safe." That made sense to Becky. She could talk all day about the 'safe' hoops to jump through.

This year, however, the school board had adopted a more conservative curriculum. That meant some pretty hefty lessons on STDs and other delightful material to help the kids make informed choices. They'd covered the requisite contraceptive topics, and now the next step was to talk about the 'alternative.' No wonder the teachers originally slotted to teach the class had bailed.

Flipping to the disease chapter, a topic she had studiously avoided in the past, Becky sat back in her chair and started reading.

***

"Anybody home?"

"Out here!" There was nothing 'out' about the sunroom, especially with the fire blazing, but it seemed like a good directive.

Maddy walked into the room with a shiver. "Hey there."

"What was it like to be a virgin on your wedding night? Or whenever," Becky amended with a grin.

"Well, hello to you, too, Becky." Maddy set her purse on the counter and slid out of her coat. "I thought we decided that conversation was off limits."

"You decided that."

"Well, it was a good call."

"Oh, please, I never really wanted details. I just liked watching you squirm."

"Nice." Maddy sat down on the couch where Becky had settled in with her book. "Whatcha doing? Or should I even ask?"

"I have to teach Friday's incredibly awkward lesson on ... waiting, and I have no idea how to do it."

Maddy peered into her lap. "Doesn't your teacher's manual give you the information?"

"Sure. It's all here. I just don't know how to sell it."

"Hmmm ..."

"Seriously, how did you do it? Or how didn't you do it?"

Maddy laughed a little. "I wish I could tell you that I had some fool-proof motivation or resolve." She sighed. "It was really only an issue with Phil. I didn't date anyone else long enough."

Becky snorted. " 'Long enough' is in the eye of the beholder. Sometimes dating someone long enough means you learned their name on the way out of the bar," *or the wedding reception* ...

Maddy was quiet for a moment, and Becky wished she'd held her tongue. No use letting her sister know the extent of her own foolishness.

"I think the fact that it was unknown territory made it intimidating for me; more so as I got older and everyone around me seemed to be ... more informed."

Becky nodded, grateful that Maddy chose to ignore her comment. "We always assume that everyone else is more experienced. I don't know why. For all of my 'practical knowledge,' I still felt like I didn't really know what was going on." She laid her head back on the couch pillow. "So you got more cautious and I got more daring."

"There's a lot of pressure out there for kids - adults," Maddy amended.

"Very young adults," Becky further qualified, feeling older by the minute. "I look at those girls in my classroom," she shook her head. "I know some of them are having sex, and it kind of breaks my heart. You'd think I'd be the first to understand, but I guess I also know the lonely road they're heading down."

"Lonely? You never seemed lonely."

"I always got a lot of attention, demanded it, even. Didn't necessarily mean I had a lot of close friends. And the guys figured out pretty quickly that I was ... daring."

Maddy sat quietly beside her, and Becky again wondered if she'd shared too much. It was no secret that she'd been 'active' early on, but she'd never confided in Maddy about any of the details.

"So what do you think made you daring instead of cautious?" Maddy turned toward her. "Maybe that's your starting point with your students."

Becky looked down at her hands. She hadn't had a manicure in some time, but they looked nice again. Maddy laid a hand on top of hers, her diamond glittering in the firelight.

The glitter began to shimmer and Becky looked across the room into the fire. "Taylor promised me ... oh, everything. He loved me, said we'd get married ... all the usual stuff, I guess, and I bought it." She swiped angrily at a tear. "He ignored me, of course, as soon as I gave in. Never said another word to me. His friends, however, were very attentive."

She could hear Maddy's soft intake of breath. Becky went on before it turned into sympathy. "I actually thought I was pregnant for a while. It was a ... a lonely, scary time."

Maddy took a hold of her hand, and Becky squeezed back. "I decided that it was the last time I'd ever be alone and afraid." She turned to her sister. "I just kind of turned off my feelings and went for the attention. I figured that once I crossed the 'sex bridge,' it didn't really matter anymore."

She closed the book in her lap. "I look at these statistics on diseases, and I can't believe what I've escaped. It makes no sense."

She ran her fingers over the letters in the title of the book. "Still, I wish I'd known this stuff then. I might have been a little more responsible."

It felt good, somehow, to dump the hurt and the awful memories on Maddy. She seemed to absorb them without anything more than sadness; no judgment or criticism radiated from her. Becky finally looked at her sister. "Sorry for unloading all of this on you. Probably not what you came over here for, huh?"

Maddy smiled sadly. "I'm glad you told me. I'm sorry you've been carrying that, and I'm so sorry I wasn't there for you."

"Yeah, well, you were a senior - getting ready for college and winning all of those awards."

Maddy took both of Becky's hands in hers. "I should have been there to help, to listen. I'm really sorry."

Becky touched her forehead to Maddy's. "It's okay. You're here for me now, helping me be done with men and all that."

"Except for the whole Tank thing." Maddy shifted to better look at her. "You never really explained that to me."

"Not much to explain. We're fake-dating; it'll all be over soon. And I haven't changed my mind about men."

Their eyes met briefly as Becky sat back and shifted her books. Maddy finally stood.

"Okay. So, one of the reasons I stopped over was to see if you guys wanted to go out Friday night." She hesitated a moment. "Frank's all excited that you're dating, so he offered to watch the boys. Might as well cash in on his enthusiasm. Is that wrong?"

Becky laughed a little and then looked more intently at her sister. "Hang on. What's up? You don't really seem all that excited."

"I'm fine. It'll be fun."

"Maddy, what's wrong?"

Maddy shrugged. "John and I just had a ... thing. We'll be fine."

Becky shifted her books to the table. "Wanna talk about it?"

Maddy thought for a minute. "Kinda, but not really. We got into it over the apartment." She sighed. "It was bound to happen. It's really not that big a deal, except that Parker and Blake saw us arguing and I think, no, I know it upset them."

She leaned over and shifted some of the pillows on the couch. "I figured I'd come over here and give us both time to cool out." She stood and looked around the room. "It all seems really silly after what you and I just talked about. I'm feeling kind of bad for walking out."

"You probably both needed the space." Becky stood and walked over to Maddy. "And it turns out I kind of needed you, so ... maybe it's okay?"

Maddy took Becky's hand. "Of course. I'm glad I came over." She gave her a hug. "I also have a bunch of paint samples ..."

Becky smiled. "Go make up with your husband."

"I don't want to rush out. You gonna be okay?"

"Yeah. I'm good. Gotta get back to work, anyway."

Maddy nodded. "Well, let me know how it all goes."

"Sure. Do you want me to take a look at those samples?"

Maddy smiled. "I'd love your input. I was feeling a little lost without it."

Becky shook her head. "You're doing just fine. But I'll look them over. I'll need a break from this other stuff, anyway."

Maddy dug the sample cards out of her purse. "Okay, so, the first one is for ..."

Becky picked up the pile. "I'll figure it out. Just go home and take care of your family."

Maddy hugged her. "You're the best."

"Fine. Whatever. Just go." Becky smiled as her sister grabbed her coat and made her way out the door.

***

Becky wanted to pour her heart into the presentation, but found herself simply spewing facts. She was no more convincing than the book. *"Don't have sex or else ..."* It was a sure-fire way to encourage them. There would probably be fewer virgins in the town of Clairmont tonight than there were this morning, and it would all be Becky's fault. At the end of the class, the kids just stared at her blankly. Some looked bored and most looked doubtful.

"And I'm sure you guys are taking your own advice." The junior laughed and looked at her derisively.

Tank lifted himself from his perch on the edge of the teacher's desk. All eyes followed him as he moved with his disconcertingly quiet style and stopped at the student's desk.

"It's not your business and you know it."

The student shifted uncomfortably. "Right, but it's a hard sell when the people teaching this stuff don't buy it."

"We do."

A hush came over the class as the students processed Tank's brief, but telling, statement.

Becky simply tried not to blush or look uncomfortable. Speaking was out of the question. Never had her personal habits - her most intimate activities - been subject to public discussion; at least not while she was present.

Tank turned toward the front of the room again, giving Becky a pained look. She nodded slightly. What else could he have done?

"Won't last."

"Excuse me?" Tank stopped and slowly faced the young man again.

The kid shrugged and smirked at another student across the aisle. Tank looked hard at him and then asked him to stand. Grumbling, he got to his feet and glanced around the room, looking for an audience. He finally looked up at Tank and swallowed.

"I don't answer to you." Tank's voice was low and unsettling. "Ms. Jacobs doesn't answer to you. What we teach is important, and if you don't want to take it seriously, get out. Now."

He towered for a moment and the student didn't move. Tank turned to the rest of the class, scanning the room to make sure he had everyone's attention.

He did.

"Ms. Jacobs and I are trying to help you with a very personal life decision. We are also dating. How we apply this class material to our relationship is absolutely and inarguably our business and ours alone. Understood?"

Not a word was spoken for the five minutes remaining of class time. The students worked quietly on their homework and then quickly left the room. Becky would have slunk out with the crowd, but she knew that she and Tank had to debrief. Their game had just gotten a lot more complicated.

She waited while he stood at the door watching every student leave. When the room was empty, he closed the door and stood against it, his arms crossed. He looked like he was trying to calm down. Becky gave him space to do it.

He finally spoke. "Can't believe that kid."

"I know," she replied, still reeling from the confrontation. "You were very cool. I'm not sure what I would have done."

He glanced over at her. "Thanks for letting me handle it." He ran his hand over his head. Becky wondered how the short, spikey hair felt running through his fingers.

"So, we made it a week, right? This might be a good time to end things," she suggested.

"Why?" He moved toward her and Becky fought the urge to relocate just because he was advancing. She couldn't begin to imagine him coming at her fast. How did those guys stand up to each other on the field?

"It's obvious that they're watching us. I feel like a hypocrite."

"Because the relationship isn't real?" he asked.

That sounded harsh. "Well, it's not really fair to claim innocence when we're not really, you know, even tempted."

He raised a brow.

"Well, because this," Becky gestured back and forth between them, "isn't real, and well, it's just not believable."

"What isn't?"

"Please. That we would be dating and not ..."

He simply stood and looked at her with his arms crossed. Why couldn't she say the words? They were teaching a sex education class, for goodness' sake.

"So, if we were really dating, you think we would ..."

He wouldn't say it either. She rolled her eyes. Good thing the class wasn't watching this exchange.

When her imagination caught up with her, she seriously blushed for the first time in a decade.

"No! I don't know! I don't think about it."

"You don't ever think about ..."

Becky's head shot up. "Don't say it!"

Tank almost smiled, which made her want to slap him and laugh out loud at the same time. It was ridiculous. She had never, *ever* been shy about this subject, but for some reason she couldn't have this conversation with this man. She'd never admit that she'd thought about him from time to time ... to time. She might be done with men, but she still had her imagination.

"I'm serious. This is getting weird," she tried to steer them back to the matter at hand. "We have to break up. You said we would, and now it's getting complicated." She walked toward the window - as far away as she could get from him. "It might get diffi-cult if we wait any longer."

"So we wait another week. We'll be old news soon, and then the kids won't care."

So naive. He clearly didn't know how the gossip mill worked. The kids would be waiting to see who ended it and why, whose heart got broken and how badly. They'd be ready to pounce like vultures; so would the teachers.

Becky felt him behind her and refused to turn around. She looked out the window at the parking lot - all the kids walking out to their cars, the busses lined up just so. She took a deep breath. The very idea of being in a relationship with the man behind her and showing restraint was ludicrous. She may not have always liked him, but she was always intensely aware of him. He had a presence that was kind of ... consuming.

She turned halfway. He was closer than she realized.

"What do you say? One more week?" he asked.

"Those P.E. teachers still giving you grief?"

This time he did smile a little. "Nothing I can't handle."

Becky walked around him to the desk to gather her things. "Alright. Since you begged me not to break up with you, I guess I can hang on a little longer."

It was possible that he growled. She turned and smiled brightly. "So, where are you taking me for dinner tonight?"

"To the grocery store. You always cook for me on Friday nights, remember?"

She grinned as she buckled her bag. "Yeah, that doesn't really work for me. You go ahead and make reservations, and I'll go home and get myself all dolled up."

"Reservations for tomorrow evening, then?"

She slowed her very sassy walk to the door.

"You are evil," she said, her eyes narrowing at him as she fought a grin. Then her expression changed entirely. "Oh, no. I totally forgot to ask if you could go out with John and Maddy tonight."

"If *I* can go out with them?"

"No, not just you - we. They want to double-date."

He lost the playful expression as he considered the invitation. "So, they both know?"

"Yep."

"Huh. And they want to go out with us?" He was thoughtful for a moment. "Oh, hold on. I can't. Alex is coming in tonight. I told Grace I'd pick him up at the airport."

"Oh, perfect! Then we're off the hook."

"When did they ask?"

"Oh, the other night. Wednesday, I guess."

"I could've worked it out with a little more notice."

She refused to be chastised. "Please, like you even want to go. I'll just tell them it didn't work out."

"We'll do it another time."

"Time's running out," she reminded him. "Only one more week and you're free. Remember?"

She turned and left the room, leaving Tank looking less than cheery.

twenty

"Tank."

"Most people say 'hello' when they answer their phone."

He'd spoken to her less than five hours ago, yet his adrenaline kicked in at the sound of her voice.

"Oh, hey Becky, I was going to call you. See if you wanted to grab a late bite." He was back from the airport earlier than expected. There still might be time to connect.

"Yeah, right," she replied.

"Can I pick you up in fifteen? How about the Pizza Place?"

"You don't sound right." There was a pause. "Oh, that's right. You're with Alex."

"Yep."

"Gotcha. Well, I was the one who called you, so we'll do my thing. Maddy and John are asking if you still want to join us for a drink or something when you get home. So go ahead and pretend I said 'yes.'"

Tank grinned. "Okay. Where do you want to meet?"

"We're at Wally's Watershed."

"Wally's what?"

"Watershed. Great spot. Off highway H, just a mile or so out of town. Head west off Main Street. Just come whenever you get in."

"Sounds great."

"They have a band, Tank. And a dance floor. You'll love it."

Tank swallowed a moan. "Perfect."

"I like your pretend nice phone voice, Tank. Very convincing."

"Okay, see you in a bit."

"Bye-bye."

Her sing-song, mocking salutation entertained him, despite the evening's threat of music and dancing. Tank tossed his phone into the center console, hoping Alex hadn't heard Becky's end of the conversation. The man beside him sat looking out the window and politely drumming his fingers to the music on the radio.

"You been to Wally's ... whatever?" Tank asked.

Alex grinned. "Watershed. Yes, indeed. You're in for a treat."

"Do they really have a dance floor?"

"Yep. Good food, though. Interesting atmosphere."

"Guess I'll find out soon enough."

"Guess so."

Tank drove for a few minutes. "So, I'll drop you at the shop?"

"That'd be great."

Tank tapped his fingers on the steering wheel, then made the expected request: "You take good care of my sister."

Alex smiled, but there was a serious edge beneath the gentle demeanor that Tank always found reassuring. "I will."

***

Tank walked into Wally's and looked around with a half smile. The place had Maine written all over it, with fishnet curtains and old lobster cages stacked in the corners. A band played on the small stage and people were actually dancing. He shuddered. Luckily, the smell of burgers and seafood ensured that he could still get a bite to eat. His stomach rumbled at the prospect.

Cautiously approaching the dance floor, Tank took advantage of his height to survey the room. He'd decided to make the most of fake-dating Becky on this particular evening. For whatever reason, and he wasn't going there, treating her like a real date sounded good. If it ended up softening her up a bit so that she agreed to the favor he needed from her, all the better. Beyond that, he wasn't going to think about it.

It didn't take long to find Becky's table, or to realize that she already had a friend with her. He wasn't sitting with them, but he rested his arm on the booth and leaned toward her in a way that indicated he hoped to stay a while. Becky's smile was all welcome. Tank blitzed the table.

John stood to greet him, Maddy glanced with concern at the intruder, and Becky just looked surprised. She shouldn't have; she'd invited him to join her little party. Tank drew a breath and shook John's hand.

"John, Maddy." He turned and towered. "Becky."

"Hi, Tank. This is Travis. Travis, Tank."

She made the introduction without hesitation, and Tank shook the man's hand. He had a few inches, maybe ten years, and likely fifty pounds on the kid, but Travis, or whoever, was definitely in shape.

"Travis," he said.

Travis gave him a measured look that spoke volumes.

"Tank Kimball." Admiration won out as recognition surfaced. "Cool to meet you."

"Thanks. Same here."

"Travis works for John during the summer," Becky explained.

Disappointment flashed across Travis' face, and Tank wondered what Becky had left out. There was definitely a history there, though he was under the impression that Becky hadn't moved to Maine until the fall.

They stood for a moment, and then Travis finally excused himself. "Good to see you guys. Looking forward to checking out the apartment, John." He turned to Becky. "Really nice to see you again, Becky. Take care."

Tank watched as he walked away, then sat down in the booth, making decided contact with his date. He leaned his shoulder into hers for good measure.

"Cheating on me, already?" he asked quietly. Playful jealousy covered any traces of the real thing.

Becky tried to get comfortable with the little space he'd left her. "Have you got enough room? Because I'm sure they could get you a chair," she replied, predictably ignoring his question.

Grinning, he nudged his thigh into hers. "Naw, I'm good." He picked up a menu from the center of the table and popped it open. "Can I still order a meal?"

"We figured you'd have eaten already." Sweet Becky made him feel right at home.

"I did." He flipped through the pages. "But I'll need something to wash my drink down."

A subtle battle continued under the table as Becky pushed into Tank in response to his nudge. The progression called for a lean, and he accomplished this with little, visible-above-the-table effort. Becky tried to make her resulting body shift look natural, but wasn't particularly successful.

"So, I hear you're teaching drama at the high school," John said casually.

Tank and Becky jerked their heads up.

"I'm sure the kids are learning a lot about acting," Maddy agreed.

Before Tank could comment, John's phone rang, diverting his and Maddy's focus. Tank hesitated only briefly before hooking his foot around Becky's ankle, locking her into place. She changed tactics by going for a leg grab. *Big mistake.* He snagged her hand before she did any damage, barely keeping a hold of his menu in the process.

With a firm hold on her, he leaned over to whisper in her ear. "If you want to hold hands, just ask." He got a whiff of Beckiness and postponed his retreat by a second or two.

"I think somebody's ticklish," she whispered back, trying to loosen her hand from his, no doubt preparing for another attack.

He admired her determination, but there was no way she'd win this particular event. Tank was extremely competitive, and, too bad for Becky, much bigger. He kept a hold of her hand while he continued to look at the menu. Becky twisted and turned to no avail. He glanced down at her after he ordered his double cheeseburger platter. "Jumpy tonight?"

She wrinkled her nose at him in a very teenager-y way. They'd spent too much time in the classroom.

"I'm sorry, we have to take off," John said, standing. "Parker's got an upset stomach, and Frank's good will only goes so far." He grinned wryly and laid a few bills on the table.

"Bummer," Tank replied, genuinely sorry for the little guy, and maybe especially for Frank.

"Would have been fun," Maddy said, eyeing them with interest. "You good with a ride?"

Becky looked at Tank.

"Sure," he said.

Maddy smiled. "Okay, well, we'd better run."

"Hope Parker's okay," Becky replied, pausing in her effort to free herself.

"Me, too," Maddy replied, slipping her coat on. "You two have fun." They said their good-byes, and John and Maddy made their way across the dance floor.

"Why don't you move over there?" Becky gestured with her free hand. "No need to crowd in on the same side."

Tank glanced at the two chairs on the other side of the table. "Why do they have chairs on one side and a bench on the other?" he asked, still holding her hand. "Who would ever pick the chairs?"

"You would," Becky replied, leaning into him and trying to shove him out of the booth.

He grinned. "Nice try."

She narrowed her eyes. "C'mon - move!" she shoved again. "I need some space."

Tank, unmoved, continued to grin at her efforts. "No, it's definitely more fun on this side."

A couple from a nearby table approached them. "Okay if we borrow your chairs?" the woman asked.

"No problem," Tank responded. "We're not using them."

Becky swallowed her objection as the chairs and the couple moved away.

"What's your deal?" she hissed.

Tank loosened his hold on her hand a little and found himself wanting to link his fingers through hers. Funny how a slightly different grip suggested a whole different kind of intimacy.

He shook himself. "Lots of people here," he reminded her. "We have an image to maintain." She rolled her eyes which made him smile. "Do your flirt thing," he suggested. "Pretend I'm someone else."

"I can't do it if you want me to," she grumbled. "It's only fun if it irritates you."

"Suit yourself. Try to look happy."

"Says the man with the perpetual scowl." Becky fake-smiled as her eyes traveled over the room, evaluating their audience. "Besides, I don't see anyone I know."

Tank finally let her fingers go and leaned back, casually putting his arm on the back of the seat. "You never know. People are always watching, or so you seem to think." He let his hand drop lightly to her shoulder, then further surprised them both by studying her very expressive eyes. "Your eyes are great when you're irritated. I think they actually change color."

"How do they look when I do this?"

Tank almost vaulted off the bench when she squeezed his leg, this time really getting a hold of it. His knee slammed into the table, rattling everything on it. He grabbed her hand.

"You'll regret it," he breathed, "if you do that again."

"Are you threatening me, Mr. Kimball?" Becky's eyes danced, delighting in discovering his weakness.

"No threat. Simply a fact." He kept his voice low, his hand firmly holding hers. "If the table hadn't been in the way, you'd be across the room right now."

"Oh, please."

"My legs are big. My legs are strong." He leaned a little closer. "You grab that area above my knee and they react without any filter. You don't want to be on the receiving end of my leg's unfiltered response. Got it?"

She looked down at his legs, no doubt measuring the threat. Her fingers twitched under his. Looking back up at him, she continued to process their proximity. With one arm around her and the other holding her hand and basically restraining her, Tank had her pretty well surrounded.

A pulse ticked in her throat as she met his gaze.

It occurred to him to loosen his grip and back away, but something held him in place. Becky's eyes, first delighted, then irritated, looked ... intrigued? He couldn't drag himself away, though he knew he should. For all of her self-proclaimed experience, she had a look of mixed uncertainty and knowing interest about her that was captivating.

"You should probably move," she whispered.

"I should," he replied.

Tank rarely allowed himself to simply stare, but now did so unapologetically. He took his time and let his eyes drift over her face. When had it become so familiar? The curve of her cheekbone, her arched brow, her nose, those lips ... It was as though he'd spent years exploring them, yet he'd never so much as touched. His eyes found hers again; they reflected his turmoil like a mirror.

"Oh, hey, excuse me, Ms. Jacobs?"

***

Tank and Becky jumped apart as though poked with a cattle prod.

"I'm sorry to interrupt, but I'm here with my family," Bailey gestured across the dance floor, "and when I saw you I just had to come over."

Becky tried to collect herself and focus on her student. "Hey Bailey. What's up?"

Tank turned toward the girl, leaving his arm around Becky's shoulder. There was only so much untangling they could do without looking ridiculous.

"Have you met Mr. Kimball?" Becky asked, noting that Bailey was staring.

Bailey shook herself. "Hey, Mr. Kimball." She blushed and turned back to Becky. "Ms. Halloway had her baby!" she blurted out. "So now we really need you next Friday. Can you come?" She looked back and forth between the two of them hopefully.

Becky's head spun. She hadn't mentioned the dance to Tank. Under the circumstances, spending Valentine's Day with him didn't seem like a good idea.

"I haven't even talked to Mr. Kimball about it. How about I talk to you on Monday?"

"Oh, but you'd be perfect!" Bailey insisted. She moved out of the way as the server put Tank's plate on the table.

"What do you need?" Tank finally asked, his curiosity apparently winning out over his desire to ignore two women talking about babies.

"We need chaperones for our Valentine's Day dance," Bailey explained. "It would be perfect if you both could do it. It won't be hard," she assured them.

Tank took in the information, seemed to think for a moment, then looked at Becky. He pulled her in a little closer. "Let's go to the dance."

She tried to keep a pleasant face while her eyes looked daggers at him.

"Oh, thank you, Mr. Kimball!" Bailey squealed. "It will be so fun! I'll give you all the information on Monday." She started to turn. "And don't forget to dress up. It's semi-formal!"

It was quiet for a moment as Bailey ran off.

"Nice job," Becky finally said. "If you're so bent on dancing in public, we could have have just done it here."

"Not dancing - chaperoning. It's different." Tank turned to his plate and picked up his sandwich. "Anyway, I was just checking with you, and she ran with it."

"You didn't check with me, you invited me to the dance. To a high school girl that was very romantic, and obviously, that meant we were agreeing to go."

Tank looked at her over his shoulder. "Romantic, huh? That was easy."

"Romantic for a high-schooler," Becky qualified, ignoring his grin. She sipped her drink while Tank turned and took another bite. How could he eat at a time like this? A few minutes earlier, he'd given her the most unguarded, heated expression she'd ever seen. Like it or not, she'd be reliving that look all night long.

She pulled at the neckline of her sweater. It was suddenly very warm. At least Tank had scooted over a little, though there still wasn't room for both of them in the small space.

He finally took a long drink and turned to her. "We actually have something else to talk about." He searched her eyes for a moment then glanced around the room. "We can talk on the way home."

Becky had had enough of the eye contact and touching. This evening needed to end. What else could he possibly need to talk to her about?

Tank paid the server and got up. He stood back as Becky slid off the bench, and walked behind her through the dance floor. Half dreading and half curious, she pulled her coat on and ducked out into the February snow.

"Wow, it's really coming down. Is your Jeep okay in this?" It was a silly question, but she felt like irritating him.

He gave her a sidelong glance, got in and turned the key. The engine didn't turn over at first, but the second time it fired up. Becky almost remarked on his infallible vehicle, but held her tongue. Tank glanced over, daring her, while he flipped on the defrost and waited for the vehicle to warm up.

The drive back to the inn wouldn't take long, and Becky wondered if he planned on coming into the house to talk. Given the events of the last half hour or so, that didn't seem like a good idea.

"So, what's up?" She tried to sound casual, as though she weren't suddenly ultra aware of their proximity. The hand on the gear shift had held hers. She'd had her own hand on that gigantic knee. They'd been touching one way or another all night and she couldn't shake the images. She looked out the window.

"Yeah," Tank finally spoke. "Carrie Lynn talked to me after school, today. She thinks she's pregnant."

"Oh, no," Becky turned back to him. There were two Carries in their health class. Carrie Lynn was also in Becky's French class. She was one of her more difficult students. *Still* ...

"Poor baby," she whispered.

"I'm sorry?"

"She's just a baby."

"She's sixteen and she's been ..." he hesitated.

"Been what, Tank?" Becky's concern for the girl was swallowed up in anger at Tank, and pretty much all men everywhere. "Guys just do what comes naturally, but any girl who 'does what comes naturally' is a ..."

"No, Becky, please don't." He flipped on the windshield wipers with a heavy sigh. "She may be young, but she's old enough to deal with this. She just needs some help."

Becky tried to calm down. "Her parents?"

"Not so much support there."

"Of course. And I'm sure the Romeo is long gone by now."

Tank cleared his throat. "Wish I could say otherwise."

Becky gave a humorless laugh.

"Not all guys are like that," he said.

She pierced him with a look.

"She needs someone to go to the crisis pregnancy center in Benson with her."

"She wants me? I thought she hated me. She's given me nothing but attitude in French." Becky looked out the window again, anxious at the thought of reliving her past through this girl.

"Well, she didn't ask for you, exactly."

Becky swung her head around. "Who does she want, *exactly*?"

"Well, she wanted me to go."

"What? You?"

"Yeah, I know. It's crazy. I tried to convince her to talk to you, but she thinks you're too ..."

Becky sighed in frustration. "Too what?"

"Well, too straight-laced. Thinks you'd judge her."

"I don't even know how to respond to that," Becky sputtered. "Why are we having this conversation? Just go with her."

Tank turned to her earnestly. "She needs a woman. Someone who ... I don't know. She needs a woman."

The Jeep was plenty warm, but still they idled in the parking lot. "Well, she doesn't need or want me."

"I told her you'd meet her there tomorrow."

He flinched.

"You *what*? Why?"

"She needs you. You have a heart for these kids. She'll warm up to you."

"Oh, thanks."

"You know what I mean."

Becky crossed her arms. "Why would you commit me like that? Never mind how awkward this is." Another wave of panic flooded over her at the thought of setting foot inside a pregnancy center.

"Well, you're usually around the house on Saturdays when I come over to work."

Becky glared at him.

"Now, don't get mad, but ... okay, you're already mad," Tank sighed. "She needs one of us; she doesn't have anyone else right now."

Becky shook her head, biting her bottom lip. She did not want to go to the front lines with this girl; a girl who didn't want her company in the first place.

"I'm surprised she was even willing to talk to me about it. I had no idea what she wanted when she walked up to me in the parking lot this afternoon." Tank turned down the defrost fan and toyed with the gear shift. "I really didn't know what to say. I told her I'd talk to you." He took a deep breath. "By the end of the conversation, she was so worked up, I promised that you'd meet her there. I'm sorry," he finally conceded. "I shouldn't have done that."

Becky looked over at him. His remorse seemed genuine. "When is she planning to go?"

"She said she could meet you there at two."

"Please take me home."

"Think you can do it?"

"Take me home and I'll think about it."

***

Tank pulled into Becky's drive a few minutes later. The snow was starting to pile up and he was glad he only had a few more blocks to go to get himself home. He put the Jeep in park and looked over at Becky.

"You okay?"

She was staring out the window. "Yeah."

His gut twisted at the sorrow in her voice. He'd hit some kind of nerve, and while he didn't want to push her to talk, he didn't want to leave her in this state, either. He also needed to know what to do about Carrie.

"So, I'm guessing tomorrow's not really an option?"

Becky turned to him with a sigh. "You don't know what you're asking."

"You're right, I don't."

She looked up into his eyes; her own wide with emotion. He couldn't see them clearly in the semi-dark, but he could imagine the gold making inroads into the soft brown. He wasn't kidding when he said her eyes seemed to change color with her mood. Half the time he picked on her just to watch them do their thing.

This was not one of those times.

"I don't know," she shook her head and looked away. "I want to help her, but ..." she shrugged. "I just have to think about it. I'll talk to you tomorrow." She opened the door and stepped out.

"Becky." Tank turned off the Jeep, jumped out, and followed her up the steps.

"Please, don't," Becky protested. "You can't be here."

"Why not?" he asked, shoving his hands into his coat pockets.

She glanced up at him but wouldn't hold his gaze. "Tonight's been too weird. I don't think you should come inside."

Tank reached for her arm but she backed away.

"Becky, I'm not here to do anything but talk. We're friends, right?" That admission had been a long time coming.

She shivered. "I guess."

"You guess?" Tank stomped his feet to keep warm.

"Yes, of course. Please go home."

"I don't want to leave while you're upset."

"Well, you can't come in and we'll freeze out here."

He sighed, exasperated. "Why can't I come in?"

"You know why." She finally met his gaze.

"You don't trust me?"

She gave him a long look. "I don't trust *me*."

He grinned a little. "It's been a long time since someone made me do something I didn't want to do."

His effort at humor didn't hit the mark.

"You'd be surprised at what I could make you do." Becky turned away and rubbed her mittened hands together.

Tank tried to interpret her comment as a threat. "I trust you."

She turned back to him. "Why? You don't know me, Tank. Don't know what I've done or what I'm capable of."

"That sounds ominous." He added a hop to his foot stomping. They were almost dancing after all.

"Okay, here's the deal," she blurted out. "I was Carrie." She took a step closer and really looked into his eyes. "Sixteen and maybe pregnant and very alone. I got through it, but ..." She pulled her coat tighter around herself. "Carrie needs someone to guide her in the right direction, whether she's pregnant or not. I'm not that person."

Becky dug in her purse for her keys, apparently ready to end the evening on that note.

Tank wasn't. He stepped forward and pulled her into his arms. She stiffened briefly, resisting his comfort, then her body slowly leaned into his.

"I'm sorry, Becky." He held her and stroked her hair. After a moment she reached around his waist. He pulled her closer, marveling at how she fit, bulky jackets notwithstanding. She took a deep breath, and Tank rested his chin on top of her head. He could get used to comforting Becky.

"You're not the only one who's made mistakes," he gently pointed out.

She burrowed in a little deeper. "There's a story there, but I'm too cold to hear it."

Tank laughed, enjoying the warmth of her against his chest. "Yeah, I gotta let you go in." With more regret than he could have imagined, he loosened his hold on her.

She backed up and looked at him a little warily. Her hair was wonderfully mussed. Tank resisted the urge to reach out and brush it away from her face.

Becky looked down for a moment and took a deep breath. Lifting her eyes to his, she regarded him, her expression suddenly hard. "I'll help her under one condition."

Tank mentally shook himself. He wasn't quite ready to switch gears, but the look on Becky's face indicated that she had. "Okay, great. What is it?"

"We're forgetting about this conversation." She backed up another step, distancing herself in every way she could. "I never unloaded on you. We go right back to pretend dating - we break up - finish out the school year - and we never have to see to each other again. Got it?"

Tank felt like he'd been kicked in the stomach. "Wait. Why? Can't we talk tomorrow?"

"No. Those are my conditions." Becky turned away and unlocked the door. She looked over her shoulder at him, all attitude.

Tank stared back for a long moment. "I think it would be great if you helped Carrie, but whether you do or don't - that's on you."

Becky's mouth dropped a little.

"I won't agree to pretending I don't really know you," he continued, stepping toward her.

She managed to close her mouth, but incredulity still played across her features.

"I don't want to pretend date, and I don't want to break up and I certainly don't plan on never seeing you again," he finished.

"What does that even mean?" she finally whispered.

"I haven't figured that out yet, but don't even think about giving me ultimatums."

Becky stepped back, her head reeling. "But I'm done with men forever."

"You're not done with me."

twenty-one

Becky wandered out of her bedroom with a yawn, then reeled back at the light bouncing off the walls of the kitchen. The snow had stopped and the sun was out, reflecting off the endless white surface. She braced herself against the kitchen counter and blinked. She'd never seen so much snow and sunlight combined.

She made her coffee and dared to hope; she couldn't possibly be expected to meet anyone at a pregnancy center today. Looking up the number for the center in Benson, she called to make sure. Their answering machine confirmed that they wouldn't be open until Monday. Becky breathed a sigh of relief.

After building a fire, she settled in with her coffee, letting the mug warm her hands through. The faint roar of an engine in the driveway caught her attention. Who had braved the roads to come to the inn on a Saturday morning? She jumped up to get dressed.

A few minutes later, Maddy called out as she walked in the front door. "Hey Becky, you up?"

"Yeah, be right out," she called back.

She met up with her sister in the kitchen. "You're daring. How are the roads?"

Maddy seemed a little disconcerted as she looked around the room. "The main roads weren't too bad. And John's truck got through the side roads without any problem." She hesitated. "I hope it's okay that we came over?"

Becky looked up from her coffee in surprise. "Of course it is. It's your house."

Maddy nodded. "John and the boys are outside, but he'll need to come in soon and get working on the apartment."

"Sure," Becky replied, wondering why Maddy looked so ill at ease. "Is Parker feeling better?"

"Parker? Oh, yeah, he's fine. Just had too much pasta. He woke up ready to conquer the world this morning."

"Well, thanks for bringing him over here to do it."

Maddy smiled a little; didn't laugh like she normally would.

"Have you had breakfast yet?" Becky asked. "I could make pancakes."

"Oh, we're all set. Thanks."

"Anyone else coming over to work today?"

Maddy looked puzzled. "John thought the others were busy."

Becky nodded, relieved. She was pretty sure she didn't need to see Tank today. "Guess we don't need pancakes then. I'll just have some cereal."

She started toward the pantry, and couldn't help notice Maddy peeking into the sunroom.

"Okay, what's going on?" Becky asked. "Are you looking for something?"

Maddy jumped. "No! I'm just ..." She looked at Becky intently. "Are you alone?"

Becky tilted her head. "No. I'm here with you," she said slowly. "Are you okay?"

Maddy looked relieved. "I'm fine, but ... Okay, Tank's Jeep is parked out front and it's covered with snow and we just thought ..."

Becky scowled. "What's his Jeep doing here?" She went to the front of the house and looked out the window. Sure enough, Tank's Jeep was sitting right where he'd left it the night before.

"That's odd," she said.

Maddy had followed her. "I'm sorry ... It just seemed like ... I'm sorry."

The more she apologized the worse Becky felt. "No, it makes perfect sense." She walked back through the house to the kitchen. "He was having trouble with his battery. Must not have been able to start it again when he left."

She turned to her sister. "And no, he didn't even come in the house last night. We talked on the porch and he said some things, and I wasn't very receptive." She sighed. "I kind of just came in and left him out there. He probably didn't want to ask me for help after that."

"Well," Maddy replied, obviously regretting the conclusions she'd drawn, "I guess I'll let John know it's okay to start."

Becky dumped her cold coffee in the sink. "Yeah, I'm gonna have to get a hold of Tank; he's gotta move that Jeep."

"Well, John will plow at some point, but there's no rush."

The more she thought about it, the more concerned Becky became. "Actually, there is. 'Ooh la la' lives right down the street."

"Wait. Who?"

Becky looked distractedly at her sister, starting to panic. "This kid in my French class; always gives me a hard time. He lives at the end of Camden. He's told me that he's seen me out running."

"So that's a problem?"

"Everyone knows Tank's Jeep at school. I can't take the chance of anyone recognizing it here, covered with snow." She got out her phone.

"Oh, right. Well, good luck."

Becky found his number and let it ring. Sincerely hoping she'd wake him, she tapped her foot and looked out the window, waiting. Of course, he didn't answer. She hit dial again, remembering Grace's frustration that her brother never seemed to have his phone with him. Her irritation locked in, Becky pulled on her jacket, grabbed some mittens, and stomped her barely fastened boots out into the snow. She'd march down to his ocean-view palace and tell him what she thought of his precious Jeep.

***

By the time she got to Tank's house, Becky was exhausted from navigating the piles of snow on the mostly unplowed side streets. She rang the doorbell and lifted the knocker, pounding it a few times for good measure.

Several minutes later, Tank finally came to the door, puffy-eyed and disoriented. Never had such a big, scary man looked so cuddly and ... *cute* wasn't the word, but whatever it was, he wouldn't like it. Becky recalled 'waking' him on another morning at the inn a few months earlier, but there had been nothing cuddly about that Tank.

This one lifted his arms in a stretch that should have been featured on the cover of some body building magazine, then blew that impressive image by letting out some sort of grumbly morning growl that was as adorable as it was alarming. Becky momentarily forgot her irritation, and simply stared.

After a moment, Tank seemed to wake up enough to realize she was standing on his porch in the cold. Apparently not questioning why she'd shown up at his house on a Saturday morning, he greeted her.

"Hey." He pulled the door wide so she could enter.

Becky refused to satisfy her curiosity about his house and remained on the porch. She would not be impressed by the needlessly large and airy entranceway, or the wide staircase that no doubt led up to the beast's lair. She glanced past the enormous, contemporary living area that stretched from the front to the beach side of the house, where it joined the kitchen. All of the windows showcasing the view of the water received no more than a cursory glance.

"No, thanks," she replied to the unspoken invite as her eyes returned to Tank. She was about to let him have it, and he stood there regarding her with a sleepy smile. Did he think this was some sort of prehistoric social call?

"Why is your stupid Jeep in my driveway?" she demanded.

Tank reeled back as though she'd struck him. He rubbed the back of his neck and blinked. Becky ignored the bicep, his traps, and that gap of muscled stomach peeking out between his T-shirt and sweats. She fisted her hands on her hips and tried to look as menacing as possible.

"Oh, right," he replied slowly. "Forgot about that. You want some coffee?"

"No, I don't want coffee! I want you to move your Jeep! It's covered with snow and it looks like it spent the night at my house, which it did. People will get the wrong impression. You have to move it!"

Becky made every effort to hold onto her anger, really wishing Tank wasn't so appealing in his sleepy effort to process her request. She tapped her boot, which was actually kind of hard to do.

"Right, okay. Gonna need a jump."

He actually rubbed his eyes. Becky looked down and bit back a smile. She came back up when she was sure she looked irritated again. "John's at the house. I'm sure he can help you. Just hurry."

"John? Good. Okay."

"And another thing. The pregnancy center in Benson is closed today. I called to make sure. Do you have a way to get a hold of Carrie Lynn? I mean, she'll probably figure it out, but since you told her I'd be there, we should follow up."

Tank nodded. "Yeah," he thought for a minute. "I have her number. You want it?"

"No, I want *you* to call her. Tell her I'll talk to her at school."

"Okay, no problem." He finally seemed to be waking up. "You wanna give me a minute and I'll walk back over with you?"

"No thanks. I'll let John know you're coming." Becky turned and trotted back down the steps. She started her jog home without saying good-bye.

***

Becky threw herself into making a snow fort with Blake and Parker. For hours, she rolled snow boulders into place, strategically placed spy holes, and otherwise perfected their abode. By early afternoon they had an impressive fort and a snowman to guard it. He was holding a fireplace poker.

Otis came out to join them, and the boys showed him the fort and its fearsome guard. Afterwards, they all worked together to shovel Otis' walkway.

Cold and tired, but happy, the four of them returned to Maddy's kitchen to warm up.

"That was so fun, Miss Aunt Becky!" Parker beamed as they thawed out with hot chocolate. "I didn't know you were so good at snow playing!"

Becky smiled, nursing her own cup of cocoa. "I have lots of hidden talents, Parker. Never underestimate me."

"Under what?"

"Aunt Becky can do lots of cool things," Blake explained, sharing his own smile with Becky.

She lifted her mug in salute. "Thanks, Blake."

"I sure do appreciate the help with my walkway," Otis added. "That was a lot more snow than I expected. Sure is pretty, though."

Maddy had spent the day helping John in the attic, but Becky didn't ask her for proof. She figured they could use a little time alone; whether they chose to use it remodeling or ... otherwise, was up to them. At some point during their snow adventure, Maddy had made a great big pot of soup, so Becky was happy.

Maddy was currently playing hostess and refilling their hot chocolate. "Your dad's gonna want to see that fort before we leave today," she said. "He might get some good ideas for the apartment."

Blake and Parker giggled. "Maybe we can live out there instead!" Parker offered. "It's so cool!"

Blake grinned and sipped his cocoa. Becky smiled at them both. "We'll have to add a room or two if you're going to live out there," she replied. "And you'll probably want a fireplace to stay warm."

"But that would make the snow melt!" Parker laughed. "I'll just bring Burt. He'll keep me warm."

The Irish wolfhound wagged his tail at hearing his name. He'd had his own adventure in the snow and was trying to sleep it off on his mat in the corner of the kitchen.

Maddy smiled affectionately. "He's gonna be wiped out for the rest of the day. I hope one of you can carry him to the truck."

Blake and Parker giggled again at that, and Becky grinned. Maddy was so good with the boys. They were lucky. Maddy was lucky. John was probably the luckiest of all.

twenty-two

Tank pulled into his driveway, revved the engine a bit, then turned off his Jeep. He'd have to look into a new battery after school sometime during the week. He got out and breathed in the clear, crisp, morning air. His only memories of Maine belonged to summer. It was kind of cool to see those memories blanketed in snow.

Cool and cold, *really cold*. He jogged up the steps to the door, keys ready. He'd love to build a garage and a workshop on the half lot next door. That bit of property was available; he'd long since had that confirmed. He just needed the owners of his house to sell. Letting himself in, he kicked off his boots and shrugged out of his coat. It was time to check in with his real estate agent again.

Grace would be happy. She'd been right; Clairmont was a great little community, and it had somehow embraced him over the past few months. It was nice to feel at home somewhere.

Dropping his keys on the front table, he recalled the scene with Becky the morning before. She'd come spitting fire and all he could think of was how much he wanted her in his house. She'd worn the same L.L. Bean jacket that he'd held her in the night before, and it was hard to focus on anything else as she'd stood there complaining about his Jeep.

She was right, of course. He shouldn't have left it Friday night, but it would have been awkward to ask for her help. Becky needed space. Tank was increasingly convinced that he needed Becky. The more desperate she was to drive him away, the more determined he was to hold onto her.

Things had definitely changed over the last few months.

He shook his head and went to start a pot of coffee. He thought about the day ahead; one that he'd been half dreading for the past couple of weeks. Frank had invited him over to watch the Super Bowl, but Grace had asked for his help at the shop. Either way, he wasn't likely to be alone for his 'farewell to football.' Though it seemed rather anticlimactic, he felt like he might actually be ready to be a spectator again after all these years.

It was nothing short of miraculous - the transformation he'd gone through since the fall. Although he knew he had to give up playing, he certainly hadn't been ready to do it four months ago. While he'd still love to play, and continued to work out as though he was on the team, he felt a kind of peace about moving on. He could never have imagined that happening.

Tank looked out his kitchen window as he waited for the coffee to brew. He wondered if Becky would be watching the game. She'd watched the Thanksgiving game with interest, and he'd grudgingly conceded at the time that she seemed to know what was going on.

He would enjoy watching football with her - explaining the plays - giving her an inside view of the action. Would she care? Would she even try to imagine what his former life was like? He wanted to think she would.

He was beginning to think that he'd enjoy doing a lot of things with Becky. He watched the water lap the icy shore and felt far removed from the cold. She'd definitely gotten under his skin. Too bad she was determined to be done with men. Based on what she'd said, her experience with men had been awful from the beginning. While the challenge to change her mind about at least one man was intriguing, a part of him acknowledged that it might not be what Becky needed.

***

Becky finished painting her toenails and tip-heeled out to the sunroom. The eternal Super Bowl pre-game program droned on.

She had about fifteen minutes to finish cleaning up the kitchen and make her salad. The chocolate chip cookies she'd made were not for dinner.

She'd always liked football, but hadn't watched much of it in the last couple of years. Ever since meeting Tank, she'd wanted to sit down and really watch a game - try to see it through his eyes. Somehow, the entire season had gotten away from her - cable problems out on the beach hadn't helped - but now she was ready to sit and watch. Besides, the Super Bowl commercials were always entertaining.

Becky had made the cookies just because she felt like it. She'd have to take them to school; no way she could leave them at home. Still, it made the house smell wonderful and it had been a way to be productive without touching her school work. She washed her baking dishes, made a salad, and poured herself a glass of wine. She put the cork back in the bottle, put it way back up on the shelf, and headed out to the TV.

Ignoring the French grammar quizzes on the table in front of her, Becky curled up on the couch. She watched the players run onto the field, and wondered how Tank felt watching the game. She hoped he was with Grace, helping her kick off her new 'sports corner' at the back of the coffee shop. Becky would have gone to help out but she figured Tank would be there for his sister. He'd be a big draw for the community, and she knew Grace was counting on him. Becky sipped her wine, hoping the evening was a success for both of them.

***

Tank hardly knew how to approach knocking at her door. Becky wasn't expecting him, and he'd probably scare her to death. *Again.* He'd call, but, of course, he didn't have his phone on him. He should just turn around and head home, but he really wanted to see her.

He finally just gave a quick knock and then opened the door. "Sorry, Becky. Just me."

He waited for her to catch her breath and put the pillow down. She'd been sitting on the couch with her back to the door. It did his heart good to see the game on, but her reaction to his entry was a high price to pay. She jumped a good six inches off the couch and then turned, ready to spring. Good for Becky; always ready to put up a fight.

"I didn't mean to startle you. Thought this door would be better than the front. Mind if I come in?"

She slumped back down into the cushions and waved her hand. That was as much of an invite as he was going to get.

Tank stepped in, closing the door quickly behind him. He stomped the snow off his boots then leaned down to untie them.

Becky managed to pull herself off the couch and pad around in her big fluffy slippers until she was standing above him. His gaze trailed from those slippers - they always got to him - up to her hands on her hips, and beyond to her less than happy face.

"Really sorry," he said again as he loosened the second boot. She looked slightly less angry and a little more puzzled. That was a start.

"Is everything okay?" she asked, her brow furrowed. "You really scared me, you ..." She dwindled off and punched him on the shoulder instead.

"Ow," he grinned apologetically. "I know. I should have called or something." He stood and towered unintentionally, and she took a step back. "I was hoping you'd still be up for a bit."

"Well, you lucked out," she replied, gesturing at the game. "Some of us like to watch football, so ..."

"Yeah, I heard there was a game on."

They stood for a moment, the irritation dissolving.

"Nice shirt," Tank finally said. She was wearing one of Grace's "Caf-fiend" shirts.

He unzipped his coat. So was he.

Becky glanced at his and a small smile turned her lips. "Great minds think alike."

He nodded, hanging his coat over one of the kitchen chairs.

"Amazing how we wear the same size, too," she observed, a smile in her voice as she walked to the sink.

He watched her retreat. His shirt was like a bed sheet next to hers; they'd had to special order it. He glanced away. *Better not to think about bed sheets right now.*

"So, what's up?" she asked, opening a cupboard. "Can I get you something to drink?"

Tank noticed the wine glass next to the sink, but Becky didn't seem liked she'd had much. "Just water would be great."

"Did you go to the shop?"

"Yep." He followed her and sat down on a bar stool. "It's going well. Good turn out."

"Good. I'm really glad. Alex had some cool ideas for her." Becky poured water into a glass and added ice. "I wasn't sure Grace would buy the whole sports bar idea."

"It didn't take much to transform the back of the shop. We'll see if the people on their computers put up with the extra noise."

"It'll be interesting," Becky agreed. "Coffee shop by day, sports cafe by night. I think it might work here. I hope it does."

"Me too."

"So ... why didn't you stay?"

"It was getting a little crazy. I decided to get out of the way. Okay if we sit?" He gestured toward the couches - and the game.

"Sure," she said. "Grab those cookies over there. Might as well eat them while they're fresh."

Tank followed his nose to his favorite dessert. His last defenses against Becky fell away. "I thought it smelled good in here."

"Help yourself."

He glanced at his water. "Do you have milk?"

"Sure. It's skim. In the fridge."

"Water's good," he replied.

Becky laughed and he followed her into the living room with his glass and the plate of cookies. He sat down on the couch opposite her. The game had given way to a commercial, so he launched into his news.

"So a guy came into the bar - the coffee shop," he corrected himself, "from ESPN."

Becky sipped her own water and nodded.

"He offered me a commentator job."

Her eyes went wide. Tank wanted to read disappointment or fear or something that would tell him she didn't want him to go, but mostly she just looked impressed.

"Wow, that's really cool. When do you start?"

He shook his head slowly. "I'm not sure." He looked at the TV screen and then back at her. "I didn't take it."

"Are you kidding?" she sat up straight. "Why not?"

He thought for a moment. "Well, I didn't say no, outright. My agent's been talking to me about it, so it's not like I didn't know this might be coming. Just not ready to commit, yet."

"That's so cool, though, Tank." Becky sat back and regarded him. "Why would they ask you now, during the Super Bowl? Aren't they supposed to be covering the game?"

He smiled. "Plenty of people covering the game. I think they chose this time 'cuz my defenses would be down. Hard to say no."

"Ah ... I guess that makes sense."

Tank shrugged and picked up a still-warm cookie. He took a bite and the warm chocolate melted on his tongue. The rest of the cookie followed. If his mouth hadn't been full he would have proposed.

He looked up to see her watching him.

"They'll last longer if you take a bite at a time," she offered.

He grinned. "These aren't bite-sized?"

Becky leaned forward and picked one up for herself. "Observe." She took a small bite of her cookie, then closed her eyes, savoring the taste. If her goal was to keep him from eating her cookies, she'd managed very well. Her baking was now the last thing on his mind.

Tank took a big swallow of his water and focused on the TV.

"You're not paying attention."

He turned back, and they looked at each other for a long moment. Becky withdrew the tiniest bit, the look on her face slightly alarmed.

Tank let out a long breath. "Becky, why are you afraid of me? What do you think I'm going to do?"

"I'm not afraid of you," she huffed, "but look at you. You think that's not intimidating?"

"What?" he asked, looking down. He was sitting on the edge of the couch, his elbows braced on his knees.

"Put one of your hands on the ground."

"Why?"

"Seriously, do it."

Tank shook his head, leaned over and braced his left hand against the floor.

"Okay, now lift your backside off the couch."

Maybe she'd had more wine than he thought. Tank looked up with concern.

"Just do it."

"You sound like a Nike commercial."

"Like this," Becky said, striking a three-point lineman pose.

Tank grinned. "That *is* terrifying." He sat back, delighted with the spectacle.

She dropped back onto the couch. "Well, that's what you looked like, practically in your football pose; 250 pounds of Tank, ready to spring."

"I'm only 240."

"Oh, sorry, *Tiny Tank.*"

He laughed. "Well, that wasn't my 'pose' as you call it, though it looked good. Except you need at least a hundred more pounds on you. And linemen don't wiggle their hips."

"I can dream."

Tank smiled and shook his head. He moved the coffee table and then crouched down and modeled the position for her. "You gotta let your hips drop a little, and bend your legs - this isn't yoga."

"Like you'd know," Becky dropped back into position.

"Okay, shift that leg back like mine," he nodded at her left leg. "Now look at me and snarl."

"I can't believe you'd have to ask."

She slowly looked up and grinned at him. They were almost nose to nose. Her grin faded and her lids lowered a fraction. She hopped back onto the couch.

Tank slowly pulled himself to standing, reeling from how close he'd come to kissing her. He'd have proved all her concerns founded. He wasn't sure he cared.

"So, what was your pose?"

"My what?" Tank rubbed the back of his neck.

"Well, if you didn't crouch like that, what did you do?"

Tank shook himself. No one ever had to ask him twice about football. "Well, I was a middle linebacker." He lowered himself into the two point crouch, arms slightly extended. "Defense. Blitzing the quarterback, lots of tackling ..." His eyes lit up.

"I think that's scarier," Becky observed, holding her pillow.

"You asked," he grinned, sitting back down on his couch.

"Oh, look!" Becky turned to the TV. "Someone's about to score."

Tank followed her gaze, for the first time in his life not really caring about what was happening in a Super Bowl game.

"Fourth and inches. What do you think they'll do?" She crossed her legs into some impossible pretzel pose, acting like he hadn't just been about to tackle her.

Tank took another deep breath and fixed the table. Becky barely looked at him, pretending to be all intent on the game. He shook his head and looked up at the screen.

Fourth and inches. He smiled and turned to her. "They should definitely go for it."

"I don't know. Too chancy. Field goal's safer."

"Safer, but not as much fun."

She threw the pillow at him and smiled.

twenty-three

Her French classes dragged on Monday, but Becky was grateful that she didn't have to deal with either of her Health classes. She increasingly liked the block schedule which gave her a break from teaching with Tank. She needed that break today. She'd seen him Friday night, Saturday morning and Sunday night - each time together more loaded.

The fact that he would come over to discuss his future was touching and disconcerting. Hanging out, laughing and watching football together was way out of her comfort zone. She couldn't dislike or discount that Tank so easily. That whole lining up against each other in between the couches? Completely uncharted territory.

All in all, there'd been too much Tank over the weekend.

Becky walked up and down the aisles while the students took a quiz. She couldn't help but see Carrie with more sympathetic eyes. The girl hadn't acknowledged her at all when she'd walked into the room, but she definitely looked sad, overwhelmed. Becky planned to check in with her after class and offer whatever help she could.

A few minutes later, they corrected the quiz and Becky wrote their assignment on the board. When the students got up to leave, Becky walked to the door.

"Carrie?" she said gently as the girl was about to pass her.

A guilty, sullen face silently answered her call.

"Got a minute?" Becky pressed. At first she thought Carrie would push right past her into the hallway, but she hesitated, then shrugged and slung her book bag onto a desk near the door.

When the room had cleared, Becky closed the door and turned to her. "So ... how are you?"

"Fine." Carrie regarded her suspiciously.

"Mr. Kimball talked to me over the weekend."

Her remark was met with silence.

"I'd like to help," Becky continued. "He mentioned that you had hoped to go to the pregnancy center?"

A shrug.

"Okay, well, I could go with you." Becky cleared her throat. "It's a tough thing to do alone."

"Like you'd know."

The lashing out shouldn't have surprised her, but it still hurt. Becky sat down on one of the desks and smoothed her skirt. "I'd know more than you think."

"What - you work there?" Carrie didn't sound particularly interested, but at least they were having a conversation.

"No," Becky replied. "I was a client."

Carrie looked at her doubtfully. "When?"

Becky stood. She didn't have to tell the girl anything; wasn't sure why she'd started to in the first place. "We'll talk on our way to the clinic. Can you go after school today?"

"I have an appointment this afternoon."

Becky raised a brow.

"Dentist," Carrie explained.

"Okay, well, how about tomorrow?"

"Track practice."

Biting back her frustration, Becky nodded. "When are you available?"

"Wednesday, I guess."

Becky mentally checked her calendar. "Wednesday after school, then?"

Carrie looked down, scuffed her boot on the floor. "I don't have a car."

How hard was she going to have to work to help this girl? *This isn't even the hard part.* "I'll take you."

Their eyes met. Carrie narrowed hers. "Why would you help me?"

Becky took the dive. "Because when I was sixteen, there was no one to help me."

***

She was tired of feeling nervous walking into her own classroom. Becky had dressed to devastate, the only way she could cope with every nerve in her body being on edge. Her dark blue pencil skirt and creme silk blouse was professional and empowering, while entirely feminine. She couldn't help but imagine Tank in his sweats and T-shirt. The mental image should have given her a distinct advantage, but it didn't help at all. Tank in a T-shirt was muscle explosion Tank. At least during the last couple of months he was generally well-covered. She even occasionally tried to imagine him being all roly-poly under his long-sleeved sweaters.

Sweats and T-shirt Tank erased that image so thoroughly, that when she walked into the classroom on Tuesday morning and saw him at the desk, Becky immediately blushed. His light blue button down was open at the neck, revealing the T-shirt she was actually seeing when she looked at him. She advanced slowly to the desk, the heels she'd routinely worn suddenly feeling like the awkward stilts that they were.

Tank smiled appreciatively, taking in her ensemble with a slightly raised brow. "Meeting today, Ms. Jacobs?"

"No, Mr. Kimball," she answered, sounding far calmer than she felt. Unfortunately, those were the only words she managed.

"Just dressing up, then?"

"I suppose."

"For me?" he asked, grinning.

"In spite of you," she replied, frowning.

"Well, spite me anytime," he said, standing and rounding the desk. "You'll definitely have everyone's attention today. Glad it's not my lesson." He stopped in front of her, amused appreciation clearly displayed in those amazing green eyes. Becky stood, immobilized, fighting to hold his gaze. If he'd picked her up, slung her over his shoulder and walked out of the room she probably wouldn't have put up a fight. Something was terribly wrong with her.

So much for dressing to devastate.

She veered around him and set her bag down on the desk. "Thanks, I think," she qualified. "We have a movie today, remember? No one's going to be looking at my clothes." She busied herself getting the movie ready to play.

"Oh right, movie day. Where are you sitting?"

She could hear the teasing invitation in his voice and fought the warm feeling flooding through her. She longed for the days when he did nothing but irritate her. Turning with her best, 'I'm in control of this situation' look, she replied, "Far away from you."

The students began filing in and Becky was more than happy to have anyone else to look at - talk to - think about. She took attendance, introduced the movie, and then sat at the front desk and watched it on her computer while the rest of the class watched the big screen. She no longer trusted Tank, or herself around him. Avoidance at all costs would be her new survival technique. It was going to be a long rest of the year.

***

Maddy and Becky walked to the back of the coffee shop and sat down at one of the new tables. Becky looked around at the renovations. The big screen TV and the pool table changed the look but not the overall feel of the place. There were several tall tables with high stools that were more typical of a bar, but nothing seemed out of place. The coffee shop in front seemed to melt seamlessly into the sports cafe in back. It really was a cool idea.

"So how was your Super Bowl party?" Maddy asked as Grace sat down to join them.

"It went really well," Grace replied. "We had a decent turnout, and there were a few people who mentioned that they liked the 'feel of the place,' which was good. I guess not everyone wants to go to a bar to watch sports, so this is a nice alternative."

"Your regulars okay with it?"

"Well, I don't have as many evening 'regulars' as morning or mid-day, so I don't really think the sports focus is getting in anyone's way." She looked around. "We'll have to see. I don't have a frame of reference from last year, but I'm happy with business so far."

"I'm just mad that you took out my booth. These tables and chairs are cute, but ..." Becky sighed.

"Yeah, those booths were about to cave in," Grace said. "I liked them, too, but they were a hazard."

"Sorry, not buying it," Becky sniffed. "Hey," she changed gears. "Are you working this evening? The pool's finally open at the high school, and we're going to go get some exercise."

"Oh, I'd love to," Grace replied. "I think I'm good. Let me check with Daphne."

She jumped up and walked to her office in the back of the store.

"You sure you want to swim?" Maddy asked, clearly regretting having committed her evening to Becky's direction.

"Of course, I do. Can't run in this cold."

Maddy tried for cheery. "Right. Okay. It'll be great."

Becky smiled at her. "We'll have fun. You'll see."

***

"I can't believe we went out in the cold to go into the water to get cold."

"Where's your sense of adventure?" Becky asked, leading Maddy and Grace through the lobby by the pool.

"Back at home, in front of the fire," Maddy sighed.

"Oh, so that's what you call him now."

Maddy and Grace laughed. "Are you sure we'll be able to do laps?" Maddy asked. "It won't be just a bunch of high school boys tormenting the middle-aged women?"

"Bite your tongue!" Becky scolded, signing herself and the other women in. "I'm nowhere near as old as you are."

Grace looked back and forth between them. "You can't be that far apart."

"Two years," Becky replied. "I will always be two years younger than Maddy," she made a face at her sister, "no matter what."

"Very mature," Maddy made a face back.

They walked down the short hall to the women's locker room, and Becky found several free lockers. She stripped down to her sleek back swimsuit. "I can't wait to move again. It's been driving me crazy not to be able to run. I feel like a slug."

"Welcome to the rest of humanity," Maddy replied, revealing a crimson colored suit under her jeans and sweatshirt. "We exercise when the weather's nice, and wear lots of layers for the rest of the year."

"Where's that yellow and orange suit we bought last summer?" Becky asked.

Maddy wrinkled her nose. "I need color for that one, and a few less pounds."

Becky considered the woman in front of her. No one ever looked great in a swimsuit in February, but Maddy pulled hers off just fine. She'd always been envious of Maddy's fuller figure, but she'd rarely admitted it aloud.

"You look great," Becky observed. "I'd love to have your curves."

Maddy smiled. "Thanks. I've always envied your ..."

"Planes?" Becky supplied with a wry smile.

"Hardly," Maddy laughed. "Sleek sophistication. And your muscular legs. But you've worked hard for those."

"Not recently," Becky pined. "Now, Grace, here, she'll run in the cold. That's why she's so fit."

"Thanks," Grace replied. Her dark blue racing suit fit well for mid-winter. "This will be good, though. I'm ready to switch to swimming for a while. The roads up here are just too icy."

They walked through the showers and out into the pool area. As they'd hoped, very few people had braved the cold to swim. Two women swam laps on one side, a couple of divers practiced at the far end, and someone finishing a lap was climbing out of the pool on the side opposite them.

Becky stopped in her tracks, and Maddy and Grace almost bumped into her.

"What's wrong? Ohhh ..." Maddy said.

Grace peeked around both of them. "Oh. What's he doing here?"

Becky tried to breath. His back was toward them but there was no question who had just pulled himself out of the water. She'd been struggling to erase the image of T-shirt Tank, and the vision in front of her effectively did so. There were no words for the problem it left in it's wake.

"Becky," Maddy hissed. "Close your mouth."

Grace looked on with amusement, but Becky's focus was elsewhere. She did manage to snap her mouth shut, but she couldn't stop staring. Tank was wearing long, baggy, dark blue swim shorts, his enormous calves the only part of his legs that she could really see. She marked his progress as he walked over to pick up his towel. He could turn around at any moment. This was her only chance to calmly run from the room.

"Huh. I bought him those swim trunks. They look good," Grace observed, far too casually, as far as Becky was concerned.

She remained frozen as Tank finally turned, toweling off his spikey hair. He stopped, one hand on his head, when he noticed them.

Becky swallowed. He was stunning.

Grace stepped from their group and walked over to her brother. "Hey, Tank."

Maddy nudged Becky. "Come on," she whispered. "You'll look really silly if you don't go over there now."

Looking silly was not an option. Becky moved her legs, attempting to keep her eyes on Tank's face as she approached.

Tank nodded. "Becky, Maddy." He reached for his neck and then changed his mind. His arm swung down to his side and Becky couldn't help but wonder how much just one of his limbs weighed.

While she mentally weighed and measured him, Maddy had the presence of mind to say hello. "Hey, Tank. Doing laps?"

"Just finished," he replied, trying not to stare at Becky and failing.

Grace continued to grin. "Well, I'm going to jump in. Maddy?"

"I'm ready."

Becky watched them leave, eyes narrowing as they abandoned her. She breathed deeply and resisted the urge to fold her arms in front of herself. She was on display, almost as much as Tank was. Normally, she embraced showing off the body she worked so hard to keep fit. Right now, she wanted to crawl back into the locker room.

"Water cold?" she managed, wishing he would settle his eyes somewhere on her. His effort not to stare was more distracting than openly ogling.

"Not too bad," he replied. He held onto the two ends of the towel around his neck. "You look ..."

"Don't. No. Don't say it."

He grinned. "Say what? That you look like you put on a little weight?"

Becky gasped. Before she could find the words to counter-humiliate him he qualified his barbaric statement. "That's not a slam, Becky. You look good."

He emphasized the word 'good' in a way that actually made her knees weak. She mentally shook herself and regained her scowl. "I work hard at keeping the weight off. Don't mess with me."

He grinned. "Well, leave some of it on. I like it."

She crossed her arms. "What do you know? When you're super-sized everyone around you looks too small."

"Super-sized. I like that."

She rolled her eyes.

Tank laughed and Becky couldn't believe the role reversal. Since when was he so cheerful?

"I work hard at putting the weight on. Different goals, I guess."

"Why do you want to put more weight on?" Becky asked. "What do you even do with those?" She glanced at his traps. It must have been an upper body workout day because they were bigger than ever.

He grinned and shrugged.

Becky pulled her eyes away from his muscles. "Impressive. Like you need twenty extra pounds on your shoulders to do that." She shrugged her own shoulders and Tank followed the movement.

"You're right. Yours are perfect," he said quietly.

She didn't like the direction their conversation was taking. It was bad enough that they were standing face to face, mostly undressed, after the tumultuous weekend they'd had. She needed to get herself in the cold water.

"Well, I should get my swim in."

"Okay."

He looked over her shoulder and then took a step closer. Every nerve in Becky's body screamed in confusion as he took the edge of his towel from around his neck and wiped her cheek. His gaze was a little too intent for a guy who'd just said 'okay' as his parting salutation.

Becky concentrated on breathing. He was very close, and while he was making contact through the towel, the motion was decidedly intimate. The corner of his mouth lifted and she was mesmerized. Then one of the other P.E. teachers walked by.

She exhaled, tried to make her voice light. "Is he the one who's after you?"

Tank snorted. "After you, more like. Watch out for him."

Becky tried to see around him, but couldn't without appearing to try. She looked back up at him. "Oh, please."

He lifted her chin. "I'm not kidding. He's no good."

He looked into her eyes. She swallowed and tried not to think about their proximity. She glanced at his jaw - his stubble was darker today. She really wanted to touch it.

"Can I swim now?" she squeaked. Clearing her throat, she backed up a step and tried to look cool.

He dropped his hand. "Sure, need a push?"

She half-smiled at him. "You'd like that."

"Yes, I would."

He walked her to the edge of the pool and watched as she lowered herself onto the ladder. She was not about to look at him from this angle. She mumbled a "See you later," to his ankles.

Ducking into the water, she tried not to whimper at the cold. She felt him watching as she pushed away from the pool on her back and then turned into a side-stroke. Concentrating on the strokes, she willed him to leave.

If avoidance at all costs meant running into Tank half-dressed, she needed a much more effective method of survival. She doubted she'd find one before the dance on Friday.

twenty-four

The ride to the Benson pregnancy center was quiet after Becky shared her own experience. She didn't give all the details, but enough to let Carrie know that she trusted her with some personal backstory. Becky hoped the favor would be returned at some point, but wasn't going to hold her breath. When pressed, Carrie had said that she'd taken a pregnancy test at home that had come out positive. She wanted another opinion and, for obvious reasons, had chosen to go to the center, rather than her own doctor. Other than that initial conversation, Carrie had said nothing. She listened, but never made eye contact; her gaze riveted on whatever was passing outside of her window.

The ride home was a bit more productive.

"So, what would you like to do next?" Becky asked, pulling out of the center's small lot.

Carrie looked up in surprise. It was amazing how attractive the girl was when she wasn't scowling. "I figured you'd probably take me home."

"Well, yeah, of course," Becky replied. "Do you have time to make one more stop?"

Carrie looked at her speculatively. "Okay?"

Becky nodded and put her car into gear. "I think we need to celebrate."

The relief spreading across Carrie's face gave way to a huge grin. "That'd be cool."

They drove down the street to a little diner, and within minutes were seated in a cozy booth padded in red vinyl. Fifties music played and neon rope signs spelled out various menu items on the walls. "French Fries" flashed in hot pink above them.

"Cool spot," Carrie said, looking around.

"Yeah, I've passed it a couple of times and always wanted to try it," Becky replied. "Fun atmosphere."

Carrie smiled and looked down at her menu. Becky did the same, but the selections blurred before her as she considered the potential of the next half hour. She'd have her student's attention like never before, and probably never again. What should she say?

Her own memories of slinking away from the clinic, wild with relief, but still utterly alone engulfed her. She'd been in such a panic; fear and uncertainty had been her constant companions for weeks. When she'd been told she wasn't pregnant, all she wanted was for her life to return to normal.

Of course, it hadn't.

She'd wanted to tell Taylor, but he'd never known of the possibility of her pregnancy. No one had. There was no one to celebrate with; no one to help her think about her new future.

Her family was there, but she'd been too ashamed to go to her parents or to her seemingly perfect sister. Looking back, she ached with regret. They would have loved her through it; she knew that now, though she couldn't believe it at the time.

Bouncing around in a sea of unstable emotions, sixteen-year-old Becky gave in to the new attention she started receiving. She'd never had problems with the boys, but she enjoyed the amped up interest they were expressing. She didn't have a lot of close girl-friends, so when the boys were ready to take her mind off her confusion, she let them.

She'd let them for a decade. Now she had the opportunity to help the girl across from her to *not* let them, and she wasn't going to waste it.

"Um, Miss Jacobs?"

Becky looked up from her unread menu.

"I don't have any money."

Becky smiled. "This one's on me." She considered Carrie for a moment. "But we're gonna talk, okay?"

***

Becky wrapped her scarf more securely around her neck. The wind was bitter cold, but there was something exhilarating about walking on the beach at night. She was alone with the elements, and the elements were doing their best to chase her back inside. She ducked her head and continued walking. They were not going to win. She needed to think.

Her talk with Carrie had been ... eventful. The girl had come down off her 'I'm not pregnant' high and begun to unload all of her fears and regret on Becky. The story was painfully familiar. At least Becky could honestly say, *'I know how you feel.'*

Once Carrie had finished venting, she seemed to feel a little better, though she also seemed lost. So she wasn't pregnant. That was a relief. What now? Her heart had been broken, of course, though she didn't say it in so many words. She felt marked, judged. Though she'd confided in very few people, she still felt like 'everybody' knew. And though it seemed like 'everybody' had been doing the same thing, Carrie's almost getting caught, so to speak, made it all seem different. More real. More permanent. She'd made her choice and there was no going back.

Becky had mostly just listened. It hardly seemed helpful to say, "Well, I slept around a lot afterward. Not sure that's the best course, but you could see if it works for you." Neither did it seem responsible to say, "Just go on with your life and pretend it never happened. Stop having sex. Stop looking at boys. You've seen what can happen!"

By the time Carrie had finished her meal and wiped her tears, she was exhausted, and Becky thought it best to take her home and let her sleep. She encouraged her to open up to her parents or one of her brothers. Carrie had looked alarmed at the idea, but Becky told her to consider it, just the same. She might find more compassion than she expected. It might be worth a try.

She wanted so much for Carrie to rebound differently than she had. So she walked the beach and she thought about her past and the kids in her class. It was late when she finally trudged up the steps to the inn. She kicked the snow off her boots and stripped off all the layers. After a hot shower, she went to bed and slept like a baby.

***

" 'Abstinence makes the heart grow fonder.' A poem."
Silence.
"Kidding. It was a joke." Becky looked around the room. "But the issue that we've been discussing is serious, and I want to leave you with some closing thoughts.

"Sex is serious business. You're young, you promise each other the world, then you find, when it's all said and done, that you don't necessarily want to spend the rest of your lives together. You may not even look at each other in school the next day."

Tank listened with interest. She was being more than fair. In most cases, the guys were doing all the promising. Becky could have lashed out at guys in general with her 'closing remarks,' but she didn't.

"What kind of a first experience do you want to have?" She looked around the room, her face serious, but Tank saw the vulnerability.

"You roll your eyes when we tell you that you need a certain amount of maturity to be sexually active, but it's true. Just because your body is capable of doing certain things, it doesn't mean your mind or your heart can deal with the aftermath.

"Our job here is to help you see that you don't have to bow to all of the pressure out there. You've heard the arguments." She continued to walk through the aisles of the classroom. "Please know that you're not alone. And I'm not talking about your having the support of your teachers, though, of course, you do. I mean that you have each other. Some of you will choose to wait. Very few of you will admit it. Who brags about not having experience in something that everyone wants experience in? But you need to know that you're not alone. No matter what they say, not 'everyone else is doing it.' "

Becky didn't make eye contact with Tank as she approached the front of the room again, but his eyes never left her face. She turned back to the class.

"However, some of you have made other choices."

She didn't look around the room; didn't seem to want anyone to feel implicated. She paused and straightened some papers on the desk.

"What's done is done, right? Turns out, what's done is fun. Now you know. No big surprise there. But does it follow that you have to or that you should stay sexually active?

"If you have taken the leap, please know that your choices are no different and no more limited. I understand that it's hard to stop. You know what you're giving up. But there's power in making that choice.

"I'm telling you that it's possible to start over; to choose something else. There are so many things to be gained: an incredible sense of self-worth, of accomplishment, of power. And hopefully, one day you find someone that you really want to give yourself to - with no fear - no regret - no looking back. Imagine what that relationship will be like."

She looked down at the neat stack of papers on the desk. Tank saw her draw a deep breath.

"If you hear me say nothing else this semester, please hear this. You can start over. Don't let anyone tell you you can't."

twenty-five

"I feel like I'm back in college decorating my dorm room."

Maddy handed Becky another lacy heart to hang in the window. "Well, I think it's a nice little touch," she replied. "I wasn't sure I could sell the romantic getaway weekend. I'm glad a few people are trying it out."

"They just heard about my phenomenal breakfasts," Becky concluded, slapping up the last heart with a grin. She jumped down from the stool she'd been perched on.

Maddy smiled as they looked around the parlor together. "I like it. The roses are a nice touch, and they smell wonderful."

"They'd better. They cost an arm and a leg this time of year."

"Hence, the potpourri," Maddy lifted one of the porcelain dishes she'd found at a garage sale. "I think we're done. I'm just going to go upstairs and check the rooms one more time."

"Good deal," Becky said, picking up the stool to return it to the kitchen. "And you still have time to help me pick out a dress?"

"Of course! Be right back."

In a matter of minutes, Maddy was rifling through the closet, while Becky sat on her bed, fighting the nerves that were finally settling in.

"So this is gorgeous," Maddy pulled a dress out and held it up to herself. "I don't think I could ever wear a red like this, but it would be stunning on you." She spun around and watched the skirt flair out.

"It's a Valentine's Day dance. I can't wear red."

Maddy gave Becky a look. "You're not wearing the grey suit."

"Why not? It's comfortable, teacherly. Kids won't mess with me if I wear that."

Maddy hung the red dress back in the closet. "Okay, I get that the red dress is a little much for a dance that you're chaperoning, but the grey suit? Really?"

Becky put her head in her hands. "I don't know if I can do this, Maddy."

Maddy sat down next to her. "Do what?"

"Be on display with Tank. We're in such a weird place with each other right now. And there are so many people invested. It's so awkward."

Maddy considered this. "Yeah. No one needs an audience while they're trying to figure out a relationship."

"Ever since we started fake dating - spending more time with each other - teaching together - he's just really started to grow on me, and, oh ..." Becky groaned, "it's making me crazy."

Maddy laughed. "Why?"

"Because I'm done with men forever and he's making it so difficult!"

"Why do you have to be done with Tank? Is he not interested? And if you think he's not, then we need to talk."

Becky smoothed the bed spread. "He's interested."

Maddy grinned. Becky could feel the happy energy coming off her sister in waves.

"Well, then I really don't see a problem." Maddy nudged Becky's shoulder with hers. "Come on, Beck, this is exciting! Give it a chance."

Becky lay back on the bed. "I just feel like I can't stick with anything I decide to do. Can't hold a job, can't settle down in any one place, can't say no to men. I'm just ... I have no conviction. I'm tired of living my life this way."

Maddy looked down at her. "Seems to me like you've already started to change that."

"What, because I've managed to hold onto a long-term sub-bing position while living in my sister's house? Yeah, I've really turned things around." Becky sighed and looked toward the window.

"You've helped me a lot since you moved up here, more than you know. You put your family first ..."

"After losing another job."

"Turning that slimy guy down was the right thing to do and you know it."

"Yeah, well, I still lost a job I loved."

"I know. And I'm sorry, but that wasn't your fault. And you've been a huge help to me here."

"Planning your wedding was fun. Cooking for your guests has been fun. Subbing has been easy. Big deal."

"Subbing with Tank hasn't been easy and you worked through that."

"And look where that got me. Ready to jump back into the first relationship that comes along."

Maddy was not about to give up the fight. "Other guys have asked you out. Did you go out with any of them?"

"No."

"Taking care of the inn involved cleaning up after people, *cleaning toilets*. Did you enjoy that?"

"No."

"Give yourself some credit, Becky."

Maddy got up from the bed. "I don't know everything that went into your decision to be done with men. If you want to stick with that conviction, then great. I'm behind you and I have no doubt that you can do it." She went back to the closet. "Just be sure you're sticking to your convictions for the right reason."

***

Becky glanced at the clock; she had less than twenty minutes before Tank picked her up. Looking back in the mirror, she tried to decide if her current dress was too clingy. It was cut more conservatively than some of the others; knee length, long-sleeved, gently scoop-necked, but the midnight blue material clung to every curve, such as they were. It qualified as semi-formal, she supposed, though why the teachers were expected to dress up was beyond her. No wonder they had trouble finding chaperones.

The doorbell rang and she glared at her reflection. Leave it to a man to cut off a woman's prep time by fifteen whole minutes. Maddy had left to run an errand, so Becky stomped into her heels and down the hall, yanking open the door.

Tank stood there, fine in his long winter coat. His look of appreciation did not gel with her look of frustration. She shivered and pulled the door open. "You're early."

Tank stepped into the front hall, making an effort to look contrite, but mostly just admiring her dress. "Yeah. Sorry. I was ready, so I came over."

Becky sighed. "Well, I'm not ready, yet."

"You look good to me."

She fought her body's reaction to his words. "Thanks, but I haven't even decided for sure what to wear."

"You should definitely wear that."

She blew her hair out of her eyes. "Okay, but I still need to ... oh, just go sit while I finish."

She gestured toward the parlor with its delicate furniture, none of which would comfortably accommodate him. *Serves him right.*

Tank took one look in the room and rubbed his neck. "I'll wait in the kitchen."

Becky turned with a sigh, feeling his eyes on her as she led the way down the hall. She slipped into her room.

"Give me ten minutes," she called out.

She heard Tank walk through the kitchen, making himself at home while she tried to concentrate on finishing her hair and makeup. Taking a deep breath, she settled into her routine. She had no problem making him wait until she was good and ready to go.

***

"How can they dance to this?"

They stood in the high school's cafeteria, trying to be cool and not cringe at the volume of the music that was playing.

"It is kind of ... different. I know it wasn't that long ago, but I think our music was easier to dance to," Becky shouted.

"Nothing's easy to dance to," Tank yelled back.

Becky laughed. It was no use talking. The students, at least, seemed to be having fun in the transformed cafeteria. Strands of white Christmas lights and strategically-placed streamers that stretched from floor to ceiling gave the room an entirely different look. They'd even brought in a small ice-sculpture that presided over a fairly elegant hors d'oeuvre table. It was all very impressive for a high school dance.

The chaperones - six of them - gathered in pairs in different areas of the cafeteria. There was little to do but make sure that the dancing was civil and that there wasn't too much PDA. Becky wasn't sure what she'd do if she had to confront someone. She decided to leave that job to Tank.

The music mercifully quieted and slowed. Two of the chaperones, a married couple, went out to dance. Becky watched to see how the kids reacted, but the adults were largely ignored. She looked up, expecting to see a panic-stricken Tank, but he was simply looking out over the crowd, a thoughtful expression on his face. He looked very handsome in his dark grey suit, his tie subtle, but classy. Becky smiled to herself. She'd always thought that dark colors made a person look smaller. Not so with Tank.

He looked over at her. "At least I know this song," he was able to say in a more conversational tone. "And you look amazing tonight." He leaned his shoulder into hers, seemingly embarrassed by his gushing praise.

"Thank you," she said, feeling ridiculously self-conscious. "Your suit is beautiful."

He smiled at her and she turned to the dance floor, wishing someone would do something wildly inappropriate so that she could go stop them.

"I think I'll get some punch," Becky decided. "Want some?"

"I'll get it," Tank offered.

"No, you're doing a great job holding up the wall. I'll go. Be right back."

She ducked into the small crowd of people getting refreshments and made an effort to have a conversation with anyone who would stand still long enough for her to engage them. It was almost twenty minutes before she got back to Tank with his drink.

He gave her a wry smile. "Good thing I wasn't thirsty."

"Well, you have to dance for that," she said, immediately regretting her words.

He raised a brow. "Do you wanna dance?"

Becky listened to the music for a moment. "This song is kind of crazy. I wouldn't know what to do," she lied. "Let's wait for another one."

Tank nodded, looked relieved. "Kind of thinking the same thing."

"Okay, well, cheers," Becky raised her plastic cup to his. The bathroom would be her next escape. After that, she'd have to get more creative.

***

The DJ announced the last dance of the night, and almost every student went out to the floor. Becky and Tank still hadn't danced, but Becky had had meaningful conversations with just about everyone else in the room, including the custodian. He was one of her favorite people at the school, so she was glad she'd found him.

Bailey interrupted their conversation about whether enough effort was being made to promote recycling at the school.

"Excuse me, Ms. Jacobs?"

Becky turned. "Oh, hey, Bailey! Great party. Are you happy with how it all came together? Great turnout."

Bailey nodded, looking a little bewildered at Becky's energetic greeting. Not to be outdone, she launched into her own.

"Yeah, it's great. But this is the last dance. You *have* to dance with Mr. Kimball. You haven't danced all night and you both look so amazing. It's not like the adults can't dance. Everybody's dancing."

Becky's head spun from the "dare to dance" challenge. She glanced toward the wall where she'd left Tank for the umpteenth time during the evening. He stood with his arms crossed, looking out over the crowd. At the very least, she needed to go over and tell him not to glower.

"I'll see what I can do," she told Bailey, as though Tank were the problem.

She excused herself and found her way over to his side as the music began. Having spent the evening avoiding him, she wasn't even sure what to say. She sure wasn't going to confront him about looking scary.

Tank glanced down at her and she met his gaze, trying not to look guilty.

"Dance?"

Eloquent Tank. Becky smiled. "Okay."

Of course, the final song was a slow, familiar tune. Tank took her hand and led her to the darkest corner of the room. One of the strands of lights had gone out, and there was a fraction more privacy.

He turned to her, keeping a hold of her hand, and placing his other at her side. Becky tried to breathe as she placed hers on his shoulder. She should have nothing to worry about. They were at the high school, of all places, with too many interested parties noting that they were finally dancing. It's not like Tank was going to make a scene.

His hand moved a fraction along her side, a very subtle caress. Becky stiffened on the outside while her insides turned to jelly. She lost her footing briefly, but Tank held her upright.

And a little closer.

She couldn't look up at him; she was not about to see what was in those intense green eyes. She couldn't rest her head on his shoulder, that would be too cuddly. Instead, she kept herself upright, as pliable as a board, and looked at his charcoal grey chest.

Tank wasn't much of a dancer, but he knew how to hold her, and they swayed gently back and forth. Becky started to lose herself in the music, allowing herself to enjoy being held in his arms for a few minutes. It was heady; the audience was probably a good thing. As the music wafted through its final refrain, she heard a barely perceptible, "Ah, Becky."

She came out of her reverie and realized that they were close and barely moving. Tank had let go of her hand and was gently holding her at the waist, his thumbs sending shivers as they stroked her sides. Becky's hands linked behind his neck. They weren't pressed against each other, but they might as well have been for the heat radiating between them. Becky pulled back a fraction and Tank resisted a fraction.

"Space," she whispered.

"What?" he leaned in, turning her away from the rest of the crowd.

She shook her head slightly. He'd only gotten closer. She looked up at him, eyes a little wider, heart beating wildly.

He smiled and brushed his lips over hers before letting her go.

***

Becky never told him that they'd have to oversee the undecorating.

"It won't take long," the girl, Bailey, promised as she gathered her fellow council members together to find the cafeteria again.

Tank looked at Becky with a sigh. "Do they have to take the lights down?"

She looked around the room, rubbing her arms. All of the students leaving the building had left the area chilly. "I'm sure they do. Cafeteria is supposed to be back to normal by Monday morning."

Tank nodded and walked to the first set of lights, setting them free from the wall. One of the students was pulling a step ladder out of a closet and stopped when she saw him. "Thanks, Mr. Kimball!" she called out.

Tank nodded and continued to pull down the lights and the tape that held them. The DJ had packed up and left, but someone had found an old eighties station on a radio in the kitchen and cranked it. The kids were tired, but worked cheerfully. Everyone seemed pretty happy that the dance had gone well.

All Tank could think about was holding Becky, and that brush across the lips that left her wide-eyed and looking like she'd never been kissed before. He wanted to revisit that moment before the night was over. He just needed to make sure Becky didn't hitch a ride home with the custodian. He liked Joe, too, but if Becky had spent any more time with him, Tank would have escorted him from the building.

He glanced toward the corner where he'd last seen her helping put the food away. She was gathering the tablecloths, laughing with one of the other chaperones. *A male, of course.* Why was she always hanging out with the men?

Tank watched as she walked away with her bundle and stuffed it in one of the garbage cans. She had no business collecting garbage, dressed like that, though she didn't seem to mind. She turned with a smile as one of the students called out to her.

Finishing his job, Tank gathered the ropes of lights that he'd bound, and set them near several boxes where the party supplies were piling up. Within minutes the whole pile was hauled away, and Tank noted that the students had started filing out. Becky was talking to Bailey. The other chaperones had left.

Becky looked up as he approached, all kinds of interesting emotions dancing across her features.

Bailey spoke first. "Thank you both *so* much for coming tonight! Everything went so smoothly, everyone behaved, probably 'cuz Mr. Kimball stood in the corner looking so scary." She giggled. "Anyway, I'm so glad you danced! Everyone was wondering if you would. It was so romantic!" She turned as someone called out to her. "Oh, my ride is here. Are you sure you don't mind turning off the lights and stuff?"

Becky glanced at Tank, then back at Bailey. "No problem. We'll see you on Monday."

Bailey left, and Becky turned, all business. "Okay, we need to find the cafeteria lights - and turn off the music in the kitchen. I'm pretty sure the doors are locked, so once we do a walk-through, check the bathrooms and stuff, we should be good to go." She barely looked at him while she rattled off her list.

"Sounds good," Tank replied.

A few minutes later, he stood by the cafeteria light switches, waiting until Becky was almost to the kitchen.

"Becky," he called out. She turned and raised a brow.

"Hang on a minute." He knew she was heading for the music. A ballad was playing, another classic love song, and Tank wasn't about to miss his chance.

"Why?" She stood with her hands on her hips, not looking quite so tough in her mind-blowing dress. Tank hit the lights and

Becky stood in relief against the light from the kitchen door. He moved fast, skirting one of the refreshment tables.

He grabbed her hand as she started to back up into the kitchen. He couldn't clearly see her face, but he could imagine a bit of panic there. He wasn't going to let the evening end on that note.

"Come on," he said, pulling her gently back out to the now deserted dance floor. "One more dance. This is a great song."

Becky dragged her mind-blowing heels. "We already danced, Tank. We need to get home."

He guided her back into position. "The song's almost over. Let's dance without an audience."

He pulled her close, and she sighed. Within seconds she melted into him, her arms around his neck and her head against his shoulder. Tank had pretty much always believed that no good could come from dancing.

He was wrong.

He held her and they swayed, the haunting lyrics floating around them. He focused on how she felt in his arms. Largely behaving himself, he kept his hands on her waist or her back, making a valiant effort to keep the dance relatively innocent.

The song ended, and another one began. Becky pulled back and looked up at him. "We have to go."

Her eyes were full of all the longing he felt, and Tank hesitated only briefly before leaning down and kissing the 'go' off her lips. Her surprise turned to gentle, yet fervent response.

Tank finally pulled back before he lost his mind completely and forgot where they were, what they'd agreed to, and everything else.

A small smile touched Becky's lips. "You are trouble," she whispered, her eyes fluttering open.

Tank physically set her away from him. "Yeah, you're right. We've got to go." He jogged into the kitchen to turn off the music. He hit the overhead switch as they left the room, following the light from the hallway leading to the doors.

Grabbing their coats, he made quick business of throwing hers over her shoulders. Becky laughed at his newfound need for speed, and followed as best she could in her heels.

"I'll get the Jeep," he said. "You wait here."

She smile and shrugged. "Sounds good to me."

She sat down on the bench just inside the door. Tank threw on his own coat, ignoring the buttons, and ran out into the cold night.

***

Becky had the door open before Tank could put the Jeep in park.

"Hang on," Tank said. "I'll come around and help you. It's slippery."

"I'll be fine," Becky assured him. "See you Monday."

"Don't get out," he growled. "You'll fall in those ridiculous shoes, and I'm not finishing our class alone."

Becky sighed. Men did not understand how women navigated in heels. She lowered herself carefully onto the slick drive and turned to him. "Seriously, Tank ..."

He was already bounding around to her side of the vehicle. Becky didn't want him walking her to the door, and she really didn't want him coming in. They were in new and unnerving territory, which heated up exponentially every time they were alone together. If that kiss hadn't happened in the high school cafeteria, she wasn't sure how things might have ended. As much as she'd enjoyed it, and oh, she enjoyed it, they couldn't play with this fire anymore.

He was at her side.

"Tank, I don't want you walking me to the door."

He sighed. "Why?"

She looked up at him. "You know why."

She could see a tiny grin by the light from the porch. Her stomach tightened.

"You afraid I'm gonna kiss you good night?"

Her eyes were glued to his, all cool disappearing. "Yes."

"You don't want me kissing you good night at your door?"

"No."

"Okay."

Becky knew what was coming. Taking her face gently in his big hands, Tank leaned down and gave her a very gentle kiss. It was over before she could even pretend to fight it.

"You don't play fair," she said, amazed that she had to catch her breath even after such a brief kiss.

He smiled and put his arm around her, guiding her up the steps.

"No way you're coming in this house."

"I know."

"Ever again."

He laughed. "Let's take it a day at a time."

She unlocked her door and turned, willing him to kiss her again; fearful that he would.

He stuck his hands in his pockets. "I had fun tonight."

"Me too."

He pushed at a light dusting of snow with his boot. "What are you doing tomorrow?"

"Lots of things. So many things. Super busy with my guests."

He grinned. Hands still in his pockets he leaned toward her. Becky swallowed her, *Come in - stay - never leave!* just as he kissed her lightly on the cheek.

He pulled away. "See you soon, Becky."

twenty-six

Becky spent the rest of the weekend in a Valentine's haze. Maddy had checked in the two couples who'd arrived at the inn while Becky was dancing with Tank. She'd stayed to make sure they had everything they needed, and based on the message that she'd pinned to the note board in the kitchen, had left not too long before Becky had returned home.

Not surprisingly, no one was up for an early breakfast on Saturday morning. Becky got up around seven, despite having slept very little. She made the coffee and prowled around the kitchen, rechecking her breakfast menu and trying to do anything that would keep her from thinking about Tank.

Pretty much nothing worked. She wiped down the cupboards, reliving their dance over and over in her head, culminating in the kiss that kept her head spinning. She'd never responded to a kiss like that. She shouldn't have responded to a kiss like that. She couldn't imagine facing Tank on Monday.

Becky pulled out her ingredients and started breakfast. She had two days to get her head straight. Despite having to facilitate two couples enjoying a romantic weekend getaway, she had to be up for the challenge. By Monday morning, Tank and his kiss would have to find their rightful place in the far recesses of her mind. She could do this.

***

"I'd like to speak to you about the dance on Friday night."

Tank and Becky exchanged glances as Mrs. Whitestone, the principal, cleared her throat and collected her thoughts.

They hadn't even had a chance to greet each other before she'd called them to her office. On the way, another teacher caught Tank and started walking with him, so Becky had taken advantage of the opportunity to hustle ahead. She didn't have much of a plan for the rest of the day.

"I understand that you two were, that you displayed an inappropriate level of affection."

Becky's mind spun, reliving for the hundredth time their kiss in the cafeteria. The memory resurfaced quite happily, jumped and flailed its arms, waiting to be deliberated on, celebrated, even. Not the brush across her lips kiss, of course, the real kiss after everyone had left. How could the principal possibly know about that?

Luckily, Tank wasn't so rattled. "We danced one dance, Ms. Whitestone, the last dance of the night. Everyone was on the floor, even the other chaperones."

"Well, the dancing is fine to a point. I was told that you were," she cleared her throat again, "that you were dancing and kissing. It made some of the students uncomfortable."

"You're kidding."

"The job of a chaperone ..."

"No, we get the job of a chaperone."

Becky looked up in surprise, actually making eye contact when Tank interrupted the woman. He shook his head, then addressed the principal.

"We spent the entire evening - gave up our free time - to attend the dance, monitor the students and make sure everyone behaved."

"Well, yes, and we do appreciate that."

"Then what's the problem?"

"Chaperones shouldn't be kissing. It's unprofessional."

Becky was dumbfounded. Their lips had hardly touched while the kids were there. She could sense Tank's frustration, and contemplated what she could say to diffuse the situation.

Tank abruptly changed tactics. "I'm sorry, Ms. Whitestone, it was all me. I didn't give Ms. Jacobs much warning, and frankly, I didn't give her much choice."

Tank being charming? Becky closed her mouth and glanced at the principal. Ms. Whitestone colored slightly and ran a hand through her hair.

"Well, it's not for me to dictate relationships between faculty members here ..."

"Makes sense," Tank interjected.

"But you should know that we generally frown upon romantic involvement," she droned on, as though Tank hadn't interrupted. "In such cases as it develops, we ask teachers to keep their private affairs discreet. In your circumstance, it's especially complicated because your class subject material is so ... delicate."

Tank raised an eyebrow and leaned forward. Becky held on to her armrests.

***

"I can't believe you talked to her like that."

"I'm just tired of people like her making the rules. She treated us like children, yet couldn't even say the word 'sex.'"

They were navigating through the almost empty halls, late for their own class.

"Stop saying that word!" Becky hissed.

"Sex, sex, sex."

Becky walked to the other side of the hall and Tank followed, continuing their conversation like Becky hadn't just tried to escape him.

"People like her make me want to go right out and do whatever it is they're telling me not to."

This logic sounded vaguely familiar to Becky, but she could hardly encourage him under the circumstances. "Good luck with that."

He didn't look down at her, but he did lean into her as they walked. Becky pushed back.

"Get serious. We have a class to teach."

"Now, there's authority I can respect." He grinned and opened the door to their room.

***

"Is it true you got in trouble for PDA?"

They hadn't even taken attendance, yet. Tank looked at Becky and shook his head, a little grin threatening. She tried to keep her face serious, but it was all very disconcerting. It had been a long time since she'd been embarrassed about a kiss.

Other students began asking what the story was and the room started buzzing. Tank dropped a large text book on the desk. The room became silent.

"We didn't get into trouble," Tank announced. "The principal wanted to speak to us about the overwhelming success of this program." His corny smile belied his words.

"That's not what I heard."

"You heard wrong, let's get started."

"Are you going to get fired?" This voice had the decency to sound concerned.

Tank sighed and Becky replied. "Nobody's getting fired. We didn't do anything wrong."

"I heard you were making out on the dance floor."

Tank's head shot up, and the class got very quiet again. He looked around the room until everyone felt good and uncomfortable. "We danced one dance. We kissed once."

Twice, Becky amended to herself. *Three times,* she recalled, starting to blush. She looked down and straightened the hem of her sweater, glad that Tank was handling this exchange.

"But it was so *romantic!*"

Tank threw up his hands, leaving Becky to deal with the three dreamy-eyed girls in the front row.

***

"Well, that was interesting," Becky slumped down on the edge of the desk as the last of the students left the room. "Everybody's talking about us. I feel like I'm in high school, again. Well, I am in high school again ... but you know what I mean."

"Is that so bad? Kind of like we're getting a redo."

Becky considered this. "Huh. There's a thought. Did you need a redo?"

Tank shrugged. "High school was all about football for me," he replied. "I guess I don't have a lot of regrets on that score. I stayed pretty focused and got where I wanted to go."

"How did the girls feel about that?"

He grinned. "Couldn't say. I didn't get them. They scared me."

Becky laughed. "I'll bet you scared them. Were you this big back then?"

"Getting there, but not quite. And I wasn't as charming."

"As charming as what?"

Tank leaned across the desk and Becky pulled back. "Not in school, Mr. Kimball. You know the rules."

"She was pretty specific about what we couldn't do in school," Tank amended.

Becky refused to look at him. She stood and gathered her things. "I never filled you in on my visit with Carrie."

Tank picked up their coats. "Right. I've been meaning to ask. Wanna head down to Grace's and grab some coffee?"

"Sounds good."

"If we hang out long enough, we can catch a few of the college basketball games," Tank replied, distracted from his earlier objective by the idea of watching sports on Grace's TV.

Becky shook her head. "Yeah, let's drive separately. Not sure I'm that committed."

Tank grinned. "Grace is gonna regret her new marketing strategy. I'm never gonna leave the place."

twenty-seven

"So," Grace walked up to their table and smiled broadly. "Where have you two been?"

Tank grinned back at his sister. "I was here last weekend."

"That's not what I mean and you know it," she replied, taking a seat next to her brother. She looked back and forth between them, her eyes sparkling. "So fun to see you two together."

Becky shook her head and fought a smile as she sipped her tea.

"So I heard the dance was exciting ..." Grace continued her monologue.

Tank groaned.

"Sorry, kids. Small town. Not much else to talk about around here, now that the Super Bowl's over."

Tank's phone buzzed and he excused himself to take a call. Grace jumped on the opportunity to grill Becky.

"So seriously, how's it going?"

Becky couldn't help a smile at Grace's determination. "You have to slow down."

Grace sat back and regarded her friend. "I'm sorry, this is just so exciting! Tank hasn't had a serious girlfriend in forever."

"We're not serious." Becky sipped her tea again. It really tasted awful. How did Grace drink it?

Grace sighed. "Okay, it's been forever since Tank's had a girlfriend. At least one that I know of. He just seems really happy ..." she trailed off, and Becky could feel her friend's regard.

"What?" She finally looked up. "And seriously, how do you drink this tea? It's nasty."

Grace laughed. "Sorry, it might be a little strong. I thought you might like it that way."

"Yeah, well, I tried to cover it with some cinnamon and whatever else you have in those shakers up there. I think I probably ruined it." She pushed the cup away.

"I'll get you some coffee. Gotta keep our customers happy." Grace stood with a smile. "You okay? I mean, besides the tea?"

Becky had another deflection ready. "Yeah. Tank and I were just talking about one of our students. She's okay, but just a tough situation."

"Gotcha." Grace gave her an appraising look. "Be right back."

Tank filled the spot his sister left almost immediately. Becky was amazed at how he dwarfed the table in comparison.

"Everything okay?" Becky asked, determined to clear the atmosphere of all relationship talk.

"Yeah, good," he replied, sitting back and regarding her.

She was beginning to feel like some sort of display at a freak show. The Kimballs and their green eyes could be so intense.

"That was Steve from ESPN. They want me to fly out and talk to them this weekend."

She perked up at that. "Wow - that's exciting! You're going, right?"

He nodded. "Yeah. I need to hear them out."

"They're pretty determined, huh?"

Tank spun his mug, the coffee dancing close to the lip of the cup. Becky waited for the spill.

"Well, I'd be good at it," he said without sounding arrogant. "And I guess I had a pretty decent fan base, especially following my final injury. They want to capitalize on that while they still can, of course."

"I never heard how you got injured," Becky replied tentatively.

Tank continued to focus on the cup. "Concussion. It happened one too many times. Doctors said one more could kill me." At this he looked up, daring her to feel sorry for him.

"Wow." She'd always thought he'd broken a bone or had a knee injury, though he never seemed to favor one leg over another. "Feel like I should know that, especially since your sister practically has us married."

That should make him good and nervous.

Tank glanced behind the counter where Grace was laughing with one of her employees. "She asking for a date?"

"No, she's pushing for details, though. As relentless as ESPN."

Tank smiled. "Don't let her hassle you too much."

"It's getting harder to be evasive. She's so happy with Alex, she wants everyone around her to be ..."

Tank looked back at her with a raised brow.

"Whatever. So what's the deal with your concussions? Does it limit what you can do?"

Tank visibly switched gears, stopping to think for a moment. "Well, I can't play football." He spun his cup again. "Have to avoid contact sports."

He looked so sad, Becky wasn't sure how to respond. "That's tough. I'm sorry."

He shrugged. "I've pretty much made my peace with it. Never thought I'd get to this point."

Grace approached the table with a mug of hot coffee for Becky. "Here you go."

"Thanks," Becky smiled, warming her hands on the mug.

"You need a refill?" Grace asked her brother.

"I'm good. Thanks."

"Okay, well, I'll just leave you to it," she replied. "You're lucky it's busy." She grinned at them before walking away.

Becky shook her head. "Another casualty of our fake relationship."

Tank extended his long legs under the table, caging hers in. Becky couldn't escape the warm pressure of his calves on hers without making a scene.

"Not so fake anymore."

"Nothing's really changed, Tank."

He increased the pressure a bit. "I kissed you."

She nodded, avoiding a direct look.

"You kissed me back."

She pulled her coffee close. "I need more cream."

"C'mon, Becky. Things have changed."

She studied her mug. Of course, things had changed. "A kiss doesn't change a relationship."

Tank considered her. "Normally, I'd agree. But that was a big deal for us. We've come a long, long way."

Becky's faced heated at the memory, *and it was just a kiss*. She was in so much trouble.

"Dangerous territory," she finally replied. She could feel his eyes on her and finally looked up. He was smiling like a contented cat. "Tank, we can't mess around with this. There's too much at stake."

"You sound like Mrs. Whitestone."

"Well, she's right. If we blow this, we've got a huge audience waiting for us to make a mistake."

"So we don't make any."

"Tank." She tried to look at him sternly.

He nudged her under the table. His intense green eyes invited her to forget all of her fears, so she looked down at his mouth.

Big mistake.

"I have to go." She pushed her chair back and stood.

Tank stood with her.

"Don't walk me out." She tried to look threatening.

Tank tried to look innocent. "Just going to my Jeep," he protested with a grin.

She eyed him warily. "Well, I'm going to get this to go, so you can run along."

Tank followed her up to the counter, not giving her nearly the space she needed to transfer her drink and add her cream. He chatted with Daphne, who seemed to find it easy to make conversation with anyone who walked in the store. She'd probably practiced a lot on Tank, because they seemed to be getting along well.

Becky fastened the lid on her cup, trying not to let that last thought bother her. Hadn't she just spent the last five minutes trying to ditch Tank? Wouldn't it be better if he stayed and flirted with Daphne?

She fixed on her Becky smile as she said her good-byes, heading out the front door with Tank in tow like a very large puppy. They walked down the street to where their cars were parked, and Becky shivered. For some reason she'd left her hat and mittens in her vehicle; not smart on this mid-February day.

"Chilly?" Tank asked, draping his arm around her.

She looked up as he tucked her in close. She was much warmer and much less comfortable. She couldn't find her disciplinary look or voice. She must have used them up at school.

Tank took her cup from her hand and placed it on the hood of her car.

"Hey, I need that, I'm cold!"

What an invitation.

He pulled her in close and smiled down at her.

"How about if I just kiss you once a day until we get this figured out?" Tank asked, leaning down and touching his lips to her temple.

Becky sighed, chills and warmth spiraling through her. She wanted so badly to stop fighting whatever was happening between them. "Okay, fine. That was it for Monday."

Tank growled a little, a sound that Becky was beginning to find endearing. It made his chest rumble.

"If I get one kiss, I'm going to make it count."

Becky sighed. Nobody had ever gotten to her this way. She burrowed her head in his chest. "I'm not ready."

She felt him laughing more than heard it. He tightened his hold on her.

"Okay, I'll just wait here; relax and plan."

"Plan?" Her head popped up and he was ready.

"That's the plan," he said as he found his target.

Becky smiled, which made for an even more interesting kiss that neither one of them was particularly interested in ending. She finally staggered back.

"That was Tuesday, Wednesday and Thursday; maybe the whole weekend," she accused him, trying to catch her breath.

Tank grinned and opened her door for her. She slid into her seat and he handed her the coffee.

"See you tomorrow," he said.

"Yeah, probably not," she replied, finding new courage when she wasn't pinned to him. "We don't have class together."

"Oh, I'll find you," he promised as he shut the door.

Becky sighed and a little shiver ran down her spine. She wanted to laugh and cry. She was in so much trouble.

***

Cleaning up after her guests wasn't quite as much fun after a long day at school, followed by too much time with the Kimball family. Becky was exhausted, but she wasn't convinced that Maddy's company was the best thing, under the circumstances.

Her concerns were well-founded.

"So, how did it go on Friday?" Maddy asked as she stripped the sheets off the bed in the Captain's Quarters.

Becky pretended to be hearing impaired in the bathroom. Maddy came around the corner, her arms full of sheets.

"So? Friday?"

Becky sighed. "It was nice. The kids did a great job. Everyone behaved. Tank kissed me." She shrugged and went back to wiping out the tub.

Maddy leaned against the door with a happy sigh. "Ohh ... You good with that?"

Becky scrubbed away. "It was wonderful, and I'm really scared."

The sheets dropped on the floor. Maddy wasn't going anywhere. "Why?"

"I don't deserve him, Maddy."

Maddy walked over to the tub. "Why is that?"

"I've been with too many guys. He deserves someone less ... used up."

There was a pause. "Is that what you tell your students?"

Becky looked up, surprised. "What do you mean?"

"Well, once they are 'used up' as you say, they no longer deserve to be in a meaningful relationship."

Becky snorted. "None of them have hit that point. They're just starting out."

"Oh, so it's a matter of numbers, then. Once you've slept with so many people. Is that in your text book?"

"That's ridiculous."

"Well, you're saying that you passed some sort of unseen boundary into the undeserving zone. That sounds ridiculous to me."

"Says the woman who saved herself for marriage."

"I've messed up in plenty of other areas, Becky," Maddy said so sincerely that Becky had to look up. "So has Tank. We all have. I hate to think we're going to reach a point where it starts to be un-forgivable."

Becky considered her sister, then sighed and shook her head. "So many guys, Maddy."

Maddy sat down on the only seat in the bathroom. "I'm sorry, Becky. Sorry for what you believed about yourself and what you allowed yourself to do. But you can't keep beating yourself up. You have to believe it can be different." She touched Becky's shoulder. "You are different now. You have to see that. And there's never a point where it becomes unforgivable."

Becky leaned into Maddy's hand. "I want to believe that."

"Then believe it. It's a faith thing."

Becky went back to scrubbing with a sigh. "Another area where I've fallen short."

"We all have. We just keep getting up and starting again."

Becky buffed the faucets until they sparkled. "Tank has an interview with ESPN at the end of the week. They really want him. I have a feeling he's going to be gone soon, anyway."

Maddy leaned back, considering. "Does he want the job?"

"I don't think he knows what he wants."

"Well, then, I wouldn't assume anything. Take it a day at a time. See what happens." She stood up and gathered her sheets. "By the way, I think John and Frank will be back working on the apartment this week. Mostly days, so they shouldn't be in your way too much."

Becky looked up, relieved. "No Tank, then?"

Maddy smiled, considering. "Not unless he comes on his own time in the evenings."

Becky narrowed her eyes at her sister.

"John loves his work with the cabinets, so I can't really say for sure."

Maddy flounced out of the room with a grin, her dirty sheets trailing behind her. Becky sighed and went back to scrubbing, all sense of control slipping away.

twenty-eight

It felt so good to hold a brush in her hand; it had been too long since she'd painted. Becky looked again at the picture she'd sketched of the Davidson's horse. She was itching to start the painting, but something wasn't right. She had Ed's reference pictures, but she needed to see the horse moving to really capture her on canvas.

Time for a field trip.

A few phone calls and an hour later, Ed was walking her through the barn and introducing her to their various livestock. Blake and Parker followed along, delighting in the sights and smells of the farm animals. Becky was happy for them, not so much for herself. She hadn't been in a barn in a really long time, and there was good reason. She tried breathing through her mouth, but that was almost worse.

She gave up and resigned herself to the experience. If Tank had been there, he'd have thoroughly enjoyed harassing her about her squeamishness. But, of course, he wasn't. Tank was back in his home state of Connecticut, on a job interview for a job he'd be crazy not to take. Parker's squeal brought her back to her pleasant surroundings.

"That cow just screamed at me! Did you hear him, Mr. Ed?" Parker giggled, giving the cow's stall a wide berth.

"She's just saying hello, Parker. She won't hurt you." Ed chuckled at the boys' enthusiasm and continued to lead the way through the barn. They had just a few animals; the cow, some chickens, a few goats and the horse, but it was all Parker and Blake needed to be completely enthralled.

"Wait 'til you see their horse, Miss Aunt Becky. He's huge!"

"He's a she, Parker, just like the cow."

Parker hopped-walked next to Becky. "The horse is so big! But I bet Mr. Tank would squish him if he got on him."

Ed chuckled. "Poor Lillibelle."

"Is that the horse?"

"Yep, and she's all girl. I don't think she'd take kindly to being called a 'he.' " He turned to Parker. "Actually, not even Mr. Tank would squish Lillibelle. She's almost fifteen hundred pounds."

Parker stopped his hopping and tried to process this information. "Does Mr. Tank weigh that much?"

"I surely hope not," Ed laughed.

"He only weighs 240," Becky offered, figuring that might be the single context in which she'd plug the word 'only' into that sentence. She looked up at Ed and immediately regretted having, and sharing the information.

"That so?" he asked, a twinkle in his eye.

Becky tried to clarify. "That's what he told me when - oh, never mind."

Ed smiled, then turned to Parker. "Well, then I figure it would take about six Tanks to squash that horse. Probably just one could ride him just fine."

"Mr. Tank might be on TV," Blake joined the conversation.

"Yeah, and we could watch him and maybe he would say 'hi' to us!" Parker burst in. "But he might marry Miss Aunt Becky," he added with much less enthusiasm.

Becky stared at him, dumbfounded. Blake noticed and tried to contain the damage. "Parker, don't say that. We don't know."

"Well, that's what Dad says," Parker mumbled.

Ed grinned again, shaking his head, while Becky continued to sputter an incoherent protest.

"We're not getting married, Parker, don't worry," she finally managed. The Tuesday, Wednesday and Thursday kisses danced on the edge of her consciousness, begging to be relived, begging her to refute her own statement.

Parker looked relieved. "Oh, good, cuz I want to watch him on TV."

"If we get to watch him on TV, then he won't live close by," Blake pointed out.

Parker and Becky frowned at this news, and Ed stepped in to distract. "Here we are boys. Let's see if we can get Lillibelle to come and say hello."

He called out and she trotted toward them from the other side of the small field. The horse really was massive. Becky smiled at the thought of the magnificent animal in front of her carrying the name that it did.

"Hey, Lillibelle," she cooed as the horse approached. She gently stroked down its long nose when it drew near. "You sure are pretty."

Parker and Blake both climbed onto the fence to get a better look, giggling when the horse snorted and whinnied at them. Ed helped them feed Lillibelle some sugar, and Becky backed up to give them some room. She smiled as the boys snatched their hands away when the horse's lips nibbled at their palms.

She stepped back again to see the animal from a slightly different angle, pulling her sketch pad out of her bag to capture some of the horse's movement. It had been a good call to bring the boys along. She figured she'd take them out to the Pizza Place for an early dinner, and really make a day of it. It was win-win for everybody, and she wouldn't mind the distraction. It would help to pass the time on the first weekend in a long while that she felt strangely alone.

***

It was late and he knew he had no business stopping to see if she was awake. Still, Tank drove slowly by the inn and couldn't keep himself from turning into the drive when he saw a light on in the parlor. It was unusual; Becky generally didn't hang out in the front rooms, but if she was there, she might see his Jeep and not be surprised when he came to the door.

It had been a whirlwind of a weekend. He'd met with more execs and sportscast personalities than he could count. His head was full of the possibilities, and the concerns. He knew he couldn't dump it all on Becky; he just wanted to see her. Somehow, if he could just say hello, he'd feel grounded. Then maybe he could go home and sleep on an incredible job offer with some degree of clarity.

He pulled as close to the house as he could, hoping she'd notice his headlights. It was after eleven and they both had school bright and early. He wouldn't stay long.

He would try not to stay long.

Tank parked and walked up the steps to the porch. For some reason, his heart pounded like he was going to see someone he hadn't seen in years, rather than three days. Just as he was about to knock, the inside door opened. He couldn't help but smile; couldn't believe how much he'd missed her. Would she ever feel the same way?

Becky looked perfect in her rumpled sweats and long-sleeved T-shirt; very cuddly looking, though Tank's very precise memory of their brief meeting at the pool always helped him fill in what wasn't evident with her winter wear. When would it ever warm up? He fought that image as he took in the sight of her, arms crossed as she all but tapped her fluffy slipper at him.

She didn't look upset or frightened, just curious, concerned. So far so good.

He opened the outside door and stepped over the threshold. He froze. That was a boundary she'd set and he wanted to respect it. He placed his boot right back down by the other one. She wasn't likely to come out in her slippers and she was equally unlikely to let him in. He searched her eyes, waiting.

Finally, Becky extended a hand and Tank took it, stepping just inside the door. Before she could say a word, he took her in his arms and held her. They stood that way for a few, very powerful moments, then he pulled back enough to take her face in his hands.

"I need Friday, Saturday, and Sunday," he said, then gave her something else to think about before she could argue.

She relaxed into his arms and he began to think the threshold boundary was probably a really good idea. Then he began not thinking at all. He slowly and very reluctantly pulled away.

"I think I need those to roll over into next week, and I'm gonna get out of here."

Becky stepped back and blinked. "Aren't you going to tell me how the interviews went?"

"They went fine," Tank replied, stepping out onto the porch.

She placed her hands back on her hips and cocked her head, and he almost came right back through the door.

Instead, he turned and jogged down the steps, not looking back until he got to his Jeep. By the time he turned, the window of the outside door had fogged up and she was a blur, still standing in the same position, likely confused and probably fairly irritated.

"I'll see you tomorrow!" he called out, doubtful she even heard him. He started his Jeep, said a prayer of thanks for his new battery, and sped off.

***

"*C'est tout,*" Becky told her class, glad that she'd made it through the day. It was almost better that she had nothing but French classes. She didn't think she'd lost track and started rambling on about her infatuation, but if she did, most of the kids wouldn't have understood. They still had a ways to go before they could seriously track what she was saying.

She dismissed the class and began pulling her things together, half-hoping and half-fearing that Tank would walk through the door. He'd been very tenacious about finding her on the days they didn't have class together, usually in her room so they could have a minute alone. Becky was beyond fighting the daily greetings, which were getting more interesting each time. If he thought she was thinking rationally about giving up men when he was kissing her like that, he was sorely mistaken. If she was going to make a coherent decision, she was going to need a break from him.

Their weekend break was not nearly long enough, especially when he surprised her by coming over in the middle of the night. She stopped packing her bag and stared out the window, thinking about the look on his face when she'd opened the door. She honestly couldn't recall a time when someone had looked so happy to see her. It melted her heart, even as it heated up the rest of her. He didn't greet her, didn't tell her about his trip, just collected on his kisses.

Tank followed his brief knock into the room. "Busy?"

Becky scrambled to pull her things together and stop acting like a lovesick middle-schooler. Tank walked over to the desk, his long strides eating up the space, and she found herself scooting behind the chair.

He laughed. "I've tackled far worse than that, Becky. You're going to have to try a little harder."

He braced his hands on the desk, looking relaxed, but Becky could tell he was ready to spring, whichever way she decided to move.

She bit back a smile. "You are such a child. Why don't you just ask me out like a normal person?"

He straightened up. "Great idea. Would you go out with me, Becky?"

"Not tonight." She took advantage of his momentary confusion to skirt the desk and make tracks for the door.

He was on her heels. "Yeah, I'm not available tonight either. I'm working my second job."

She turned, holding her book bag as a barrier between them. "What job?" Her mind spun with the possibilities. Was he going to work remotely for ESPN?

Tank drew a finger down her cheek. It was almost like a drug. Her feet felt sluggish and she couldn't think about moving.

"My carpentry job," he reminded her. "Boss wants me to finish up the wainscoting tonight."

Her breath caught and she narrowed her eyes. There was no way she was going to be in the house alone with him. Of course, she wasn't going to tell him that. Better to just not be there.

"Okay," she finally said. "Guess I'll see you later then."

She gave him a saucy little look and reached for the door knob. Tank stepped close. "Just in case I miss you ..."

***

"It was so great of you to stop over and spend time with the boys, again," Maddy said, walking Becky to the door.

"Yeah, well, I figured they'd get a kick out of painting with me, and I have to finish up my horse, anyway."

"They had a blast."

"Sorry I kept them up so late."

"It's okay. It doesn't hurt to push back bedtime once in a while."

"Right, well, I'll let you get to your bedtime stories."

"You don't have to leave."

Becky looked at her sister hopefully, then shook her head. "No, you need your time with your husband."

Maddy laughed. "Yes, I do. But he's over at the house tonight. Didn't you know that?"

"He is? Oh, well, then I can go home," Becky replied cheerfully.

Maddy smiled. "So, not only did you want some last-minute bonding time on a school night with your new nephews, you mostly wanted to avoid being alone with Tank?"

"Absolutely," Becky conceded, setting her oil paint case down.

Maddy stiffened. "You're not afraid of him?"

Becky looked up in surprise. "Oh, no! Well, yes, but not in that way." She zipped and then unzipped her coat. "He's as gentle as can be, and while he's compelling," she felt a silly grin tugging her lips, "he's not pushy. Well, he's pushy," she amended, "but it's adorable, and I just don't trust myself alone with him."

Maddy laughed. "Never thought I'd hear the words 'adorable' and 'Tank' in the same sentence, especially coming out of your mouth."

"Yeah, I wouldn't have bet on that, either," Becky grinned.

***

Tank always enjoyed working with John. They were both detail oriented, and John had really come to trust Tank's input and decision-making on the projects they were working on. He'd wondered if John would ask about his relationship with Becky, but, like usual, they threw themselves into the work and kept the conversation project-related. It was different when Frank was around. He often made the work more interesting, but he sometimes derailed them with his story telling and cutting up. It was a good time either way, and Tank knew that he'd really miss working with them if he took the ESPN job.

He prowled around his kitchen, knowing he had to get to bed after a long day at school and then working at the inn. Somehow, the day was incomplete, because he hadn't really spent time with Becky. That brief moment in her classroom was all they ended up having. She'd made herself scarce while he worked on the apartment. No surprise there.

He pulled out supplies to make his lunch for the next day; he'd be too tired to do it in the morning. He pictured making lunches with Becky by his side, giving him a hard time, telling him he ate too much. He'd hassle her for eating like a mouse. Then they'd forget about the food ...

He shook himself. He was a goner. They were going to have to really talk and figure out where their relationship was going. It was one thing to tease her about being done with men, and he really enjoyed the daily reminders that he wasn't going away. But she was going to have to figure out if she was ready to trust him and give their relationship a chance. The pressure was on with his job offer. ESPN wasn't going to wait forever, and how Becky felt about him leaving was a much bigger factor than he cared to admit.

Four sandwiches later, he packed up what he'd made, figuring he'd finish in the morning. Tomorrow was health class. Tank liked health class. One of the other P.E. teachers was going to be leading a two-day CPR unit, so there wasn't any significant prep.

Tank smiled. It was fun to mess with Becky during class. The CPR unit would give him all kinds of opportunities to do it.

twenty-nine

"If one more kid would have asked us to demonstrate mouth to mouth ..." Becky stormed through the classroom, shoving the desks back into place.

Tank grinned. "Well, if you'd have just cooperated, they wouldn't have had to keep asking."

She looked up at him with a glare that had no chance of lasting. She pursed her lips to keep from smiling. "And you needed to encourage them."

Tank threw his hands up defensively. "I said nothing."

"You smiled and gave me that ... that look."

"What look?"

Becky turned back to her desks, knowing better than to make eye contact. She knew exactly what she'd see in his eyes, and how it would affect her breathing, her coloring, her ability to focus. He had no business giving her that look in front of a roomful of teenagers.

She shoved another desk over. "You could help."

"Yeah, I was kind of afraid to get in your way."

She scowled at him and quickly looked away. "Are you ever going to tell me what happened over the weekend?"

"Are you ever going to give me five minutes alone with you?"

Becky kept shoving. "We're alone now. Tell me what happened." She looked up from a safe distance across the room. "I really do want to hear about it."

Tank finished shutting down the Smartboard. "I have a meeting tonight." He thought for a moment. "Helping Grace at the shop on Wednesday. How about pizza Thursday?"

Becky considered the offer. It seemed safe enough. "You working at the house anymore this week?"

He smiled a slow smile. "I could get called in any time."

She'd never seen him smile so much. It made it really difficult to stay irritated with him.

He pulled his jacket on. "I won't be over tonight. You're safe."

"Good," she replied, pretending she believed it.

"So I'll need to walk you to your car."

Becky sighed and gathered her things. It was a funny game they were playing, really fairly childish. Still, she knew her part. She'd make a fuss and continue to pretend like she wasn't dying to find out how he'd give her his daily greeting.

She'd never had so much fun kissing in her life.

Trouble, trouble, trouble.

***

The students finished their French test, and for once, sat quietly doing their homework until the period ended. Becky found herself distracted as always. Would Tank come and find her after school? She was like a Pavlovian dog, her heart racing because the clock hit 2:45. The image did not please her.

She did get a visitor on the heels of the kids departure, but it wasn't Tank. Ed Davidson walked in and greeted her heartily, as he always did.

"Hello, Ms. Jacobs! How are you, today?"

Becky smiled, internally switching gears to talk to the tech ed teacher. "Doing just fine, Mr. Davidson. How are you?"

"Fine, just fine. I talked to old Mrs. Brindle, and I think she's finally going to retire."

Becky cocked her head. "Mrs. Brindle? Do I know her?"

"The art teacher," Ed boomed. "Gotta be a hundred and fifty years old. Time for her to retire and make room for some new blood."

"Ed!"

"She's been waiting for someone 'worthy' to replace her. Someone who loves the kids and loves Clairmont. Won't leave her kids 'til she knows they're in good hands." Ed sat on the corner of Becky's desk. "I showed her your painting of Lillibelle and she loved it!"

Becky tried to process everything he was telling her. "I'm glad she liked it, but I don't want her to feel like I'm after her job."

"That's the only thing that's gonna budge her."

"Well, I don't even know what I'm doing next year, if I'll even be in the area," Becky hedged.

Ed raised an eyebrow. "You don't see yourself staying in Clairmont? Sure seems to suit you."

Becky pulled her coat on. "I do like it here. More than I expected to. But it's all very temporary. I'm living in my sister's house, remember. As soon as they finish that apartment, her family will be moving in and I'm going to have to figure out my next step. It may be here. It may not," she shrugged.

She could tell that Ed was itching to say something about Tank, but he seemed to think better of it and returned to his original tactic.

"Well, we sure could use a young, talented art teacher around here. We're going to need one soon, if I have anything to say about it."

Becky laughed nervously. "Thanks Ed, but it's not really your decision. There are a lot of steps to the process."

"Right. We start by getting her out of the building."

"Ed!"

"Oh, I've known her forever. All my kids had her. She knows I like her. It's just time, that's all." He leaned in and whispered dramatically, "She's even older than me."

"Shocking! And is she also working with power tools like you are?" Becky asked.

Ed chuckled. "You never can tell with those artsy types."

"I'm an artsy type, Ed."

"Exactly! And we need you. Now why don't you run down to the office and see if there's some sort of paperwork you can fill out?"

Becky shook her head. It had been a long time since Ed had applied for a teaching job. "The job will be posted after she retires. I'll look into it then. Meanwhile, why don't we let her finish her year in peace?"

"If you'd just go and say 'hello,' and tell her ..."

"Ed," Becky used her stern teacher voice.

"Fine, fine," Ed grumbled good-naturedly.

Becky followed him out of the room. "Thanks for thinking of me. I do appreciate it."

He grinned. "We're going to get you to stay in Clairmont, one way or another," he replied. "Once we get attached to someone, we don't let go easily."

***

Becky felt every muscle in her legs as she made her way through the halls to her classroom. She'd run the afternoon before and hadn't taken the time to stretch like she should have. She'd be feeling it all day. Shifting her book bag, she opened the door to their classroom. She'd arrived earlier than usual, hoping to be the first teacher in the room. It helped her equilibrium the tiniest bit if she could get in and nest before Tank arrived.

Strong arms enveloped her the minute she walked in, and Tank did his best to cover Becky's squeal of surprise. Her pounding heart continued to pound for all kinds of reasons, and she finally broke free.

"You're crazy!"

Tank lifted her book bag off her shoulder. "I missed you yesterday."

"Well, that was no greeting. That was an assault."

Chastised, he set her bag down on the desk and turned to her. "I'm sorry. I would never hurt you."

He was so serious, Becky was taken aback. "I know. You just surprised me, that's all."

"I had just walked in, myself." He shrugged his big shoulders and grinned a little. "I couldn't resist when you kind of backed in like that."

Becky smiled and shook her head. "You're lucky it wasn't Mrs. Whitestone."

Tank groaned in horror. "And you look so much alike, I just might have made that mistake."

Becky smacked him. "Nice."

"Now look who's assaulting."

"Poor baby," Becky said. "We've got one more day of CPR, right? Do we need the Smartboard?"

"Nope. Just lots of resuscitation practice."

She rolled her eyes. "You're just ... trouble."

"With a capital T," he grinned.

***

"So, would you do this year-round?" Becky asked as she helped herself to a second slice of pizza. Tank was on his fourth, and he'd eaten most of his salad. He'd also done most of the talking.

He'd caught her up on the people he'd met, some of the details of the job, and then taken off on sports analysis. Becky marveled at how it animated him. When she compared the Tank that she'd first met and the man sitting across from her, she could hardly believe they were the same person.

"There's work that I can do year-round, of course, but the air time would be late summer through early February."

"And you'd move, of course."

He looked at her intently. "It would make sense. I'd probably keep the beach house, that is if I can ever buy it so that I can keep it."

Becky nodded and took a bite of her salad, chewing thoughtfully. "And what are your options if you don't take it? I mean, I'm sure you will; that makes sense, of course, but I'm just curious why you're even deliberating. What else would you do?"

Tank took a break from eating and sat back in his seat. "They talked to me about the P.E. position."

Becky smiled; that was no surprise. "I don't suppose they're trying very hard to replace you. I'm sure they'd love it if you stayed on."

"Thanks," Tank replied. "I do like working with the kids. And I like the town." He looked around the pizza place like it was all right there in front of him. Then he leaned forward. "They asked me to join the coaching staff." His eyes snapped with excitement.

Becky marveled at how much she enjoyed seeing him so happy. "Oh, how great is that? Is somebody leaving?"

"Defensive coordinator would appreciate the break. He came on a few years back when the staff was short. I don't think he'd planned to do it long-term."

"Wow, that would be perfect for you."

"Yeah, I have some pretty sweet options."

Becky pushed her salad plate away. "So, how long do you have to decide?"

"School's giving me time. ESPN wants to know yesterday."

"I'm not surprised."

Tank reached over and traced Becky's fingers on the table. It tingled right up her arm. "Do you know what you're doing next year?"

It made sense for him to ask, of course. No one was talking about commitment, just looking ahead to job prospects. Still, they were forging new territory.

"I'm not sure. Ed Davidson's trying to kick the art teacher out so that I can have her job."

Tank laughed. "Good for Ed."

Becky smiled. "Yeah, it's not quite the concrete job offer that you have, but it's something to think about."

"She close to retirement?"

"According to Ed, she is. I haven't met her."

"How about French? They hiring a new teacher?"

"Yeah, I think they're looking for someone part-time. I'm going to need to go back to full-time with benefits - the whole deal. This year was a little off the beaten path for me."

"You've been a big help to Maddy."

Becky grinned. "There was a time you wouldn't have admitted that."

Tank leaned back and stretched. "I was determined not to like you."

She watched and enjoyed the stretch, then tuned in to what he was saying. "Really? Why?"

"Because you're beautiful, smart and funny. All of those things bugged me."

Becky wasn't sure if she should be flattered or offended. "Do tell."

His lips twitched. "It's a deadly combination, and not many people handle it well." He leaned back in and took a hold of her fingers, playing with them more than holding them. "But you've figured out what matters and there's a really cool woman underneath all the rest of it that I really want to know."

"So you'll put up with 'all the rest of it.'"

He grinned. "I'll do my best."

She blew her hair out of her eyes. "I haven't figured out what matters," she objected. "I think I just finally realized what doesn't."

"Men?" He gave her fingers a tug.

She looked at him wryly. "You've made it really difficult to stick to my plan."

"Maybe there's a better plan."

"Maybe you just want me because I'm fighting you. You probably never had a woman say no before."

Tank considered this for a moment. "Guess the only way to find out is to have you throw yourself at me." He leaned back, keeping a hold of her fingers. "Then we'll see from there."

"Oh, that's great for me," Becky said dryly. "And when you decide I'm not such a big deal and move on, I'll just ..."

"You're a big deal, Becky," Tank gently interrupted.

She looked into his eyes, lost herself a little. "You should never have kissed me," she whispered.

"Can't say I'm sorry. Don't know if I can stop."

Becky swallowed, tried to concentrate. "You kiss me and I get stupid," she protested. "It's a good stupid, a better stupid than I've ever felt before, but I don't feel any control."

Tank spun the pizza pan, then sat back and regarded her. "I don't believe I've ever kissed anyone stupid before."

"You probably have and you just don't know it."

He grinned and stopped the pan. "Who feels control when they're kissing?"

"Oh, please, you never look flustered after you kiss me - just all smiling and pleased with yourself."

Tank laughed. "Well, I am happy when I kiss you, but it doesn't mean I feel any kind of control. This is a ride for me, too, Becky. I'm in it now, and I want to see where it goes."

"I just feel like this is all happening to me. Like I'm not choosing it."

Tank sat back, concerned. "Don't like how that sounds."

"I'm not saying this very well," Becky conceded. "I think what I really need," she stopped and thought for a moment, "is to stop letting men define me."

"I'm not men, Becky. I'm one man. I'm not everyone else you ever dated."

"I know. I know." She looked at him longingly. "I just need some time."

He sighed. "Okay. I get that."

She looked at him. "I need you to be my friend."

He squeezed her fingers. "Of course."

"And I need you to stop kissing me."

thirty

The snow was falling so hard Becky couldn't see the ocean from the kitchen window. She looked with relief at the pile of wood next to the fireplace. She hadn't thought to stock it after her long day at school on Friday. John must have done it when he arrived to work on the apartment. What a guy.

She glanced outside again before joining Maddy in the kitchen. "Don't you worry about the boys out there in that blizzard?"

"I think they're safe with John and Tank. I'm sure they're having a blast."

"I meant all four boys."

Maddy laughed.

"Seriously. They're probably half frozen."

"Aren't you the little worrier today?"

Becky opened the oven to check the double chocolate chip cookies. The edges looked crisp and the chips were nice and shiny; just about ready. "It's just coming down so hard."

"Maybe we should go out there; make sure they're okay."

Becky slipped on the oven mitts. "Are you kidding?"

Maddy washed her hands. "No, I'm not. That's the last batch of cookies. Let's go surprise them. It'll be fun!"

Becky groaned. "Did you not hear me say that I was trying to get some space from Tank? It's enough that he spent the whole day working here with John. Why would I go out there and play in the snow with him?"

Maddy rolled her eyes. "Then go out and play with Parker and Blake. They loved it the last time you did it. Talked about your fort all week." She hovered as Becky pulled the cookies out. "They smell heavenly." She squeezed Becky's shoulder. "I'm going out."

Becky scowled at her sister, but hesitated only briefly before stomping to her room to get her boots. No matter what was going on with Tank, she was still working on being a fun aunt. She'd go out and mess with the boys.

The little ones, anyway.

Finally bundled from head to foot, she tottered onto the porch, following Maddy's prints out to the snow blown beach. She could hear the boys yelling and laughing, with the deeper laughs of John and Tank mixed in. She headed toward the voices, her movement slowed by all of her layers.

"Ahhhh! The monster's got me!" Blake squealed, followed by what could only be Tank roaring. Becky couldn't help smiling. Blake was usually pretty reserved; it was fun to hear him letting loose in their snow monster game.

"I'll save you!" Parker yelled.

Becky caught movement ahead as Parker ran straight for a very large, dark mass - could only be Tank - and tried to tackle him. The big form, with a smaller, floppy one on his shoulder, dropped back a step and then roared again, leaning down to scoop up Parker.

With both boys flailing on his shoulders, monster Tank climbed into the snow fort that she'd built. *Of all the nerve ...*

Becky jumped at Maddy's voice.

"We're going in for the rescue. We need a diversion!" She and John were wrapped around each other, grinning, cheeks red from the cold.

"You hardly look ready for a rescue," Becky replied with a half-smile. "You divert, I'll go in."

Laughing, they split apart. "I'll approach from the back," John suggested, suddenly all business. "Maddy, you sneak down around those rocks. Well, you can't see them, but you know where I mean. Becky," he pointed, "straight out on the beach. You're the only one who can cause the kind of distraction we need," he grinned.

She rolled her eyes, but smiled. "Yes, captain." She offered a mittened salute and turned, trying to jog out to the beach. Her waddling through the snow drifts would probably make Tank fall over laughing; perfect distraction.

She circled around until she was fairly certain she could pop up within view, but not too close to Tank's lair. She could tell the moment he saw her. Both boys were climbing on him, apparently not trying too hard to escape. He slowly peeled them off and leaned over; gesturing with his hands for them to stay put. Then he turned and threw out his arms, letting out another terrifying snow monster roar.

Becky stood, shocked and immobilized, her heart slamming into action when he started running toward her. She looked wildly around at her options. It made sense to draw him away from his poor, helpless prisoners, so she started run-waddling down the beach.

She could hear him pounding in the snow behind her, and couldn't help her own shriek when she looked back to see him close on her heels. She turned back, laughing and trying to make headway in the deep snow. *So this is what it's like to be blitzed by the linebacker.*

She didn't have a chance, of course, though she'd like to take him on in her sneakers and about five less layers. She'd give him a run for his money then.

His steps thudded right behind her and she felt his hands on her waist. She squealed and twisted before he brought her down in a pile of snow, rolling her until he had her good and truly pinned.

Becky lay there laughing, trying to catch her breath.

"Surrender," he growled.

"Never!" she gasped back.

He got very close and repeated his request.

Their noses were almost touching. "I'm on a mission," she protested. Tank lifted his head a bit, and they could hear the boys laughing and horsing around with John and Maddy. Becky grinned. "Mission accomplished."

Tank smiled back, watching as the snowflakes started covering her cheeks. Becky shook her head back and forth. "My face is cold."

He leaned close. "Want me to take care of those for you?"

Becky closed her eyes, and tried to breathe. "No?"

She could feel the cool air rush in when he lifted his head. She dared to open her eyes. "You don't play fair."

"I always play fair," he replied with a grin. "I just play better." The glint in his eye was as heart-stopping as his warm breath on her face.

Becky tried to draw a calming breath. It wasn't easy with a Tank on top of her. "You have over a hundred pounds on me. How is that fair?"

"I figured closer to fifty."

She tried to shove against his chest. "You're a horrible snow monster!"

"I'm actually a very good snow monster. I have you pinned."

"Yeah, about that," Becky twisted. "You should move. You're lucky there's snow all around me."

"*You're* lucky there's snow all around you. Although," he added, looking around, "without it, I don't think I'd be in this position. Without permission, that is." He grinned wickedly then spun her around so that she was free to go.

She stayed a moment, perched on top of him. Looking down at the teasing gleam in his eye, she wanted to forget all her fears, lean down and warm up those perfect lips.

Becky brought her eyes back to his. He knew perfectly well what she was thinking. Her face warmed and she watched the snowflakes gather on his lashes. She never noticed how thick they were before. He blinked several times to clear them and she shifted so he could get up.

"Before you leave," he cupped her shoulders without restraining her. His eyes lost their teasing and became very serious. "I want you to know that I want this, Becky - I want us - more than any job - more than anything."

Her heart started pounding again.

"I'll give you whatever time you need, but I'm not going away." He stroked her cheek with his gloved finger and her face tingled. "You can be done with men. I'm good with that. In fact, I'd have to insist on it," his eyes glinted through the snowflakes. "But don't be done with me. We're a good team. We could stay here in Clairmont - teach together." He paused and ran his finger over her lips. "Raise a family together."

He spun her around one more time, bracing himself as he looked down at her. "I love you, Becky." He looked deeply into her eyes and Becky wanted to cry. Then he slowly leaned down and brushed her temple with his lips.

Becky didn't trust her voice. How could she possibly respond? Who pours their heart out in a snowbank? She lay there, looking at him helplessly, longingly. He didn't seem to mind that she couldn't find anything to say. A moment later he jumped up and held out his hand to her.

Becky took it, wide-eyed and overwhelmed. He grinned and pulled her up, and they started back to the house. She walked along next to him, her mind spinning with what had just happened in the snow. When they reached the porch, Becky pushed ahead. Stepping to the top step, she turned and put her hands on Tank's shoulders, holding him in place several steps below. He immediately reached around her waist and pulled her close.

Pushing back, she tried to regain her balance. "This isn't a hug," she told him. "I want to look down at you."

He grinned, loosening his grip a bit. Becky looked into his eyes, sighed, and then reached up and pulled his hat down over his face. She could still see the grin, but she forged ahead with what she had to say.

"When I asked for space to think, I wasn't expecting you to tackle me in the snow and tell me you love me." The grin continued to play across his lips. She smiled and shoved his shoulders. "Seriously!"

He pushed his hat up and pulled her close again. "You told me to stop kissing you," he reminded her. "I did what you asked." His lips hovered very close to hers. "I could kiss you now, but see how much space I'm giving you?"

Her argument all but forgotten, Becky could only think of closing that space. The door *banged!* and Parker slid out onto the porch.

"Hey, you're finally back! Dad wants to know if Tank-monster can stay for dinner."

Becky and Tank slowly separated. The snow monster stepped up to the porch and towered over them both. "I'd love to stay," he replied, fist bumping Parker. "This monster's hungry."

Parker giggled and grabbed his hand, pulling him into the house. "You can come, too, Miss Aunt Becky!" he called over his shoulder.

Becky shook her head with a smile and followed them into the house.

thirty-one

Becky rolled her eyes. *Another fire alarm?* They hadn't told the staff about this one. Maybe one of the kids had pulled it.

She hushed the class. "Alright, everyone, settle down. Line up calmly. You can't stop at your lockers, so once we get outside, find a buddy and stay warm. But stay close. Taking attendance is hard enough out there."

The school buzzed with chatter. The students were anything but quiet as they headed out of the building, happy to be freed from their classes, even if it meant standing in the snow.

Becky led the group to their appointed spot on the football field between what she guessed was the forty and fifty yard line. She took attendance with a growing sense of unease. There wasn't the normal chit-chat between teachers as they tried to keep their respective kids quiet. One of her students stood shivering in her sleeveless sweater. Becky tossed the girl her jacket.

"Put this on," she called. "Everybody line up!"

"Smoke!" one of the students yelled, and everyone followed his gaze to the shop wing. About a hundred students soon fixated on the area as smoke began to billow out in earnest. Becky's heart sank; that was Ed's territory. She found herself praying that he and his students had gotten out safely.

A moment later, one of the assistant principals appeared from around the corner of the building and jogged over to the group. He gathered the teachers and updated them.

"We need to move the kids over to the middle school. Nobody's going back inside today." He gestured over his shoulder.

"Is everyone alright?" one of the teachers asked.

"Don't know yet. Fire in one of the shop rooms. Everyone's evacuating."

Amidst murmurs of disbelief, the teachers turned to gather their charges.

"Ms. Jacobs."

Becky turned back to the assistant principal. She'd forgotten his name. "Yes?"

"Just thought you should know," he hesitated, looking back to the building before continuing. "Mr. Kimball was in the shop wing with Ed Davidson's class. That's where the fire started."

Becky felt the blood drain from her face. "Is he, are they alright?"

"Like I said, I'm not sure. I just know he was helping out with some demonstration. I talked to them about a half hour ago."

Becky nodded, looked over at the building. The smoke was even thicker now, and she could hear the sirens as emergency vehicles started responding.

"Can I go - is it - am I allowed to go over there?"

"The best thing you can do is get your students safely to the middle school."

"But I can't ..." she looked helplessly over his shoulder. She tried to breathe. "Of course. Okay."

She turned to see her students watching their exchange. They were huddled together, looking concerned, the adventure of the fire alarm having lost its thrill. One girl started to cry. Becky kicked into automatic mode. She simply couldn't think about Tank being injured.

"Alright, let's go. It's going to be okay. Let's follow the others to the middle school."

She started to lead the way across the football field, when an explosion shook the ground. She stumbled and turned to see flames and smoke shooting from the building behind them. She watched, frozen, imagining Tank trapped somewhere inside. Then she thought about Ed - so much older and less agile. What about the students? Helplessly she watched, praying like she hadn't prayed in years.

"Alright, everyone, let's go. We need to keep moving."

Becky hardly recognized her own voice as she turned and made herself walk away from the fire.

***

The back parking lot was full of emergency vehicles. Becky called Grace and left a message, hoping she'd get it and would be able to find her way in through the throng. People were milling in all directions and Becky tried to find someone she could talk to, to get some information. She finally noticed Ed sitting on the tailgate of an open ambulance. Relief swept over her as she ran up to him.

"Ed? Are you alright?" she called through the group of people surrounding him. She noted that he had some minor scratches on his face, but except for his clothes being rumpled and messed, he looked like he was okay. She dared to hope.

The group parted so that she could approach.

"Becky." His haggard expression spoke volumes as he looked up, and her heart dropped back into her stomach. "Tank's in there."

She took his hands and mustered some strength on his behalf. "I know." She looked back toward the building. Two EMTs were intercepting a student who'd just exited the building with a fireman. They helped her over to a waiting ambulance.

"He was helping me with a drilling demo," Ed said hoarsely. He hung his head mumbling, and Becky squeezed his hands.

"It's okay Ed. They've got lots of help in there now," she tried to comfort him.

"Wall of fire - students panicked. They were blocked in by the drill press. Tank just shoved the whole thing over - and the kids got out. One girl backed into the corner; too afraid ..." He shook his head and drew a shuddering breath. "Tank went back for her."

Becky kept her eyes glued to the door of the building. No one else had come out since she'd arrived. She glanced around her, taking in a few more details of the unbelievable scene. Two firetrucks and about half a dozen firemen battled the blaze outside. An ambulance pulled out of the lot. Teachers and administrators were everywhere, trying to account for students and deal with anxious parents.

Her attention shot back to the entrance as two firefighters wheeled a gurney out of the building. It was slow going. She didn't have to strain to see that the heavy load they were pushing was Tank.

***

Becky adjusted her position on the hard chair. She'd actually dozed for a bit, which was probably a good thing. It had been a long evening of waiting, hoping, agonizing. Grace was the only one allowed in the ICU with Tank, so Maddy, John, and Frank had kept watch in the ER waiting room with Becky.

Six other students had been treated and released, including the girl that Tank had gone back to rescue. The other teachers and students in the wing had all evacuated without injury.

Not Tank.

Becky felt the tears surfacing again. She reached for the box of tissues on the table beside her, glad that the others were dozing or distracted for the moment. She didn't want the focus on her. They had their heads and hearts full thinking about Tank.

She jumped, her heart slamming wildly into her ribcage when the door to the ER opened. Grace walked out, looking drawn and worn. The doctor followed, and the others quickly roused to hear the report. Grace sat next to Becky and held her hand.

"Mr. Kimball is in critical condition," the doctor began, cutting right to the chase. His voice was professional, but there was an edge of compassion to it. "He's suffered an injury to the back of the head, which is further complicated by like injuries sustained in the past. He's unresponsive, though his vital signs are strong."

Unresponsive. The word hit like a physical blow. Becky couldn't imagine Tank lying in a bed, *unresponsive.* She tried to tune into the details of what his medical team would be watching for in the days ahead. *"We're doing all we can."* Of course, they were. Becky squeezed Grace's hand, trying to offer strength she wasn't sure she had.

The doctor finally excused himself, and the group in the waiting room gathered together. Becky listened as they immediately launched into prayer on behalf of their friend and brother. She listened quietly, trying to believe that the words spoken in this tiny, stark country hospital waiting room would somehow make a difference in the life of the man lying helpless down the hall.

***

Becky prepared for school in a daze on Tuesday morning. The damage caused by the fire had been contained in the shop wing, so the school opened its doors after only one day off. Maybe it was best for everyone; Becky could hardly say. She'd spent the weekend at the hospital - half of that time sitting and talking with Ed - and she had no energy left to face her students. The school would surely be buzzing with news of Friday's fire and Tank's injury and she wasn't sure how she was going to handle the kids' distress on top of her own.

He hadn't improved over the last three days, but at least he wasn't technically worse. Grace had requested clearance for Becky, so she'd been able to go in and sit with him for a few minutes at a time. She fought the tears as she recalled watching him lie there, immobile, so not like Tank.

Becky took another swallow of coffee and packed her lunch. She hadn't eaten much over the weekend, and knew she had to make herself eat if she was going to field the physical and emotional demands of the week ahead.

Maybe more than a week.

Or it could end today.

A sob escaped as she allowed herself to think about really losing Tank. He'd said that another concussion could kill him. Concussions were why he'd had to give up football. If he didn't die, he could be paralyzed or ... She willed herself to stop. She couldn't take on the 'what ifs.' She barely had the strength for what was.

Throwing her sandwich and an apple into a bag, she dragged herself out of the house. Her students needed her.

***

Grace was sitting with Tank when Becky arrived at the hospital late that afternoon. They had moved him to the neuro ward, which essentially meant that his vital signs were stable and his coma score had improved somewhat. Becky wanted to jump at this good news, but held back her enthusiasm. Grace didn't look particularly cheery.

"How are you holding up?" Becky asked, trying to focus on her friend and not on the man lying in the bed.

Grace sighed. "I'm okay. Tank seems to be ... okay. Did they explain why they moved him?"

Becky nodded.

"I was so hoping for a change that I could see." Grace rubbed her temples. "He hasn't moved; he just ..." She looked down at him lying peacefully between them.

Tank was never peaceful. Becky swallowed. "Have you heard from Alex?"

"Yeah, he's coming out tomorrow. Not that it makes a differ-ence," Grace sighed helplessly as she picked up her brother's hand.

"It will make all the difference," Becky protested. "He'll keep you going, and you'll keep Tank going."

Grace looked up. "So will you. He needs you, Becky."

Becky nodded. "I'll be here."

"No, I mean he needs you. For the long haul. When this is over," she gestured aimlessly around the room, "when he's better," she amended with more determination, "he's going to need you." She looked at Tank with mingled concern and affection. "Some-one's gotta keep him out of trouble."

Becky looked down at Tank and picked up his other hand. "I'm not sure anyone's ready for that job."

They shared a sad smile. "If anyone can do it, it's you." Grace sighed. "Oh, and just so you know, you can stay with him a little longer now. I guess they'll let you know if they need you to leave."

Becky patted her book bag. "I brought plenty to do. I'll just camp here 'til they kick me out."

"Sounds good. I'm going to go home and shower and then head back to the shop for a bit." Grace walked around the bed and gave Becky a hug. "Take good care of him."

"I will."

Grace left and Becky set her book bag down, pulling the chair close to the bed, as she'd done over the weekend. At some point she'd try to correct her French papers, but first she'd hold Tank's hand and watch him sleep. She liked to think of him simply sleeping - resting. When he was strong he would wake up and terrorize her again. She was counting on it.

Not that he'd terrorized her during the last week. He'd respected her wishes and not come around for his daily greeting. They'd taught their class together and he'd been friendly and professional. He'd worked on the apartment on two of the evenings and had only said hello and good-bye when she happened to be around.

She'd been intensely aware of his presence in the classroom and in the house. His giving her space only made her feel him everywhere. His respecting her wishes only made her long for him more. She'd never been taken so seriously; wasn't sure how to respond.

Becky stroked Tank's hand. It was a big hand. They'd never really held hands during their whole, odd relationship. He'd helped her up, taken her briefly by the hand, but they'd never just walked hand in hand together. Whatever else they did when he woke up, she wanted to walk with him and hold his hand and just be.

Her gaze traveled up to his lips. They were gently parted in sleep. There was a cut and significant swelling on the lower left, but otherwise, they were perfect. She released a long sigh. There was nothing in the world like being Tank's sole focus when he kissed her. A shiver ran through her. It had been almost two weeks since their last kiss.

Unless I count the kiss on my forehead when he told me he loved me.

Becky closed her eyes, not fighting the tears. She'd been blown away by that confession in the snow.

No one had ever wanted her like that. The variations of love talk were familiar, but they were usually connected to a demand of some kind. She'd never had someone just tell her they loved her and not even expect a response. She felt ... delighted in. It seemed odd to describe it that way - it was a such foreign concept - but that's what it felt like.

Looking at him now, she could kick herself for deliberating and making them both wait.

She sighed; if she were honest, she knew that just because he lay there helpless, needing healing she couldn't imagine possible, it didn't change the fact that she needed healing of her own.

Well, now she truly had the time she'd asked for. What an unwelcome gift.

thirty-two

Becky got through health classes better than she would have imagined. The students were subdued - they'd run out of questions the day before and seemed to understand that she had enough on her plate. The unit on community health was probably a little dry, but they managed to cover the material.

Carrie hung out after her first class, and when the room was cleared, asked how she was doing.

"I'm okay. Thanks for asking," Becky responded.

"You look tired."

"I am. Hard to sleep." The night before she'd fallen asleep next to Tank's bed. She'd awakened in the middle of the night, surprised the hospital staff hadn't kicked her out. She never did grade her French work.

"We could watch a movie in French. Give you a break."

Becky gave her a tired smile. "I was thinking the same thing."

Carrie picked up her books. "I know there's nothing I can do. But if there were ..."

"I know. Thanks, Carrie. That means a lot."

Carrie nodded. "Well, guess I'll see you after lunch."

"See you later."

Becky watched her student leave the room, marveling at the change. She sat down with her lunch and forced herself to eat. Maddy promised to come by the hospital and sit with her after school. That would be a good thing. She needed her sister.

***

Becky glanced at her watch. It was just before suppertime; not that Tank adhered to any kind of meal routine. She studied the giant form lying so still under the covers. Was he losing weight? He had to be. They were feeding him intravenously, of course, but there was no way they could keep up with his real appetite.

She considered the workouts he was missing. He'd be furious; Tank was religious about his weight-lifting routine. Becky reached under the bar and ran her fingertips along his forearm. She'd never seen forearms like Tank's. His fingers twitched slightly, and Becky's heart soared with hope that she knew would be dashed in the same breath.

She reached up to stroke his cheek. He needed a shave. Who's job was that? She decided that she would like to do it. That would be another thing when he woke up. She'd hold his hand and she'd shave him. Becky smiled wanly to herself, wondering what other things would make the list.

It was so strange - he was completely accessible and inaccessible at the same time. She could stare at him all she wanted, touch his face, his arms, his hands. She'd run her finger over his Adam's apple at one point, marveling at the size of his neck. More than once she'd laid her hand on his chest when she wasn't sure he was breathing. Then she'd been weak with relief when she felt the big mountain move again.

She remembered when she first met him, and thought his size was off-putting. Not so much anymore.

She ran her fingers back down to his hand and held it. What she'd give to have him squeeze hers in return.

***

Maddy met her with soup and biscuits half an hour later and forced Becky to eat. It actually tasted good. She couldn't even remember what kind of sandwich she'd made for her lunch, but Becky was pretty sure she'd eaten it. At some point in the afternoon she'd had a few carrots. That was about it.

"His color's better, don't you think?" Maddy asked, ever the optimist.

Becky looked at Tank's face again. As long as he was so still, it was hard to notice improvement. "Could be." She took another bite of soup. "Thanks for dinner. This tastes great."

"Of course." Maddy sat down next to Becky and folded her hands in her lap. "You getting any more sleep?"

"Not so much last night. I'm going to try to get home a little earlier tonight. I haven't been much good at school. Doesn't help anybody."

Maddy nodded.

"You know what's crazy?" Becky pulled the biscuit apart and dropped some pieces into her bowl. "In the middle of trying to figure out what I'm supposed to do about men - in the middle of trying not to just be attracted to Tank because of his, because he's so ..." She stopped and swallowed. "For the first time I looked at a man and saw him as a father. I've never done that before. I think Tank would make a really good dad. I think he'd be gentle and firm ... and fun. The other day in the snow ..."

That was as far as she got. She set the bowl on the bedside table and put her head in her hands. She'd never cried so much in her life.

Maddy stroked her back and let her cry for a while, handing her a tissue when she guessed Becky was ready to pull it together.

"That's not crazy," she finally said. "It's wonderful. I got that view of John from the beginning. It was one of the first things that I loved about him."

Becky blew her nose and went into the bathroom to wash her face and hands. She walked back out and stopped at the foot of Tank's bed. It occurred to her that apart from all the devastation, she knew that she, herself, was in a better place than she'd been in in a long time. Whether it was a good enough place to survive losing Tank, she didn't know.

***

The hospital corridors were looking too familiar. Becky made her way to Tank's room, greeting the attendant at the desk, who gave her one of those 'be brave!' smiles. Becky smiled back the

'I'm a trooper!' smile. It had been a week since the accident. It seemed like a good time for Tank to wake up.

She met Grace and Alex just outside of Tank's room.

"Hey, Alex," she reached for his hand. "Nice to see you."

"Hi, Becky," he replied, taking her hand in both of his. "I'm just so sorry for ... everything. Tough time."

"Yeah." Becky turned and hugged Grace. They were beyond words at this point.

"He's strong. He's young. There's a lot in his favor."

Becky and Grace exchanged glances, wondering who should field the comment. Becky finally did. "Well, we're not going to let him go without a fight."

Everyone stood for a moment, embracing the sentiment. Grace finally spoke up. "We were just leaving - Alex has a flight to catch - but if you're going to be here, I'll come back for a bit."

"Sounds good. Take care, Alex."

"You, too." Alex touched her gently on the shoulder then picked up Grace's hand as they walked down the hall. Becky watched them walk together, trying hard not to be envious. She finally turned and walked into the hospital room.

"Okay, Tank. Time to get up. I want to walk with you and hold your hand." She walked over to the bed, feeling the familiar hole in her heart at seeing him lying so still. She reached out to touch his cheek. "Seriously, you need a shave. And I want to go get pizza with you at that place with the amazing cheesy garlic bread. It's time to wake up."

She sat down in her chair and looked at him. "Ms. Whitestone talked to me about the art job today, Tank. Potentially full time."

She reached up and ran her hand over his brow, brushing the top of his head. "I've always wanted to do this; touch your spiky hair." Stroking his head gently, she watched him sleep, or whatever he was doing. She didn't think it was possible for him to be so still. If Tank was anything, he was barely harnessed energy. She figured he probably slept hard under normal circumstances, too.

"I will never admit this to you when you wake up, but I was afraid of you when I first met you. And I'm not afraid of anyone." Becky pulled her hand back and picked up his.

"You were big and scary and you didn't like me." She rubbed her thumb across his knuckles. "And I thought your muscles were a bit excessive, I mean, seriously, what? How big do you need to be? Though I was always fascinated with your traps." She glanced at his shoulders, impressive even beneath a hospital gown. "I always wondered what I did that night that you found me, um, a bit inca-pacitated. You must have carried me to bed, though I don't really remember. I just have this idea that I was ... that I might have made my secret obsession known. Probably best that I don't know." She gave his hand a squeeze and sighed. "Just squeeze back, Tank, let me know you're fighting."

Becky sat there, trying to imagine his fingers moving. "Come on, Tank. Let's go home."

"Yes, please," Grace said, walking into the room. Becky looked up with her hospital smile. Grace smiled back at her, blinking back tears.

"I think we need to start threatening him," Becky said. "I'm tired of this. I want him to wake up. I want to marry him and re-decorate his beach house."

"Wait, what?"

Apparently, the distraction worked. "Tank pretty much said he wanted to marry me, or at least have kids," Becky replied. "Maybe it was just the kid part."

Grace walked over, the biggest smile Becky had seen since the accident hovering on her lips. She threw her arms around Becky.

"Well, we haven't really talked too much. He just said," her effort at sounding light faltered a bit, and Becky cleared her throat. "He said that we were a good team. That we should stay in Clair-mont and teach and raise a family together." She nodded her head, affirming that she'd captured the gist of it.

Grace was dumbfounded. "Tank said that?" She hugged Becky again. "You know, I've never seen him so happy. I thought he'd be thrilled about the ESPN job, and all he could talk about was whether you'd care if he left."

Becky processed that for a moment, then said, "Maybe if we start planning the wedding, he'll wake up and object." She picked up Tank's hand again. "I'll call him on his offer and raise him one.

Come on, Tank," she said, "I'm going to start re-arranging your house while you sleep. Lots of flowers. Lots of pink. Maybe turn one of the rooms into a nursery. What do you think?"

Grace warmed to the conversation. "That sounds perfect! I'll tell Mom and Dad. Mom would love to help plan the wedding."

They both watched his face, willing him to react.

"I haven't even met your folks," Becky replied. "Will they like me?"

"Yeah, probably, not," Grace replied. "Tank has notoriously bad taste in women. They never liked anyone he brought home."

Becky stared at her friend for a moment, then realized that Grace was simply throwing herself into their 'wake the Tank' game.

"And there have been sooo many, right Tank? Girl after girl after girl."

Becky started to lose interest in their little game. "That many, huh? Do tell." She gave his hand another squeeze.

Once again, they both waited, allowing him the opportunity to break into the conversation.

"Maybe Tank would rather I told you about the time he asked the most popular girl in school to the junior prom."

"Really?"

"Yeah. As a freshman."

"Oh, that was gutsy. Did she go?"

"No. She was a junior - too old for him. He just always thought he was hot stuff, 'cuz he was bigger than most of the guys in school. He played for the varsity team as a freshman, so he hung out with the big boys. Got a little full of himself."

"Wow, Tank. Did you get your heart broken?"

"Hardly. I think he did it on a dare."

"Well, no girl wants to be asked to prom on a dare."

Grace smiled. "It took him down a notch or two - for a couple days, anyway. Of course, she came running back to him the follow-ing year, when he was more socially acceptable to date, but he wouldn't have anything to do with her."

"Wow. This is very informative. Sure you don't want to put a stop to this, Tank?"

They both stopped and looked at him, their game on pause while they waited for him to recover from a life-threatening injury. Apparently, Tank wasn't interested in playing along.

"Excuse me?"

Both women jumped as a third woman entered the room. The nurse, petite and very pretty, walked in like she owned the hospital and everyone in it.

"Hi there. You must be ..." she looked back and forth between the two of them. "Let me start over. I'm Melanie, the RN in charge of the floor. I'm assuming that one of you is Ms. Kimball?"

Grace extended her hand. "I'm Grace, Tank's sister."

The nurse nodded, friendly, but all business. "And this is?" She looked at Becky inquiringly.

They'd been through this before. Grace had had to clear Becky on more than one occasion.

"This is my friend, and Tank's girlfriend, Becky Jacobs."

Becky was given a very measured look. "Okay, well, we're going to need a few minutes alone with our patient here. Can I ask you both to step outside?"

Grace and Becky stared at her as though she'd asked them to jump out the window. Somehow, it felt very odd to have a complete stranger, and a very attractive one, come in and order them out of Tank's room. Becky was particularly unwilling to move.

"Of course," Grace finally replied. "How do you think he looks?"

The nurse was already bustling around the bed, checking machines and IVs. She lifted Tank's wrist to take his pulse. Becky had an unreasonable urge to slap his wrist out of the woman's hand and tell her to go away. Of course, she wasn't about to do that. She wouldn't slap Tank while he was defenseless.

Melanie wrote something on Tank's chart. "His vital signs are good. The doctor will be in shortly. He can give you a better idea of his progress."

Becky latched onto the word 'progress' as she allowed Grace to guide her out of the room. Another nurse entered and closed the door behind her.

"I don't like her!" Becky hissed.

"Which one?"

"The first one - either of them."

"She's just doing her job," Grace replied, leading Becky to a bench a little way down the hall.

"I don't want her alone with him."

"She's not. That other nurse just joined her."

"You know what I mean."

"What do you think she's going to do?" Grace asked, a little grin touching her mouth.

"I don't know, but if she's not done soon, I'm going to go in there and ..." Becky trailed off.

"No, you're not." Grace laughed. It was a good sound to hear. "Whatever she's doing needs to be done. She can't help it if she's pretty while she's doing it."

Becky gasped. "You think she's pretty? She's so tiny. She hardly looks old enough to be in high school, much less be a registered nurse."

Grace continued to smile at her friend's expense. "My, my, look who's jealous."

"I'm not jealous of a child."

"She's no child. And she's probably changing his gown. Seeing Tank in all his glory."

Becky jumped up and Grace laughed, reaching an arm out to restrain her. "Leave them, Becky. Seriously," she laughed again.

Becky narrowed her eyes at her friend. "How can you sit there while some stranger disrobes your brother?"

"Well, I'm sure not going to do it."

Feeling helpless, and raging with a completely unreasonable jealousy, Becky stared down the hall toward Tank's room. Of course, the nurses had to take care of him. Of course, they were trained to do it. Becky knew these things, but she didn't have to like them.

The minute the door opened, she jumped, ready to spring down the hall to make sure Tank had survived.

"Easy," came Grace's quiet voice, the laughter subdued. "Don't need to run them over on their way out of the room."

"I'm not going to run anyone over," Becky snipped, her nose in the air as she calmly made her way down the hall.

The machines were blinking, his heart was going strong. Tank had survived whatever the nurses had done to him. Becky walked over and held his hand. Now, he just needed to wake up.

***

On her way out to the parking lot, a familiar figure passed her.

"Evening, Becky."

"Oh, hi Pastor Rob."

"I'm so sorry about Mr. Kimball. Has he improved at all?"

She sighed. "Nothing's really changed, though he doesn't seem worse."

He nodded. "Well, praise God for that."

"It's nice of you to visit him," she offered lamely. She'd forgotten that Tank went to his church.

"I'll keep checking in," he assured her. "And of course, we'll keep praying."

Becky was surprised to hear that he'd visited Tank already. She'd been in such a vacuum of her own sorrow, she hadn't really thought about all the others who were affected. *Except the kids.* She always worried about how the students were taking his injury and absence. *How they would feel if he didn't come back.*

"How are you holding up?" the pastor asked, concern evident on his face.

"Okay," she responded, afraid to go into any kind of detail; afraid that he would turn it into an opportunity to badger her about going to church.

"Folks are praying for you, too, Becky, and of course, for Grace."

"Thank you," she replied, anxious to get away, yet somehow drawn to the peace that seemed to surround him.

"Well, I'm going to go in and see if I can tell Tank a few bad jokes; get him to try to throw me out or something."

Becky looked up in surprise and was further startled by the uncertainty on his face, as though he wasn't sure if his joke was appropriate.

She couldn't help but smile. "Well, I already threatened to redecorate his house. Can't hurt to try another tactic."

Pastor Rob smiled back and put a hand on her shoulder. "Take care Becky."

She nodded. "You, too."

He turned, then stopped and called back to her. "God's got this, Becky. Either way, God's got this."

"I know," she called back, somehow, a small part of her starting to believe it was true.

thirty-three

She'd dreamed it a dozen times: Tank squeezing her hand, Tank stroking her hair, Tank waking in some sweet, gentle way, letting her know that he was okay. Becky felt the hand on her shoulder and willed it to be Tank, nudging her awake.

"Ms. Jacobs."

She sighed. He wouldn't call her that, or at least he hadn't for a long time. She kept her eyes closed, waiting for him to get it right.

"Becky?"

Slowly opening her eyes, she focused on the nurse who ran the world. Becky lifted her head from the side of Tank's bed where she'd apparently fallen asleep.

"The doctor's on his way in," the nurse said gently. "Just thought you might want to ..." she gestured at her face, and Becky touched her own cheek. She could feel the indent of the blanket and whatever part of Tank she'd been sleeping on.

"Right. Thanks." She shuffled to the bathroom, glancing back at the bed as the nurse pulled the railing back into place. Tank continued to rest peacefully.

Becky grimaced at her reflection in the mirror. She had two lines down the side of her cheek that were not going away any time soon. She splashed some water on her face and reached for the paper towel. She heard the nurse talking quietly and wondered what kind of doctor brought out that meek tone. Becky imagined the doctors and pretty much all of the hospital administrators groveling to this delicate little nurse with an aura of authority unlike any she'd ever seen. She had to concede a grudging respect for the woman.

Pausing and looking in the mirror, she listened again to the gentle tone the nurse was using. Becky's heart began to race as she considered the possibility that the nurse was using her bedside voice. Daring to hope, and fighting an unreasonable pique that Tank would wait to wake up to the beautiful little nurse instead of her, she leaned out of the bathroom door.

Tank's head was turned away. That didn't really mean anything, although she didn't recall him facing anywhere but straight forward before. She looked over toward the nurse, who returned her glance with a look of such unaffected delight, Becky didn't even try to tamp down her hope. She bolted to the bed.

"Tank?" she whispered.

He turned his head slowly, cringing from the apparent pain before settling his eyes on her. He smiled as well as he could with his cut lip. "Hey," he said hoarsely.

Becky's pulse roared in her head. He was awake. He was looking at her and trying to smile. She wanted to launch herself on top of him and get every bit of him awake and moving. Instead she picked up his hand and started to cry.

"Don't ..." He tried to lift his hand to her face, but the effort seemed to drain him.

Becky lifted it for him, resting her cheek against his big warm hand, smiling through her tears.

"I'll give you a minute," the nurse said to Becky a moment later, "but the troops are on their way." She stepped quietly from the room.

"What," Tank tried to clear his throat. "What happened to your face?" He ran his thumb along the indents on her cheek.

Becky turned her head and nipped at him. "You would ask that." She leaned down and grazed his lips with hers while they were still alone. "Those are Tank dents," she said, lifting her head so she could look at him again, take in the glory of his green eyes. "I fell asleep on some part of you," she explained, picking up his hand again.

"Which part?" he tried to grin.

Becky grinned back. She could hear hospital personnel hustling down the hall toward them. "I have to call your sister, and everybody," she said, hating to pull away. "The doctors are probably gonna want some time alone with you."

"Don't leave," he said, trying to grip her hand. Becky's heart leapt into her throat.

"I'll be just outside the door," she promised. "I'm not going anywhere."

The doctor walked into the room, barely waiting for a response to his light tap on the door. A trail of medical staff followed him.

"The big guy's awake," he said, beaming. "Miracles do happen." He smiled at Becky. "They're calling his sister, but you might want to try to touch base, yourself. If we could have a few minutes with him?"

"Of course," Becky replied. She squeezed Tank's hand again, marveling at the fact that he was looking back at her, helpless as a baby, but looking back at her. She leaned down and kissed his knuckles. "I'll be right back," she said, then reluctantly withdrew her hand from his. She backed from the room, eyes glued to his as she ran into the partially closed door.

She jumped, turned, and darted from the room. When she got into the hall she fell on her knees and cried.

***

While tests were run and the medical people were doing whatever else they needed to do, Becky pulled out her phone and started making calls. Her conversation with Tank's sister involved mostly squealing on Grace's part. Somehow, Becky had gotten through before the hospital staff did. She was pretty sure the conversation ended with Grace's promise to beat it down to the hospital.

Her call to Maddy was almost as fun. She wished she could call the students in their class. She wanted the world to know that Tank was awake. Next on her list was Ed Davidson. He choked up immediately, thanked the Lord, then thanked Becky for calling. She smiled as she hung up. Tank had touched a lot of lives. A lot of people were going to be smiling and thanking the Lord today.

By the time Becky got permission to see Tank again, Grace was running down the hall toward her. They grabbed each other in a fierce hug, then turned to the doctor for a debriefing. It sounded as though Tank's coming around when he did was a significant factor in his positive prognosis. Full recovery would likely take six months or longer. The doctor made several references to the need for Tank to take it very slowly. Grace and Becky were fully on board for keeping Tank in line, at least in theory.

In her excitement, Becky felt like she missed half of what the doctor said, but figured there would be time to sort through the information. Surely, they wouldn't release Tank without someone having a clear idea of his care in the coming weeks. Once the doctor excused himself, Becky pulled back and urged Grace to go in to see Tank by herself.

"I'll give you two some time," she offered.

"Are you kidding?" Grace said, grabbing Becky's hand. "I want to get this wedding thing settled. You're coming with me."

"Don't!" Becky laughed. "Let him wake up."

Grace grinned and all but flew to her brother's bedside. "Hey, you big jerk. Thanks for putting us through hell this week." She leaned down and kissed his cheek. "You need a shave. Have a nice sleep?"

Tank grinned and looked past her to Becky. "I want to get out of this bed," he growled.

"And there he is. Sorry, you can't." Grace pushed on his shoulders for good measure. "Getting flabby, Tank. You're going to have your work cut out for you."

He shifted underneath her, his powerful frame itching to move and prove her wrong. "Give me three days," he mumbled, lifting his hand and then letting it drop to the bed.

"Ha. We'll see about that," Grace replied, deep affection lacing her flippant words.

"When can I go home?"

Becky noted that his voice was stronger. He'd lost most of the rasp from earlier.

"The doctor will check back in sooner or later. I'm sure we'll find out then."

Grace turned and gestured for Becky to come closer, so she rounded the bed and stood on the other side. Tank followed her movement, squeezing her hand when she took a hold of his.

"Mom and Dad send lots of love. They fly in tomorrow. Nice timing for them. They had a hard time getting out of Aruba once they really started trying." Grace rubbed his arm. "I think they were hoping you'd come through this faster. Well, we all were." She sighed, smiling. "So ... how did it happen? What did Becky do to wake you up?"

Becky glanced at Grace and grinned, then looked back into Tank's eyes. She couldn't get enough of them.

"Well," she answered for him, "Tank, being the charming guy that he is, waited until he could be alone with that cute little nurse to wake up." Becky narrowed her eyes at him playfully. "Not sure what she did to inspire him. I'd stepped out of the room."

He grinned back. "Yeah, she asked me out."

Becky rolled her eyes, linking her fingers through his.

"Wow. Not cool, Tank. Becky's been here all week. Should have timed that better."

He turned slowly to Grace. "All week? How long have I been out?"

Becky and Grace exchanged glances. "Eight days," Grace replied. "The fire was a week ago yesterday. You remember that?"

Tank closed his eyes. "Yeah." He took a deep breath and blew it out. Becky watched his chest rise and fall, every movement a new miracle. "Doctor was checking my memory, so I just relived that a bit."

He kept his eyes closed and Becky grew nervous. She wanted to poke him and wake him up again. Instead, she rubbed his hand with her thumb. He turned toward her but didn't open his eyes. "What day is it?"

"Saturday," the women answered together. They exchanged tentative smiles over the bed.

Tank grinned a little himself. "I'm tired," he said.

"We should let you rest," Grace said. "I should, anyway. If you're going to be all recovered and everything, I might as well go back to the shop."

Becky held onto his hand. She didn't want to go. She didn't care if he slept, she just wanted to be there when he woke up again.

"See ya, Gracie," Tank said sleepily.

His sister looked down at him, the tears finally starting to fall. She leaned down and kissed his cheek and then just stood and stared at him. "I can't believe it," she whispered.

"I can't either," Becky replied. She finally looked up at her friend. "Guess I should head out with you?"

Grace started to shake her head and Tank squeezed Becky's hand. "Don't go," he mouthed, barely making a sound.

Becky looked sheepishly at Grace, who only beamed in response.

"I'll stop by later," she said. "And bring coffee."

"That would be great," Becky replied, pulling her chair up close to the bed.

Grace gave them one last affectionate glance and left the room.

***

It was an effort to open his eyes, but Tank was tired of being tired and done with being prone. The sooner he could get his wits about him and get a little strength back, the sooner he'd be home again.

Before his eyes finally obeyed, he felt a hand in his. *Becky.* He turned his head gently in her direction and forced his eyes open. She was folded into the chair right next to the bed, one hand holding his, the other propping a book against knees that were somehow bent so that she fit sideways. Tank grinned.

"Hey," he greeted her.

Becky dropped the book and he winced at the *clunk!* as it hit the floor. "Oh, sorry," she said, jumping out of the chair. "How are you?"

"Better. I wanna go home."

She smiled tenderly down at him. *Becky. Smiling tenderly.* He blinked. He must have really scared them.

"You need to rest. You'll get home soon enough."

"You coming with me?"

"Where?" She looked puzzled.

274

"Home. Someone's gonna have to take care of me." He wished he had the strength to pull her down next to him. He just wanted to hold her. Then he wanted ...

"I think your parents will do a good job of that."

He jolted out of his daydream. "When are they coming?"

"Tomorrow, Grace said."

He closed his eyes. "When did I talk to her?"

"Late this morning."

"Right. She left to get us coffee."

"She's bringing me coffee. Not sure what your diet is right now."

He could hear the teasing smile in her voice. He really wanted to see her, but he was so tired. He finally forced his eyes open.

"I'm gonna rest for a few minutes, then I want to talk."

"Sounds good. I was really excited to read again."

He smiled, then winced. "Ow. It hurts to smile."

She reached out and touched his chin below his lip. "So sorry."

He wanted to kiss her fingers, but he just couldn't find the energy. "Thanks for hanging out."

"Thanks for waking up."

He squeezed her hand. He really wanted his strength back. "I'm going to be really well-rested when this is all over."

"You'd better be."

"I hope you're ready."

"For?"

His smile was his only response before he drifted back to sleep.

***

"So, are you done?"

Becky was slightly less startled when he woke the third time. She managed to keep a hold of her book as she turned to him and squeezed his hand. "Done with what? My book? Hardly."

"Nah. Not your book. Are you done being done with men?"

She put her book down and turned fully to him. She wrapped both of her hands around his big one. "I don't know. Are you done with that nurse?"

He grinned. "Depends on your answer. She was cute."

Becky sort of lunged at him and he grabbed her hands. His strength was definitely returning.

"Let's get married, Becky. You wouldn't say no to a helpless man in a hospital bed."

He wasn't looking or acting so helpless anymore.

"Nice - add some pressure. Play on my compassion."

"Whatever it takes."

"You should ask me when you can stand and kiss me properly."

"I'll haul you into this bed and kiss you properly."

He still had a hold of both of her hands and he gave her a little tug. She didn't doubt he could do it. She leaned in and kissed him on the forehead.

"So, yes?"

"So," she answered slowly, "strong possibility."

He pulled her hands wide, effectively toppling her onto his chest. He let out a huff of air, and Becky scrambled to right herself.

"Are you okay?" she asked, looking for any kind of leverage to lift herself off of him.

He smiled and wrapped his arms around her. "I'm good."

"Tank, I can't stay like this. The door's wide open."

"Then kiss me and I'll let you go."

She looked at his lips and back into his eyes. It was all the invitation he needed.

"Tank, you can't ..."

Turns out he could.

thirty-four

Six weeks after the fire, Tank was pretty much back to his regular schedule. He took it easy during his P.E. classes, but other than that, he was working full time. He'd even stopped over at the house on several occasions to check out the apartment. Tank knew that it would be months before he was fully recovered, if he was lucky, but he felt good. He felt very lucky. *Blessed.*

His parents had come and gone during the first week of his convalescence. It was enough time for all of them. He loved his folks, but even his big house couldn't contain all of the personalities in his small family. They'd been as incensed as they could reasonably be with an invalid when he told them he'd turned down the ESPN job. Their subsequent attitude toward Becky was barely civil.

Tank just hoped that she didn't sense too much of their disapproval, and was grateful that Grace more than made up for their lack of enthusiasm. He also suspected that Becky had been so busy picking up his slack in their classes and teaching her own that she didn't have a lot of time to think about his parents' behavior toward her. She'd visited, of course, and they'd shared a meal together one evening, but other than that, she'd tried to leave them to their family time.

While he appreciated the gesture, what he really wanted was time with her. He was thankful that his parents made the effort to visit and help him out, and really, it was nice that they were the ones to get him through that first week. Once he started feeling more himself, however, he was anxious to reconnect with Becky. She was ready for him.

He hadn't revisited the whole proposal thing. It was enough that they were finally, openly enjoying getting to know each other. They spent afternoons and evenings at the coffee shop or at the inn. With all of the activity surrounding the finishing of the apartment, there was little peace at Maddy's. It was the perfect place to hang out and behave.

As their spring break approached, Tank decided it was time to celebrate. He made plans to take Becky to a restaurant that John had recommended, and afterwards, they'd make one more important stop before returning to the inn. He'd build a fire - the evenings were still plenty cold - and hold her until she agreed to be his wife. It seemed like a good plan. He'd just started back to the gym, easing into his workout. While it would be some time before his strength fully returned, he figured he should be able to hold Becky still long enough to get a life-long commitment out of her.

He jingled the extra set of keys in his pocket as he walked up to her door. He was ready to take this next step; never been so sure of anything in his life. He hoped Becky was ready, too.

***

"That was wonderful," Becky said, leaning back against the headrest in his Jeep. "I haven't had a meal like that in forever. Thank you." She turned to him with a grin, and he leaned over and kissed her soundly.

"You're welcome. You look beautiful, by the way. Did I tell you that?"

"You did mention it, I think," she replied. "Once or twice."

"It's true. That red is fantastic on you. I could hardly concentrate on eating."

"And yet you finished that entire seafood platter for two. Poor baby. We should probably stop somewhere on the way home."

He gave her a sly glance. "Good idea."

***

Becky couldn't imagine what business Tank had at the high school on a Friday night.

"Seriously, you needed to stop here on the first night of spring break? Did you forget a basketball?"

Tank leaned over and kissed her until she did her little sigh/groan that told him it was time to retreat at all costs. He got out of the Jeep, walked around to her side and opened the door. "Come in with me."

"Ew. No. I don't want to go back in there for a week. Make that ten days."

"Please? I need to do one thing and I don't want to go in there alone. I'm scared."

Becky laughed, and while she was distracted, he lifted her out of the car. She threw her arms around his neck.

"Sure you're recovered enough to carry me?" she asked, snuggling into his shoulder.

"And then some." Tank shifted her and supported her with his leg while he got the keys out of his pocket. "Here we go."

He unlocked the door to the front of the school and carried her into the cafeteria. He set her down at a table. "Don't move."

Becky pulled her coat around her and sat perfectly still.

"Hey, don't leave me here," she called out as he walked into the kitchen.

"Be right back," he called over his shoulder.

She sat in the dark, non-plussed and cold. "I'm cold, you big dumb football player!" she yelled. "Come back!"

He returned a moment later with a candle and two balloons. "So impatient, Ms. Jacobs."

She watched as he lit the candle and set it in the middle of the table. The heart-shaped balloons looked like they could have been leftovers from the Valentine's Day dance, except that they were new. By the light of the candle she could read, "I love you," on one. The other said, "Be Mine."

Tank moved a table out of the way, creating what she could only imagine was a tiny dance floor. When he attached a small speaker to his phone and started a slow romantic tune, her suspicions were confirmed.

He finally turned toward her and took off his coat, tossing it on the table next to him. He walked up to her and slowly unbuttoned hers; that in itself almost had her in a puddle on the floor. She waited, hardly breathing, while he gently removed it and set it carefully on the table. He pulled her into his arms.

He led her around their little dance floor, Tank style, which basically meant that he simply swayed, doing more dancing with his hands than his feet. Becky sighed and melted into him, tucking into his shoulder.

Tank kissed the top of her head and made an effort to keep his hands still, splaying them across her back, keeping her close. They danced like this for several minutes, until Tank finally brought his hands around and tilted her face up to his. He kissed her gently.

"I didn't forget anything."

"No. Really?"

"I also didn't forget that you said 'strong possibility.' "

Becky's heart raced. "I did say that, didn't I?"

He kissed her again. "Yes, you did. And," he pulled a little box out of his pocket, "I would like to turn that possibility into a certainty. Tonight. Now."

Becky laughed nervously. "Wow. No pressure or anything."

"Lots of pressure. I want to marry you, Becky. I want us to spend our lives together. Please be my wife."

He opened the box, and Becky gasped at the size of the diamond he held out to her.

"That's obscene."

He laughed. "The response I always hoped for when I asked the woman of my dreams to marry me."

She looked up from the ring. "I'm the woman of your dreams? Really, Tank?"

"Really, Becky. Please marry me."

"Don't you want to know if you're the man of my dreams?"

Tank thought for a moment. "I just want you to marry me. I want you to be happy. I can't imagine I'm the man of anyone's dreams, but I think you're at least used to me by now."

Becky laughed. "Used to you? You think that's it?" She threw her arms around his neck. "I don't deserve you."

"I know," he said, holding her.

She reared her head back and he laughed. "Please put this ugly thing on your finger and say yes. We can exchange it on Monday."

"Yes, Tank." She let him slip the ring on her finger and she stared at it in awe. "Maybe we can exchange it if we need a new car or something."

He smiled. "I just want you to like it. I want you to be happy. You make me happy, Becky."

She cupped his face, and the crazy ring sparkled in the candlelight. "You make me happy, too, Tank."

She reached up and kissed him and they lost themselves in the music in the middle of the high school cafeteria on the Friday night before spring break.

***

"I've been thinking," Becky said as they walked along the beach several days later. The air was cold, but most of the snow had melted. The rest of the country was starting to think about spring. Maine was trying.

Tank pulled her close. "Yeah?"

"I'm not sure I want to have your children."

"Excuse me?" He stopped in his tracks.

Becky kept walking and looked over her shoulder. Her blonde hair blew across her face as she called out over the waves. "I said, I'm not sure I want to have your children."

He jogged to catch up with her.

"Well, look at you," she said, continuing backwards across the sand. "You're *huge*," she huddled into her jacket, her hands in her pockets, a grin on her face.

"It took me thirty years to get this big, I wasn't born this way."

"Yeah, well, I want to see baby pictures." She turned back into the wind.

He enveloped her in a bear hug from behind. "We'll take this one step at a time," he growled in her ear. "It may take some time and ... effort before we have to think about kids."

Becky leaned her head back against his shoulder. "Hmm ... time and effort."

Tank turned her to face him. "How much time 'til we make that effort?"

She smiled. "How soon do you want me in that big, beautiful house of yours?"

"Tomorrow."

Becky laughed. "You never caught on that I'm marrying you for your beach property." She looked out over the water. "I think I finally get the ocean."

Tank pulled her close. "Start planning the wedding."

She sighed happily. "A winter wedding, I think."

"Spring."

"Spring is like, now."

"I know."

"Well, we met in the fall. That would be nice," Becky offered.

"How about Cinco de Mayo?"

She laughed. "Lots of people get married in the summer."

"Too hot."

"You are hard to please."

"You have no idea."

Becky smiled and turned toward the inn, taking a hold of Tank's hand. Linking her fingers through his, she swung their arms and grinned at him.

"It's warmer the other way," he pointed out.

"I know. I just really like holding your hand."

He smiled and they walked up the steps to the porch. "Finishing up on the apartment tomorrow. Gonna be a long day. I should probably go."

She sighed. "I guess."

"So, we'll start making a plan?"

Becky smiled. "We'll start making a plan."

He leaned in and kissed her. "I'll be back early."

"You let me sleep."

"We can sleep when we're married."

They gave each other a long look, a quick smile, and then Tank reluctantly turned to go.

He was halfway down the steps when she called after him.

"Um, Tank?"

He turned. "Yeah?"

"What's your name?"

He grinned and walked slowly up the steps. He stopped and looked down into her eyes. They were bright with curiosity.

He pulled her close for one last kiss. "I'll tell you when we're married."

The End

About the Author

S. Jane Scheyder, a firm believer in romance, lives with her husband and five children in Connecticut. Born in Michigan, she graduated from Valparaiso University in Indiana with a degree in Music Merchandising. Her first book, *The Other Side of the Pulpit*, was published in 2006.

For Jacob, Michael, Daniel, Mary and Hannah